Creeping Beauty

Creeping Beauty

ANDREA PORTES

HARPER TEEN
An Imprint of HarperCollins Publishers

HarperTeen is an imprint of HarperCollins Publishers.

Creeping Beauty
Copyright © 2023 by Andrea Portes

Library of Congress Control Number: 2023931285

ISBN 978-0-06-242247-7

Typography by Corina Lupp
23 24 25 26 27 LBC 5 4 3 2 1

First Edition

FOR JACK COULTER.
You would have made an amazing king.
I wish I could have saved you.

"To die, to sleep;

To sleep, perchance to dream—ay, there's the rub:

For in that sleep of death what dreams may come."

—*HAMLET*, SHAKESPEARE

Creeping Beauty

Prologue

A KING'S JOURNAL

What folly!

And yet my beloved wife, the queen, has insisted. She believes it will help me with my temper. Poppycock, I say! But she is my queen, my jewel, my heart. So here I sit, writing in this godforsaken book.

A funny thing: the past two nights, I have had the same odd dream. I can't quite figure it.

It starts with a feeling of panic.

There is an old man, alone in a clearing in the forest.

The sky is turning to night. Dusk. The worn old man is tending his sheep. He whistles to himself, seemingly without a care.

Then above him, the old man hears something. He looks up to see a swarm of blackbirds, hundreds of them, flying in the sky, their screeches deafening. His eyes widen as he realizes what is to come. He mutters something to himself, dropping his tools, and races toward his humble little stone home.

"They're coming!" he yells out, rushing to the house. A young woman, pretty, peeks her head out, realizes the danger, and hurries into a hidden storm cellar.

Then the sky turns black above them . . . and the old man looks behind him in terror. He rushes to the storm cellar door, latching it behind him.

As the door shuts, there is a different kind of dread. The feeling that something terrible is about to happen.

WHOOSH.

And that is when the dream ends.

I wake up, each time, in a cold sweat.

A terrified king. A king no one should ever see.

And then, both nights, as the dream ends and I startle awake, for a moment, I see a dark figure at the foot of my bed. Hovering there.

Then I blink, and the entity is gone.

I have not told my wife, because she might think me quite mad.

So, I reserve it for you, dear journal.

A useless thing, I think, a king's journal.

Part I

1

NOBODY IN MY world believes me.

About the other place.

They think it's the raving of a crackpot; the delusion of a child.

But you, in your world. Perhaps you can understand. Perhaps there will be something familiar. Foreign, yes. But familiar.

Like a whisper or a flash or the last glimmer of a thought before falling asleep.

Come.

Come with me.

I'll show you.

Come, we'll float down from the sky, a robin's-egg blue. Lower now, over the tops of the golden king holly trees. Like lollipops: round at the top, gold and green. The trunks like narrow sticks. Then there are the long triangle trees. The pines, tall and spiky. Dark green, sometimes almost blue.

But we're flying past them now, over the hills and valleys. There's a brook there, babbling. Cross it. Now the bright green grass is shooting up, the hill is rising, and there—there at the top of it . . .

A castle.

A castle in pastels. Every color represented. Lilac. Baby blue. Periwinkle. Aquamarine. Azure. Lavender. Lime. Mint. Buttercup. Iceberg. Diamond. Peach. Pearl. Seashell. Snow. Sunset. Tea rose. Thistle. Topaz. Vanilla. Wisteria. Volt.

There is even a pastel named after our castle.

Roix blue.

Originated in the region of Roix.

A shade somewhere between azure and aquamarine, with a little dust thrown in.

I quite like it.

It's on the crest. All over the castle, in each of the four turrets, the entry, and the dining hall.

Now that we've landed, you will see there is a blinding light from the morning sun, coming through the arched windows.

In front of that, there, see me? I am standing in my knickers, arms in the air, like some kind of flying squirrel.

All around me buzz the royal dressers, tucking this there, latching that there, and squeezing every extra scone, muffin, and cupcake relentlessly tighter, into this ruthless little thing they call a corset.

This entire operation takes place every morning, exactly at eight. And the entire undoing of this operation takes place every night, exactly at ten, unless there is a ball or a gala of some kind, at which point everything is higgledy-piggledy.

Across from me is my mother, who is much better-looking than me, much skinnier, much fairer. Her hair is the color of the noon sun shining on wheat. My hair is dust mop. Her eyes are sparkling blue sea. My eyes are swamp.

It's not a stretch to say I'm a bit of a disappointment. I always have been, from the minute I debuted before the court at the royal rite of spring. There's always that *look*. A look of pity, peppered with amusement. A shaking of the head.

I am not perfect. Not even close. Just a mouse-haired princess with eyes that can't decide whether to be blue, gray, or green, not as svelte or as beautiful as her mother, the queen.

When I was a baby, my mother held me in her arms for an entire month. The experts told her I was too small and was destined for the grave. They advised leeches and bloodletting. But my mother decided to just hold me . . . for an entire month. And somehow, miraculously, this simple plan was a success and I did not perish. Because, you see, she is perfection.

At present, my perfect, miraculous mother is standing before me, bathed in morning light, lecturing me about something very important I should do. Something I *have* to do. Something that simply *must be* done.

"Darling, Bitsy, don't give me that look . . . it's time to face it."

Yes, she calls me Bitsy, short for Elizabeth.

"We must strike while the iron is hot! This spring is perfect. You've already had your debut. And the cherry blossoms are about to bloom. We could have the wedding at the summer estate. Just think of it! Cherry blossoms, all around!"

"Can they be my bridesmaids?" I nod toward my two royal dressers, Rose and Suzette, who I've known since we were little girls, splashing around in the cloisters, making mud pies down at the lake, playing hide-and-seek through the endless labyrinth of the castle corridors.

"Certainly not!" Then, taking into account their presence: "We all love our dear Rose and Suzette quite . . . obviously, but they are not of royal blood and therefore—"

"But why does it matter? I mean, truly?" I ask.

My mother exhales in annoyance. "Bitsy, we've talked about this a thousand times. I didn't make up the rules. Nor did your father. They are passed down through ages and ages. To live in this way, to be a monarch, to have these titles . . . it is a privilege."

I grumble. "How much privilege is there if I can't even choose my own bridesmaids?"

My mother contemplates. "Elizabeth Clementine Roix. You are the princess of this castle and you will behave like one. It's bad enough that—"

She stops herself.

"It's bad enough that what? That I'm ugly?"

"Ugly! Heavens no! You are a gorgeous little princess who any prince in any of the kingdoms would be lucky to wed."

"Then why do I feel so hopeless? About everything? As if nothing is either bad or good but just *there*. Neutral. Unchanging. And that's the way it will be for all eternity. Flat. Colorless. Just a glass sheet of boredom."

This stuns even Rose and Suzette, who stop primping and preening, seeming to look to my mother for assurance.

"Oh, my sweet daughter, you are one for drama, aren't you? But don't worry, I'll do whatever I can to find you the right prince.

Mayhap, a wise prince who can help you answer some of these existential questions. I had such feelings once, although never quite as bleak . . . but certainly odd. Odd feelings, I suppose."

"And what changed?" I ask.

"You." She smiles, coming close to me and tapping my nose once. "Boop."

I can't help but smile.

"The very moment I looked into your eyes . . . all of that fell away. It was like looking at a little miracle." She reminisces. "A day that changed my life. And your name, Bitsy, is my favorite word in all the world. Bitsy. It means light and love and home."

"Oh, Mother." I roll my eyes and pretend to be unmoved, but really I quite love it when my mother goes on about me. It's like a warm cup of tea at bedtime.

She glides toward the door, having succeeded in distracting me from my woe. "Now don't forget, this afternoon is tea with your cousins, and then after that—"

"No. No no no no no. Nay. Nyat. Nont," I protest.

"They are your cousins!" she answers. "Your flesh and blood."

"But they're terrible! They're rude and vain and superficial. All they ever do is have their portraits painted. Portraits in the garden. Portraits in the turret. Portraits by the pond. Did you know they even made over a hundred commoners wait at the foot of Mount Pontmillierre whilst they sat there having their portraits painted in front of the Emerald Falls!"

"Well, no, I hadn't," my mother acquiesces.

"Well, it's true! And it's not just that," I continue. "They never even go to the theater or the opera. All they ever want to do is watch the most mindless, short little ditties by whatever vulgar or contrived preposterous troupe is passing through. They laugh at a donkey breaking wind!"

Rose and Suzette stifle a laugh.

"They—they never *read*. And do you know why they can't watch an entire three-act play?" I go on. "It's because they are conceited, superficial, and most of all . . . they're mean. Mean to each other. Mean to their parents. Mean to their friends and, yes, very much mean to me."

"Darling. Not everyone in the world is going to be to your liking," she advises. "Think of it as a way to learn patience. And tolerance. A queen must be tolerant, you know. When a visiting dignitary from a far-off land offers you a delicacy of boiled lizard feet . . . you have to smile and nod. And then pretend to eat it but really spit it out into your table linens and hope no one notices. Not that this has ever happened to me personally—"

"Um. Mother. That is awfully specific for a hypothesis," I chide.

"Well, perhaps. But the point is that a royal must be tolerant. And such tolerance includes tolerance of idiots. Not that your cousins are idiots." She notes my expression. "I didn't say that!"

"Oh, of course. You absolutely did not just call my cousins idiots," I tease.

"Now, this is not the only thing on your agenda, dearest. As I was attempting to tell you when I was so rudely interrupted"— she scruffs my hair—"is the small matter of this evening. The king's consul is coming—"

"Oh, heavens no. No. Nont. Nya—"

"Aaaand . . . he will have a list of appropriate suitors, a painting of each, and a sort of summary of their accomplishments, traits, and general demeanor. I know you think this is all quite silly, but it's important that you pick one. Tonight. We'll have no more lollygagging, delaying, or excuses. Just try to pick one. And remember, they all snore in their sleep eventually. Maybe you can find one who adores three-act plays, novels, and extremely boring lectures on the ancient techniques of basket-weaving. Allll the things you love and prize."

She winks, then strolls out, the door closing behind her.

"I wonder if that's true. Do they all inevitably snore?" I turn to Rose and Suzette.

Suzette frowns, thinking. "Our father snores, so . . . our mother sleeps with us. And our uncle sounds like a dying bear, come to think of it. And don't get me started on our grandfather; you could hear him in the next village!"

"Ah, so it is true." I sit down, deflated. "If only I didn't have to get married. Then I wouldn't have to listen to anyone snore."

Suzette chides me. "You know what happens to old maids, don't you? They grow warts on their noses and hair on their chins and die alone."

"That can't be true," I protest.

Rose chimes in. "Well, it may not be true, but . . . if you don't wed, well, you won't ever be a . . . person. Or at least a person of value. Do you really want to spend the rest of your life with the entire court whispering about you and feeling sorry for you?"

"Would you feel sorry for me?" I ask them both.

They share a look. And continue cinching me into my clothes.

2

PRISSY AND BOLANDA, my two terrible cousins, sit across from me, both of them looking as if they spent five hours in their dressing chambers, ready to attend a coronation. Prissy with her dark brown hair and large eyes, blessed with looks I could only dream of. Bolanda with her auburn hair and green eyes, like some kind of autumnal doll. The green hill behind them sets off both their features. I would not be surprised if they insisted on the table being placed right here—to take full advantage of the backdrop.

"Oh, Bitsy. Did we catch you at a bad time? Perhaps you've been out horse riding," Prissy purrs. "It's so brave how you go out looking so."

"Ah, yes. Brave. That's the effect I'm going for, clearly," I reply.

"Do you know . . . the funniest thing." She shares a devious look with Bolanda. "There was a troupe coming through from the Claffordine. And we thought it would be fun to bring them to tea!"

"You mean, here?" I ask. "Now?"

"Of course!" Prissy replies. "Don't worry, you'll love them. They are just hilarious. Aren't they, Bolanda?"

"Yes, yes. Quite hilarious." She nods.

"Hallo! Halloooo! Over here!" Prissy smiles, waving off into the distance, where a scruffy-looking man drags a wooden easel up the green. She turns to me. "Now, you don't mind. We're both having our portraits painted. We thought it'd be fun. Here on the green. You know, a lush, floral, spring kind of thing . . . maybe some flowers in our hair."

"Yes, yes, flowers in our hair!" Bolanda claps her hands together, jumping in her seat like a toddler. "Someone bring the flowers!"

"We'd offer to have your portrait painted, of course, but . . . look at you!" Prissy laughs.

The put-upon painter starts unpacking his supplies.

"No, not there!" Prissy commands. "It must be this way, as to catch my cheekbones in the light properly."

She winks at the painter, who doesn't notice.

Now it's Bolanda's turn to wave off into the distance. "They're here! Oh, look, they're here!"

We turn to see the Claffordine troupe bounding up the green. One of them wears a giant fake nose and a feather hat. The others twirl brightly colored ribbons, while another trumpets a regal tune.

"You will absolutely adore them." Prissy turns to me. "They are just beyond hilarious. But don't worry, I told them not to make any jokes about how plain you are."

"Oh, I am most grateful," I reply. "But you see, I cannot tarry. Tutor and I—"

"Dear Bitsy! How I admire the way you persist with your books and maps and whatnot!" Prissy trills. "And when nothing you study will be of use to you as queen."

Bolanda chimes in, "I don't see how you have time for your tutor when you have so many important dress fittings and appearances—oh, look! They're beginning! What fun!"

The troupe has set up a makeshift stage. Behind it is a colorful landscape painted on canvas, held up by two poles. One of the troupe members is extraordinarily small and one is extraordinarily tall.

"Isn't it cute? The little one?" Prissy says, gesturing to the small man.

"Oh, precious!" Bolanda explains.

"*It?*" I ask. "Surely you mean *he*."

The painter inquires, "Should I wait until the end of the festivities, then? So you will be able to pose in a still manner, otherwise it might be quite difficult to—"

"Oh, I suppose." Prissy sighs. "Why don't you just find some flowers for our hair or something."

The painter smiles through gritted teeth, walking off toward the rose garden.

Before the festivities have even begun, the large man leads an enormous pig, dressed as a horse, in front of the brightly painted backdrop. Now he blows a little whistle and a tiny monkey, dressed as a knight, comes hurtling out from backstage, jumping up on the large pig's back.

"Oh heavens, just heavens!" Prissy and Bolanda clap and laugh as if they might die.

The hefty pig walks around, the monkey still on its back, now juggling an apple.

"I just . . . I might perish from the amusement!" Prissy exclaims, holding her stomach as she laughs. Bolanda snorts and dabs the corners of her eyes as though the spectacle has brought tears.

And this is when I decide: I will sink into the green behind me . . . and creep backward, undetected. Creeping is a trick I learned playing years upon years of hide-and-seek in the castle with Rose and Suzette. We are, all three of us, expert creepers. Our exits and entrances undetectable! First, I fade behind the topiary. Then I slide backward, silently, toward the trellis of the rose garden. Bolanda and Prissy are still guffawing with witless abandon. But I am sneaking away, invisible to their eyes. From behind the rose trellis to the castle walls. Now the trickier bit. I slither myself sideways, toward the castle, where a delectable novel about the ancients awaits me in my study . . . one my stellar tutor has gifted me, one I can't seem to put down. My tutor is quite controversial, entre nous, always inspiring me to be curious, to analyze, to reach conclusions whether they align with those of previous scholars or not.

"Oh, do it again! Do it again!" I hear Prissy commanding in the distance. "I believe this monkey has magical powers. Yes, yes, indeed!"

"But if he's a magic monkey, is he a minion of the dark arts?!" Bolanda suddenly seems filled with fear. "Oh, Prissy. This monkey may be a warlock!"

It's clear Prissy and Bolanda are not students of my tutor, or any tutor.

"Get this evil monkey away from me!" Bolanda howls. The

troupe members scurry about to remove the offending animal, who, of course, has done nothing more or less than what he has been trained to do.

I have a pang of sympathy for the tiny creature.

I manage to creep all the way up the turret stairs, up to the landing above. From my vantage point, I see that outside the window below, the painter seems to have passed out in the petunias.

Farther off, Prissy squeals with laughter as Bolanda runs, screaming bloody murder, whilst the demonic monkey, who has escaped from his handler, chases her into the fountain.

At last, something this afternoon worth seeing.

3

AFTER DINNER, AND long after Prissy and Bolanda's harried departure, my father, the king, takes the opportunity to scold me once more about my lack of manners. He is, indeed, a professional scolder with his natural gravitas, posture, olive skin, and enormous onyx eyes . . . eyes that can eviscerate worse than any dagger. Luckily, those sharp looks aren't usually aimed in my direction, as he happens to have a soft spot for me, his only child.

"Bitsy, you cannot just abandon your cousins in the middle of tea! It is rude. When they finally noticed you were gone, I think they were quite hurt. You cannot insist on sitting all day with your face in a book whilst the world passes you by! You cannot wander aimlessly around here your entire life. Tradition is the plan. You follow, because you are a royal. You have been given great privilege. You don't make a fuss." He sighs, then continues. "My dearest, I know it can be scary. This idea of growing up, of marrying. But you cannot give in to fear. Fear leads to misgivings, misgivings to confusion . . . confusion to—"

"—confusion to madness," I chime in, as I've heard this a hundred times.

"Darling. You must marry. You are of age. This is just *what's done*." He looks at my mother for assurance. There she sits, decked in her Roix blue brocade and velvet dress, strands of pearls overlapping on her delicate collar, and a diamond tiara atop her platinum head.

My mother's maiden name is actually DeBoudas. Contessa Alexandra DeBoudas, to be exact. But she married up, partially because of her legendary, fall-off-your-horse good looks.

And, although it is said he was constantly surrounded by duchesses, baronesses, and marquesas, the moment my father laid eyes on my mother, he literally tripped down the stairs. True story. He actually managed to tumble down into the knight's armor prominently displayed in the entryway.

Apparently, it made quite a racket and startled the horses. Rumor is that one of them bolted, never to be seen again.

Of course, when he tripped, no one was allowed to laugh. Which, really, was a shame.

From that moment, any previous interests were chucked into the fire immediately and my parents were wed in under a fortnight. In the spring, inside the great chapel of LeSousse, two lengths west.

Forthwith, they were the King and Queen de Roix, of the royal line of LeBrazeiux. Arguably, one of the oldest dynasties in the kingdom. Of this, I have been reminded infinitely.

And it should have been perfect. *I* should have been perfect. But somehow the arrow of enchantment missed me and I was born in this state, which is "rather plain."

Nevertheless, I persisted. In being fluent in not only Fricella and Gurbath but also Lilcott and High Rovelle, two languages considered rare and exotic. I've been taught to play both the pianette and the flauth. But, quite frankly, I spend most of my time reading dusty books and fantasizing about the ancient world. A world of strange, exotic gods, who seem to be cast in marble and who spend an inordinate amount of time bathing and eating grapes.

There is the small matter, too, of my profound wish to liberate Rose and Suzette from their station as royal servants to actual royals, which I am told can never happen but which I am determined to somehow make happen. Even if by royal decree, perhaps, if I'm ever crowned queen.

At present, however, I am being shown an array of portraits of would-be kings, also known as princes, from lands both far and near.

"Father, how can I possibly choose whomever I intend to spend the rest of my life with from a tiny painting, smaller than a napkin, etched in a few scribbles? It's impossible," I say, pleading my case.

My father and mother share a look. Clearly, they are up to something diabolical.

"Indeed." My mother looks to the ground.

"Yes, indeed. In that case . . ." My father steers himself over to the landing, nodding down below to someone, probably the king's consul. "Perhaps we should try it this way."

My mother is upon me now, flattening the wrinkles on my dress, pinching my cheeks.

"Mother! What exactly are you—"

"Your Majesty!" Here is the king's consul now, in the doorway, announcing, "May I present to you the Imperial Son of Vankrauken, Prince Wencesslont the Third!"

The king's consul nods to someone outside the doorway, but continues to stand, unmoved, leaving no trace of his opinion.

The three of us wait in anticipation. A moment. Then a moment more. We look at each other; it's an absurd silence.

But then—there he is.

And this is the moment I promptly deflate.

4

YOU SEE, THE Imperial Son of Vankrauken, Prince Wencesslont the Third, is not exactly the type of man you would want to listen to snoring for the rest of your life.

It's not that he's not handsome . . . it's just that you can't really tell because he must weigh exactly five hundred stone. Indeed, he is about as wide as he is tall. The general impression is one who could possibly be rolled out of the kingdom, if necessary. If that weren't enough, he also has skin the color of mottled pork, a face seemingly swimming with port or spirits or some other poisonous concoction.

My mother gives my father a look. Then I hear her whisper, "You can't be serious."

I look to my father for a cue. He ushers me forward.

"Young Prince Wencesslont! Why, I remember when you were just a little boy, playing knights and blackguards in the garden!" my father exclaims. "May I present to you my lovely daughter, Princess Elizabeth Clementine DeBoudas Roix."

Even though it's quite difficult to make oneself move forward in this situation, it's not possible to disobey my father's pushing me on. Nope. I have to at least pantomime this unfortunate charade.

I advance minutely and, out of the corner of my eye, see my mother glaring daggers at my father. She is not pleased with this match.

Thank God for mothers.

"Wonderful, delightful! B-Bitsy, isn't that your nickname? You see, I've done my research. Look here, I've brought you a gift. I heard you play the flauth! Here is a lovely little book of flauth compositions, transcribed by the monks of Vitmore! My father gave it to me for Noel, actually. But it is the thought that counts, isn't it? Anyway, if you don't like it, you are free to give it back . . . as I am sure it could fetch quite a high price on the market. Quite high, quite high."

I accept said book gracefully, as I have been trained. "Oh, how kind of you. How very thoughtful. I find it quite enchanting. Thank you ever so much," I purr. Purring is what princesses are bred to do!

"Yes. Yes. You're very welcome, Elizabeth. Bitsy. Shall I call you Bitsy? Or is that impudent? Oh dear. I never quite know what to do in these situations. Heavens. I hope I have not offended you. Have I offended you—"

He seems to be working himself into a lather.

"Dear Wencesslont, you've done no such thing! Indeed, our beloved Bitsy is as kind as she is . . . intelligent. Let us go for an after-dinner constitutional, shall we? It's a full moon tonight! Quite lovely this time of season!" My father is clearly hoping this little arrangement will work out.

My mother is clearly not. "Are you sure it's not too cold, dear?"

My father meets her gaze. "Of course not. It's perfect, my lovely queen."

And with that, the four of us are led down the grand stone staircase to the entry hall below, where Rose and Suzette come rushing to me, draping a scarf over my shoulders. Neither of them dares to meet my eye, knowing how humiliating this is for me. Like being asked to marry a mushroom.

A well-tempered mushroom, perhaps. But a very large, nervous, sweaty one, nonetheless. Mayhap you find me conceited. But I pray you, ask yourself, would you like to spend your wedding night drowning in mottled mushroom sweat? There. You see. You wouldn't.

As we cross through the arched doorway of the castle, my mother and father drop back, attempting to give us room—space in which our anticipated love affair can blossom.

We are not even halfway across the moat before Wencesslont turns to me and says, "What a fine match we will be! And you're certainly not as plain as they say you are!"

This hits me like a lash. Yes, I know, I *do* know this is the way in which I am spoken of . . . but to hear it. In such straight language. I can pretend it doesn't sting, but it brings back every disappointed look and pitying glance I've collected from childhood.

"Would you excuse me for a moment? I seem to have forgotten my scarf." I turn and hide behind the very large gargoyle statue, part of a set adorning the front gates.

"No, but you, silly girl, you're WEARING your scarf!" He turns, shocked now at my disappearance. "Wait. Where did you go?"

Now I creep, tiptoeing backward, I meld into the night sky, slithering back toward the moat. Creep, tiptoe, creep . . . blending myself into the darkness.

"Oh, you minx! Where have you gone, my little poppet?" he calls out, peering around. "I've got you!" He clumsily lunges behind the gargoyle, tumbling to the ground.

But I am vanished, now under the bridge of the moat. This is a challenge, this bit. You see, you have to grab the slats, without putting enough weight on them to creak. So you must distribute your weight by using your toes in the slats behind you. This took me about three winters to master.

Now my mottle-faced companion seems to grow a bit miffed. "This is quite unusual, I must say. Pray, Princess, is this some kind of game?"

This final creep, behind the portcullis, is the toughest bit. You sort of have to swing yourself from the bridge to the shadows. This must be done within milliseconds, or you're sure to be discovered. Happily, my companion seems to have grown winded with the excursion. He leans up against the massive gargoyle and wipes his brow with a silk scarf.

"Well, my dear princess." Huff puff, huff puff. He catches his breath. "You are either very strange or very stupid. No matter, you belong to me now."

At this I hurry behind the portcullis, into the entry hall, and beyond to the labyrinth of corridors.

I don't care. I don't care if I'm impertinent. I don't care if I seem like the silliest girl in all the kingdoms. I can't stand it. I won't! I can't marry this blotted-face, vulgar, gargantuan prince!

Down down down below I hurl myself, past the kitchen, past the storerooms, and down farther still, down to passages I haven't visited since I was a little girl playing hide-and-seek with Rose and Suzette. Passages cobwebbed and spidered. Passages where my footsteps provide the only noise, echoing off the stone. A maze of passages, a labyrinth, but I don't care. No matter. I don't care if they ever find me again. I'll die here, below, lost in some dusty room crawling with millipedes, my only companions a coterie of rats.

I make a wish to myself, almost a prayer . . . *Please, gods above, please do not force me into a life in a gilded cage, please free me of this fate. . . .*

At last, there is a small wooden door, a door fit for hobbits! Set there, at the end of the endless passage.

Yes, of course, I must open it. It calls to me. Beckoning me with what feels like a pulse.

I stop there, in front of the funny little door.

Reach my hand out. Then open it.

What a strange little room this is. There's nothing in it. Well, there's nothing in it except one thing. The room itself is at the bottom of a tower, a turret. Above, almost seven stories it seems, are tiny little windows.

But here, down below, just this room. With nothing in it. Except in the middle of the room, somehow lit, even here, by the light of the full moon, is a little modest wooden stool, and next to it . . .

A spindle.

5

HOW QUIET IT is!

In here, with nothing but the sound of my breath to accompany me.

I look above, at the light coming in from the tiny windows, up so high it seems impossible.

My feet seem to have decided to take themselves toward the little stool and the spindle.

My arms seem to have decided to reach out to them.

My body seems to have chosen to sit here, on this tiny modest wooden chair. A chair almost built for a child.

And now, in the shaft of light, almost a kind of moon dust surrounding my hands, my fingers have decided to reach out to the spindle.

To touch it.

Prick.

6

THIS IS THE time of falling, but not falling as one usually does . . . a quick moment of panic, a bit of embarrassment, possibly a look around to see if anyone noticed. No, that is not this. This is falling as time. Time stretching, elongating, and so, too, it seems the tower is stretching, stretching down down down as the little windows above are flying up.

Farther and farther away.

The light from the tiny windows getting dimmer and dimmer and the tower getting deeper and deeper, colder and colder, until it chills to the bone.

There is a kind of smell now, like moss. Mildew. The air filled with water and something green.

What will it be, this place? I smell it before I see it. It wafts up over me, past me, and now, somehow, I am in it.

The little moonlit windows above are gone. Replaced somehow. The stone walls of the tower now gone, too. Replaced with something . . . alive. Something breathing, something sweating, something organic. Like the forest, but not dry. No pine trees. No golden holly.

Walls of vegetation, as if the trees themselves are towers, towers with hanging leaves and trunks like sculptures, going this way and that. Trunks doubling up over themselves. Trunks made up of hundreds of little trunks within. From the trees, hanging vines, weeping from the branches.

Down, farther still, the smell of earth. The smell of mud.

And then . . .

. . .

SPLAT.

A funny thing occurs when something terrible happens to you. For a moment, you can't see it. The thing takes place, and you notice it, and then there is a moment before you realize that this terrible thing has happened to . . . *you*. And your situation (dire as it is) becomes clear.

In this case, the situation is that I am covered, from the top of my head to the tips of my toes, in mud. My face is a mud pie. My mouth fills with the taste of dirt.

From here to there, there to here, it makes no difference. This is an impossible thing. A dream, of course. This can't be what we call real. That would be preposterous.

A seat in a tower and the prick of a spindle cannot lead to a splash in the mud. The tower must have a floor. The tower is *inside*. The mud is *outside*.

Yes, certainly, this must be a dream.

Collecting myself, I hear the sound of an exotic bird, one with a clicking kind of call. Then another bird, with a call more like a shriek. The air so wet, yet it is not raining. And the mud surrounding me feels ready to engulf me.

"Wake up. Wake up. Wake up!" I command myself, a whisper through the wet air.

I've done this before, roused myself from a dream. It's a trick I have if the dream is becoming too frightening. A quick defense against what my mother calls "Perversions of the mind. Proclivities toward darkness. Despair."

Again, I kick myself in the brain. A jolt.

"Waaaaake UP!"

This is usually the time when I shoot up in my bed, gasping for air.

But there is no bed, no covers, no jolt out of nightmares.

Okay, let's try this again. "Wakey-wakey, overimaginative princess! Wake up NOW!"

SWOOSH!

What was that? That sound? Something fallen? A branch?

And now, in the darkness, I look around me. Everything gleaming a bit with the damp . . .

That thing, the swooshing thing, the fallen thing, the thing from above . . .

Was a kind of rope, a kind of sturdy, muddy rope, in the form of a grid. Wait, I know what this is! This woven thing!

It is a . . .

A net!

A trap.

And I am in it.

7

IT'S A DESPERATE feeling to realize that you, yes you, are indeed in some kind of trap. First there is the panic. Following that, there is bargaining. In this case, my case, the bargaining takes the form of grasping at this woven, inexplicably strong thing, and trying to somehow break it or break out of it, muttering *no no no no no no no!*

Below me is mud, but somehow the cage has formed a kind of claw around me. How do I know this? Well, dear friend, I know this because shockingly, and suddenly . . . the clawlike cage begins to ascend. Just so. In little jolts, and then more and then more . . .

Until now, here I am, a mud-soaked girl in a woven cage of odd strength, hoisted above the muddy swamp, leveled out at about the height of a grown man. What would you call it? In your world? The height of a gentleman? Perhaps the height of a horse? There, you see, this is how we may talk to each other.

There are many questions ricocheting between my ears. . . . How is this woven cage so strong? Why does it exist? For what purpose am I in this cage? What kind of cage is built to hold an entire person? Who built it? Why? And, of course, when are they coming? Or are they coming? And if they do arrive, what will they want?

Mayhap this is a relic left over from some ancient faraway time and now no one is coming, and I shall be forced to live my life forevermore in this swinging fortress.

The questions reverberate, bouncing off each other in such a way as to not create any kind of understanding but only further aggravate my confusion.

The good thing is, this confusion is wiped out, hurled to the side, as two figures begin to appear through the flora and fauna, speaking to each other in a kind of rickety-tickety language that has nothing to do with the language of any of the kingdoms I have studied. It's a language, as far as I can tell, consisting of long strange syllables that seem to change several times in one breath. Like eeee-ooo-aahh, ooo-aaa-eeeaah.

Yes, I should be scared, and I am. But there is also the feeling of wonder. A new language!

My tutor and I would delight in analyzing tales of epic adventure and woe written in antiquated old tomes, some on dusty scrolls. The pain and suffering, the many contradictions, the allure and cruelty of the ancients. Each tale would seem to end horribly, but horribly with a kind of lesson involved. Do not be greedy. Do not be jealous. Do not do a bad thing or a bad thing will happen to you. My tutor instilled a curiosity about faraway peoples, customs, and lands. That, I think, has been his greatest lesson. To thirst always for knowledge.

So, yes, I should be terrified. But there is, in me, that which is always peering into curiosities, wondering, analyzing. And at this moment the fear for my life and the wonder at this new language, these new beings, in this peculiar place, are in balance.

Let me describe these creatures to you. First, it's very difficult to actually SEE them, because they are camouflaged in the trees and the flora and fauna surrounding them. It's a kind of paint, all over their wiry bodies, in various shades of green and brown. So that if they stand still, it is nearly impossible to see them.

They seem to be about the same size as the people from my world, but with much less extra flesh from indulging in perhaps too many macarons, petit fours, and custard pies. No, these creatures' lithe muscles wind their way around their bones, sinewy. Each one of them a sculpture.

There is a difference in tone between the two figures approaching, despite their shared language. Tone, you see, is something that can be discerned in any language. One of the creatures is conciliatory, measured. The kind of tenor, perhaps, my mother would use with the king, or even the consul. Thoughtful, sage.

And the other? Quite the opposite. Angry, impatient. As if he can't be bothered to wait out the very sentence his calm companion is speaking.

I observe, in inquisitive suspense, as the two painted beings fight it out in clicks and clacks until one of them, the impatient one, finally raises his hands in the air in exasperation, exhales his breath, and marches over to me.

It occurs to me now, with him glaring up at me, barking commands, that I may be in danger. I tell myself this must still be part of the dream and assure myself I will wake up shortly.

But now the peaceful one hurries over to the aggressive one

and suddenly bops him on the head with a kind of club. Well, now, that wasn't very peaceful, was it? I suppose you can never really judge a book by its cover.

Immediately, the angry one falls to the ground. The sage one stands over him, as if waiting to see if he'll retaliate.

And it seems like this moment will just last forever, with one swamp man standing over the other one until the sun explodes and the moon falls, except that now there is the sound of a horse.

The minute the sound of the hooves on the ground echoes through the swamp, the sage being is on alert. He pricks up his ears and turns toward the sound of the horse. And I can see now that he, too, perceives a danger.

The angry being is now rubbing his head in a daze. Yet he also takes poignant note of the sound of the hooves, despite his confusion. The sage one and the brute share a look.

Again, this look needs no language.

This is a look of fear.

The two beings now whisper to each other, seemingly making a decision in desperate haste.

And, having made that decision, the two feral beings simply bolt off into the trees, leaving me dangling there, caged, underneath the treetops.

There was, indeed, a moment when I was afraid of them. Then there was a moment when they were afraid of something else. So, it occurs to me that this calculus logically points to the fact that whatever it was they were afraid of . . . I should be afraid of it, too.

8

———◆———

THE SWAMP BRUSH must be hindering said horse, because its pace seems to be slowing down a bit. And now even slower.

Yet, even though I feel the horse must be near me, there is no sound other than the birds high above in the canopy of branches and leaves.

Can it be the horse went in the other direction? Perhaps there is nothing to be frightened of. Perhaps those painted beings were merely scared of horses?

It's just as I've begun to convince myself that everything is perfectly fine that the hanging vines open up like a theater curtain, revealing the star of the play.

Dear reader, I don't know who you are, or what you look like, or the customs of your world. If I did, this would be easier to describe.

In my world, the men are quite thin and very much . . . *adorned*. In fact, some of the men take more time to prepare themselves for a gala than even the vainest countess. A ball, for a man, means brocade, imported silk, and hand-sewn lace. The rarer the silk, the more intricate the lace, the better. There is an unspoken competition for the oddest of sartorial curiosities. And, of course, the greater the expense, the greater the status.

With that in mind, the appearance of this particular man on horseback can only be described as a shock to the system. Similar to the white marble statues of the ancients, he is adorned with next to nothing. Not a scarf, not a hat, nor even a shirt. His legs seem to be fashioned with a kind of sandal made of leather, reaching upward, forming a kind of boot. And there, again, just a skin. The slightest bit of leather, in an irregular shape, separates him from the wildest animals seen in storybooks.

His hair is not hidden with a primped and powdered wig, but left stringy and unwashed down past his ears. It's only the moment I catch his eye, *that* moment, that I see something there less than primitive.

He, on the other hand, sits high on his horse, inspecting me as one would inspect a scientific text in the library. Quizzically. The wheels in his head seem to turn as I look to him for some kind of sign that he is not going to eat me or sacrifice me to the gods.

They are gray, his eyes. The color of an overcast day.

There's something else, too. Something in his bearing or, perhaps the space he takes up between the trees, that holds me still, frozen.

Idiot. Little girl. What are you thinking? This is some brute stranger! You must find safety!

He looks down at me now, his expression inscrutable. I believe he is about to speak, although I'm sure I'll have no way of understanding him. But, instead, he appears to hold his tongue.

Ah, strong but silent. I've heard of this in books but, quite frankly, have never seen it in action. Most of the men from the kingdoms spend all their time blathering—boasting about their vast lands, their many triumphs, their excellent jousting. A never-ending stream of braggadocio.

Much to my surprise, seemingly in one gesture, he slashes the woven bars of the trap, pulls me out and up, and hoists me onto the back of his horse. *Swoosh.* And there I am, thrown over the horse's rump like a blanket.

Dizzy with the quick movement and the strangeness of it all, I don't have time to protest as he begins to lead the stallion out of the mire.

All my life I have felt that I was living in a glass case, a kind of ornament, protected. I strained against the boundaries. And now, in this place, it seems that glass has been shattered.

I hold on for dear life as the horse begins to gallop.

I have been freed. I have been captured yet again.

9

―――◆◆◆―――

THE SUN HAS dropped down from the sky, casting a long shadow, by the time we reach what appears to be our stop.

How to describe it? At the edge of the trees lies the side of a mountain. An entire panorama, to be exact. And on that panorama, scattered throughout, are men operating some kind of exploding thing, shooting dust and dirt out with the sound of each blast. And these blasts are not soft, mind you. Each one forces you to wince and want to take cover. The danger of the blasts seems completely unimportant to the men on the mountain as they each scurry around, taking this thing here and that thing over there. Collecting, dividing, collecting again.

At the foot of the mountain there are women and children up to their knees in what appears to be a muddy river, sifting and separating whatever it is that is being blasted off the mountain and quickly spirited down to them. The whole operation is a frantic, rushed, toiling affair, and that is why no one seems to notice as our horse approaches.

I take the opportunity to adjust myself on the stallion, so that I am at least upright. Of course, this means now I am sitting behind my new flimsily dressed companion, but I refuse to be draped over the back end of a horse any longer.

My companion takes note of this.

I catch his look. "What? You didn't think I knew how to ride? I can assure you I've been riding since I was only five winters."

He only reacts with a confused look.

Yes, of course, why would he speak my language?

My companion now turns to the scene before us and whistles to a man by the side of the muddy river, who comes dashing over.

"Jaika?"

The man points to the other side of the clearing.

My companion nods and takes the reins, leading the stallion in that direction. As we reenter the forest, I look back, watching the men scurrying around and the children with their bare legs in the muddy water. What on earth could they be doing in there? And why? These poor children, some no taller than a fowl, not a smile among them.

Of course, I am wondering what this word *Jaika* means. I decide to test my companion, investigating further.

I tap him on the shoulder. "Jaika?"

He looks back, stunned. And then a sort of vaguely amused expression comes over his bronzed face. He turns back around and proceeds in the direction of "Jaika."

Is it a person? A place?

It seems no difference if I wonder or not; I shall find out soon enough.

10

―――◆―――

IT'S ALMOST NIGHTFALL. The sun has already gone down below the horizon and there appears to be one star out already, despite the fact that the sky has not yet turned itself black.

In this light, it's difficult to tell exactly what this place is. There are many little fires about. Candlelight. Torches hung. But *here* isn't a place fixed horizontally, but rather vertically. Here is the side of a cliff, a wall of stone. And within that wall of stone, carved into it . . . is a rather elaborate collection of dwellings. Lit up by hearth and candle, a shimmering village in the sky. The cliff and the firelight reach far beyond, into the dimming horizon. There must be hundreds of them, each one, each opening containing a little hustle and bustle within. A scurry here. Little legs there. A loaf of bread there. These are dwellings. Homes.

I look up in wonder at this enchanting elevated village, like something out of Scholar Gwilt's myths. My companion looks at me, smiles to himself, taking me in. Now he says,

"Jaika."

He dismounts our horse and then gently helps me down.

From somewhere in the trees I hear the hoot of an owl, *whooo-whooo*, a gentle heralding of nighttime.

Yes, I should be getting back home. But instead, my heart seems to soar out of my chest as I look around at the twinkling hamlet in the sky and, for the first time, wonder if maybe this isn't a dream after all.

This thought is somehow compounded by the two little effervescent girls, dressed in some sort of rough fabric, now giggling and barreling toward me. They don't seem to mind running around barefoot, with dirt on their cheeks and under their fingernails. They are both adorned, it seems, with a myriad of bracelets made of vines and wildflowers.

The way they come running over, it's as if I'm their long-lost sister! I stand stunned as they both lay hands on my devastated blue velvet dress. They peer inches away from every gold thread, every embroidered flower, every bit of lace. They find something new, then alert each other promptly, both of them staring in awe at the gown, commenting, nudging, giggling.

My companion looks on, taking the measure of my reaction. But the girls are so sweet and exuberant and curious that it's contagious, and I find myself laughing and smiling back at them. Maybe I *am* their long-lost sister. One of the girls takes off her wildflower bracelet and proffers it to me.

"Oh my goodness. Thank you. That is so kind of you." I take the bracelet and place it around my wrist.

But the moment is gone, as my strange language seems to have startled them. They look at each other, then at my companion. He gives them a reassuring nod, and they seem relieved.

Now they look back at me and, suddenly shy, run away out into the darkness, presumably up to whatever tiny dwelling in the wall of stone belongs to them.

My companion comes forward, taking me by the wrist. We go, past the glimmering lights above. We walk farther and farther, hearing the voices of the children in each of their suspended abodes, giggles, songs, and even a bit of crying. The smell of something like bread and pungent, sweet spice punctuate the air.

At the end of this promenade, my companion stops, motioning up to a set of steps carved into the stone. Is it another trap? I hesitate, the wheels turning in my head. I hardly know this man. If my mother were here she'd grab me by the hand and whisk me away. If my father were here my companion would probably already have his head on the chopping block, or at least be shackled by the royal guards.

But they are not here.

And at the thought I feel a lightness in my chest, an expansion of my breath that I have not felt ever before.

My companion throws his hands in the air in exasperation and makes his way up the stone steps, leaving me all by my lonesome. I look around me at the possibilities . . . not much here. The many different families all seem to be tucked into their respective dwellings, happy to draw the day down together. And out here, with only the owl to keep me company, I fear what could be lurking. For instance, those wretched brutes that ensnared me in their net. Are there other cages and traps set about? Are there more of those camouflaged creatures? Of course there might be. Why wouldn't there be?

The moon is waning tonight, offering little light and less solace. I exhale, knowing what I am going to do before doing it. My feet seem to make the final decision with their movements up the steps, and suddenly I am scrambling to find my companion.

At the top of the stairs, in one of the highest caverns, there he is in a rather spartan yet not entirely unpleasant little abode. There's a wooden table and one wooden chair. A fire in a kind of amber-colored furnace. My companion turns to me and points to the other side of the dwelling, where there is a little bench with woolen blankets piled high, a sort of mattress. What is he thinking? But he points over next to him, another such bench, and points to himself . . . as if to say, "Here's where I sleep."

He hands me a piece of bread, a rather large one, and I am now just realizing I am famished. I take the bread, trying not to look too greedy, and walk over to my designated bench. If I were by myself I would devour it in one swoop, but, alas, I've been trained never to do so. I eat my bread like a lady, except when he's not looking, in which case I gulp it down.

Now he offers me a metal cup with a reddish sort of drink in it. Quine? But no, I taste it; it's sweet. A slight taste of strawberry. He doesn't seem to be considering me much as he extinguishes the fire and unceremoniously lies down flat on his bench, on the other side of the room. Now it is almost pitch-black.

It's an odd thing, to just decide to fall asleep in a faraway place with a stranger. It's surely not advisable. But what other choice is there? I have to assume he has some sort of plan. Isn't that always the way it is? There is a plan and you follow it, hoping it's a good plan. Never wanting to make a fuss.

Yes. That is the way it has always been and that is the way it will always be. They make a plan. You follow. You don't make a fuss.

From the other side of the room, I can hear the sound of my companion breathing deep, drifting off to sleep. And here I will do the same. The length of the day, the ride, finally weigh down on me.

And yet. I cannot help but wonder when I start off to dreamland, will I not wake up back home, back in the pastel castle surrounded by servants, my mother, and possibly a doctor or two by her side? Will I be sad then? To have left this world of hanging vines and twinkling lights and little girls with bright eyes and wildflowers for adornments? Will I want to be back there, where the ladies embellish themselves like peacocks and the members of court spread vile gossip in snickering whispers?

And what of my companion? Would I be relieved to be rid of him? Surely I would. That's the reasonable emotion. But somehow, I'm not so certain.

There is something comforting about his silence. Undoubtedly it's better than the endless warbling of my cousins, Prissy and Bolanda, back in Fairyland. What would they make of all this? Prissy would probably have perished by now. Or been eaten. I smile to myself at the thought.

Outside, the owl *whooo-whoooo*s me to sleep as my eyes grow heavy, dimming down in the moonlight.

Alas, sleep overtakes me. The dream is over.

11

MY EYES ARE still closed when I hear it. The voice.

"Can you hear me? Do you understand me?" It's a female voice, lilting and gentle.

My language! My language is being spoken! The comfort of it stirs me up from my slumber. I am home!

"Yes. Oh yes. I do understand! Oh, thank God. I could kiss you!"

But I do not wake up back in the pastel palace. Far from it. The woman above me stands unmoved, certainly not desiring me to kiss her.

"I am Keela. Guardian and steward of the Cliffs of Grey. And you? What is your name? Where are you from?" she asks, and there is a definite accent in her voice. Not the sound of my mother tongue, but somehow alluring.

Unlike the rough, makeshift clothes I've seen, she is draped in a kind of woven robe. The yarn of this attire is braided this way and that way, leaving a great deal of her golden skin exposed, but there's an elegance to this gown, despite the fact it would elicit gasps in the court of my father. Her hair is long, braided. Her skin is painted a kind of metallic shade, somewhere between pewter and gold. She looks much like a kind of golden statuette.

There's another thing about her, too, a kind of intangible aura. A sort of taciturn wisdom to her, as if she is not just herself, but all her ancestors who came before her. A presence large enough to jump centuries.

"My name is Princess Elizabeth Clementine DeBoudas Roix. I am from the Roix Kingdom. Do you know where that is? Or how I could get back there? Could you possibly take me there? Or could someone guide me . . . home?"

It's at this minute I notice my erstwhile companion, standing near the door, respectfully. Ah, I can see by his stance the woman before me is a person of honor, of great prestige.

Above him!

Yes, that's right. He is looking up to her the way subjects back in my world look up to my father, the king. But she is not a king. She can't be.

This world becomes more intriguing by the minute.

"Home? Where is home?" she inquires.

"The Roix Kingdom. In the middle of Glen du Monte. Between the Carvathine Sea and the Willow Forest."

She wrinkles her brow a bit. "Curious." She looks back at my companion.

"Svan, fel ash est plack?"

It's at this moment I realize my companion's name is Svan. Yes. It suits. He is definitely a Svan.

The pewter-gold empress turns back to me. "I have never

heard of this place. And, you see, I've heard of all places."

She pauses, perhaps to let that sink in. It's certainly not a good sign.

She comes closer to me forthwith, sizing me up in a way that is exceedingly uncomfortable, as if I am a dress on a rack.

She backs up now, having taken my sum. "No. You cannot return to . . . *Roix*," she says, the word odd on her tongue. "You will stay here and fight."

She looks back at Svan and gives a definitive nod. Her decision made, she strides out of our little dwelling on to who knows where, perhaps a dip in a gold-gilded lake.

Svan looks at me and gives a kind of shrug, as if to say, "The leader has spoken."

"Fight? Fight whom?" I ask Svan.

But of course, he can't speak my language any more than I can speak his.

Now the two little girls come rushing in as if they were sent, both of them grabbing a respective hand and leading me out of the cave abode into a kind of clearing, where there are a few wooden tables arranged in a circle.

At each table sits an assortment of families: mothers with their babies, fathers with their boys, sisters next to sisters, whispering into each other's ears. It's a sweet feeling, these families at table. Warm. Homey. As if a kind of invisible blanket is wrapped around us.

I'm inclined to join them, but suddenly I am led forward by the two little girls and placed purposefully in the middle of the circle.

Wait.

The knives on the table seem to glimmer in the morning sun.

I have a fleeting, absurd thought:

Are these blades meant for me?

12

IT'S AN INTERESTING feeling, trying to figure out if you are the main course at a festive brunch. I can honestly say it's not one I've experienced ever before. The closest I can come is the feeling of playing hide-and-seek right before you are tagged. Just raise the stakes by approximately one million.

Before I know it, there begin to be what sound like questions; questions being thrown out into the air by Keela, commanding the crowd. After each question, there is a general looking around, a few nods here, a few shrugs there, culminating in a kind of simultaneous pounding on the wooden tables, either with fists or with the metal cups everyone is drinking from. It's all quite a raucous affair and I find myself looking over to my only possible advocate and friend, Svan, for some kind of reassurance.

Svan does not disappoint. He nods at me with a half smile.

It's possible there may also be some kind of sparkle in his eye, but, of course, he is an almost-naked wildling in a faraway land so, obviously, I am not noticing any of that.

"Do you mind? Terribly sorry to interrupt . . . but what exactly is being discussed?" I summon up the courage to ask the pewter woman, Keela.

"They are wondering where you came from," Keela answers.

"As I told you, I—"

"But how? From which direction?" she prods.

"Well, I suppose . . . from up? I guess?" I gesture, pointing to the air.

At this gesture there are gasps and a collective murmur. Somehow, it means something.

Keela quickly quiets everyone down. "Gehn si nekt! Da wan auldveisen!"

The group goes silent, continues to confer in looks and glances.

"Sorry?" I ask her. "What precisely . . . were you saying just then?"

"They have magical notions." She shrugs. "They wonder if you are The One Who Fell from the Sky."

"And . . . what does that, indeed, mean?" I ask.

"It is a prophecy . . . a fairy tale. It means they are foolish," she admonishes.

This appears to be the end of the discussion. Now the two sweet little girls come giggling back, leading me by the hand to sit next to them on one of the wooden benches. There appears to be a kind of semicircle formed in anticipation of some kind of event. Perhaps a stage? Or a performance?

One of the tiny girls runs off and returns quickly with something that looks like mashed legumes and some bread. The other girl returns with some beverage, a cider of sorts, more bitter than

I'm used to. But manners dictate I must be grateful and savor every bite. The two girls wait to see my reaction. I nod and smile, rubbing my belly in the universal gesture of *delicious*. They look pleased and their effervescent bright eyes seem to carry all the sunlight in them, shaming the sky.

I notice a small boy with ash-colored hair walking quite purposefully around the camp, collecting pails and bowls of differing sizes and weights. He somehow seems to feel my eyes upon him and comes over without prompting.

"Do you happen to have a pail, or even a bowl?" he asks in my language! "A bucket?"

"H-How do you know my language?" I ask the wee boy.

"Why shouldn't I know it?" He squints. "Do you have a pail, then?"

"No . . ."

And with that, the young boy is off, clearly possessed by his bucket-collecting mission.

Before I can call after him, Keela returns and seats herself next to me. "I see you've met my son." She smirks.

"The boy?" I turn to her.

"Yes. The boy," she answers. "His name is Wyeth. My son."

"He's certainly . . . preoccupied," I tell her.

"Yes, well. He's much more interested in his experiments than anything else. Trust me. There's no use in stopping him once he becomes fascinated."

"A wonderful quality, I should think," I ponder.

"You are in luck." She changes the subject. "Today is a rare event. Today is Gottlek, a celebration of the divine. The great creator and the source of all light."

She pauses to gauge my reaction.

"Then I am, indeed, lucky," I assuage her.

"Yes. Do not be scared," she advises. "It involves a lot of fire."

At this I hesitate but feel rather grateful to have her next to me, an interpreter for the events.

The celebration does not disappoint. And there is no lack of chimes, drums, and most of all . . . flames. Hurled through the air! The opening is a dance to commemorate the first light. The second, a dance to commemorate the creation of humans. And, my personal favorite, a dance to commemorate the divinity of all women, as earthly manifestations of the great creator. I can't help but marvel at this. In my kingdom, outside of the nobility, women are seen as pitiable, something to be tolerated but certainly not respected.

And yet here, the idea is that women are somehow . . . something else.

"This is an important part of the celebration," Keela tells me. "It is called the Lonely Man."

As I watch, the stage is taken by none other than . . . Svan! Most of the dancers are men, strangely. And I note that even the young men, boys of not fifteen winters, are included in some of the choreography.

Svan starts the scene solo . . . I'm assuming he is the titular "lonely man." But now he does something peculiar. He begins to pantomime looking out at the audience, out at all of us, searching . . . searching . . . for something. Or someone. At last, he finds his subject and happily lurches out to the crowd, throwing what he has been searching for over his shoulder. Can you guess what it is? Yes, exactly. A woman.

And can you guess who it is? Well, that is a surprise . . . as the woman is me.

Before I can protest, I am in the middle of the dirt stage whilst the audience, and especially the two little girls, is laughing and cheering. Even Keela herself deigns to give a slight look of amusement.

But it's dangerous! I can't help but shrink a bit as Svan begins to throw the flaming objects all around me, now to some of the other performers emerging from the wings, now to more of the performers, as the fire dancers seem to be multiplying onstage. The flames are everywhere. I could not step one tiny baby step to either side without being engulfed. My countenance must give away my nervousness, as the audience continues to chortle and guffaw. Whether they are laughing because I have nothing to fear or whether they are laughing because I might die, I do not know. Whatever the case, the fire throwing continues but now, mercifully, begins to abate. As this flaming showstopper dwindles down, the performers begin exiting the dirt stage one by one . . . now, finally, leaving only Svan and me.

He smiles and gestures for me to leave the stage. Which I do, gratefully.

Now he sits alone on the stage again, seeming to contemplate the woman he somehow discovered, then lost. Now he devolves into a dance of sorrow, a denouement dwindling down until he is sat there, huddled up in the middle of the dirt. Now, gently and without sound, the other performers tiptoe in and cover his body with a kind of thistle blanket, disguising him as part of the dirt, returning him to the dirt. And now there is no more fire, and now there are no more drums . . . no more chimes. Just silence.

And the only thing you can see is the shrunken pile of dirt, and the only thing you can hear is the wind whipping off the cliffs.

It's . . . astonishing.

Finally, after the poignant moment has offered itself in full, Keela stands, gesturing to the dirt stage. Now Svan comes up from within the dung-colored blanket and the other performers come out. I erupt in applause, jumping to my feet. The rest of the audience also applauds, hooting and hollering. The two little girls, who climb up on the bench next to me, start clapping their hands against my body, as if this must be part of the applause as well. And even though it's silly, this dance with me at the center of it, and not at all what one would expect, it is somehow thrilling.

Svan looks at me across the mass of cliff dwellers and gives me a kind of nod. Before I have time to interpret this, Keela is in front of me, her commanding presence not something to be avoided.

"Now you must rest," she informs me. "Tomorrow you will begin your training."

"Training?" I say, robbed of my delight.

"Yes. Training," she adds. "You must learn to fight."

And with that, she nods and simply glides away, disappearing into the gathering.

The two little girls look up at me, both of them patting my hand gently, as if to console me. Forthwith they giggle and begin leading me out of the throng. Now away, along the side of the cliff face, to a cave farther down the canyon, away from Svan's dwelling. A flash of disappointment comes over me as I realize I don't know if or when I might see him again.

The abode the girls now lead me to is, impossibly, even more Spartan than my accommodations last night. Furthermore, in a neat row next to the door is an array of wrought-iron tools that upon closer inspection appear to be . . . weapons. One seems to involve a ball fastened to a chain. There is an assortment of clubs of various sizes—some spiked, others bumpy on the end. A greater assortment of knives, and some very rudimentary but sinister axes.

The two sweet girls hand me some kind of wool bedding, leading me to the mat on the bench at the back of the cave. I make sure to keep my countenance pleasant. Never mind about the grisly tools of death hanging just nearby.

The two precocious girls return my smile and then leave me to my musings.

The golden woman, Keela, said I begin tomorrow. To train. To fight.

But what? Or whom?

And as I have specifically been raised NOT to fight, and do not care to harm anyone, this has all suddenly become a bit too . . . settled. And, judging by the gruesome decor, a bit too real.

And yet, these people, these strangers, have welcomed me in a place where I have nowhere else to turn. What do I do?

As if in a kind of cosmic answer, I hear something below, a stirring and then a commotion. At first, I mistake it for simple chatter . . . but now the edge in it becomes apparent. Aggression, and even fear. As I look below, I see a confrontation. On one side, a few men from the Cliffs of Grey. On the other side, two of the swamp men, painted in their many shades of green and brown.

They are having a kind of argument, escalating at each moment, their hands gesticulating madly. Finally, one of the Cliff people has had enough. He steps forward and, before I realize what exactly is happening and certainly before I can avert my eyes . . . he attacks both swamp people at once. This would seem like an impossible match, but, swiftly, they are dispatched to the ground. I gasp in astonishment as the heads of both swamp men roll off their bodies.

I am propelled backward by my repulsion, my hand covering my mouth.

How could this be? Did I just imagine it?

Beheaded!

What kind of depraved company am I keeping? What manner of place is this? Violence is always wrong, and *murder*? I want no part of such activities!

I step forward tentatively, peeking out down below, hoping to realize this was some sort of illusion. Or perhaps a play of some kind. Theater.

But no, the appalling sight remains below, with not even an attempt from the Cliff people to move the two ghastly bodies.

Horror!

I cannot believe I have allowed myself to be lured into such an inhumane coterie. Why have I been fooled by just a few kindnesses? Is that enough to win me over, even to the most barbaric of clans? What have I done?

I lean against the cave wall, somehow unable to stand or muster the decision to sit.

No. No. I cannot stay in this place. What if these wild folk turn on me? What if I am the one to be next beheaded? To what other beastly acts are they prone?

And is this what is meant? When I am asked "to fight"? Am I meant to decapitate strangers and then carry on as if nothing happened?

No, I need to find my way home—back to Roix—somehow.

It's a guilty thing to be welcomed so warmly to a place and then have to sneak away like an ungrateful prowler. It certainly doesn't feel like an honorable course. Much more like a betrayal.

And yet.

If I do not creep away, I may find my own head on the ground sooner than later.

I resolve to wait until the sun sets itself down in the trees and the waning moon has hung for a few hours.

In the wee of the night, in the witching hour, I will take my leave. And I will, I *must*, find a way home.

13

A KING'S JOURNAL

This particular writing, these scribbles, happen to come in quite different circumstances than my last. There's rather a panic here, I'm afraid. My consul has informed me that my daughter, the princess, was found sometime in the wee hours of the night, in some dreadful corner of the castle . . . asleep.

Asleep. For lack of a better word.

An otherworldly slumber.

Perhaps a trance.

For she will not wake. Not with a forceful nudge or a blast from a trumpet or even a pail of cold water thrown about her head. It is a kind of sleep I have never before witnessed.

Of course, my wife, the queen, is in a terrible state. She refuses to leave the side of the princess, and I suppose I don't blame her. She is a woman, after all.

I have told her we will find the finest healers and soothsayers in all the kingdoms. We will spare no expense. We will search far and wide for a cure.

However, each time I try to calm her, she simply sobs more, as if my words somehow add to the problem. To make matters worse, of late, she not only has lost all her mirth . . . but she seems to be blaming me for the bewildering, unfortunate occurrence. She has even dared to blame me for my insistence on an early marriage for our dear princess! As if I had a choice!

But, of course, I could not tell her.

The secret.

In her current state . . .

How could I tell her . . . about the curse?

14

IN MY MIND, I envisioned my daring escape in graceful terms—a swirl here, a pirouette there—but in reality it seems to be playing out in a much clumsier fashion. I hug the side of the mountain full of cave dwellings, my already-ruined dress snagging here and pulling there. Obviously, this frock of mine, constructed for long castle promenades, was not built for hanging brambles and clinging vines. Having said that, I do surprise myself by somehow scrambling my way down nearly to the ground before slipping and falling in a most unroyal way into a pile of hay. Here I take a moment to sigh in humiliation, catch my breath, and see if anyone heard my most inelegant fall.

Happily, the night has decided to give itself only to me, and I am on my way into the thicket of trees and God only knows what else.

How I ache to be home, safe, surrounded by my books, the giggles of Rose and Suzette floating to my ears as they peek out the window down below at whatever new male of the species they find handsome or devastating or ridiculous. How I long for tea with my mother, who held me for two fortnights as a baby. . . .

How I wish she could hold me now. Keep me someplace without all this barbary. Bring me home.

The moon now makes its small arc across the sky as I continue away from the cliff dwelling. Forthwith I realize something is following me. A twig snap here, a swish of a branch there. Yet every time I look back, there is no one behind me. Nothing.

But there is the *feeling* of someone—watching me, stalking me in the forest—a viewer of my elaborate tale of woe.

I come to a rest, standing upright against a tree, holding my breath just to listen, to try to capture the sound of this mysterious watcher.

It's not quite whispering that I am hearing. More scuttling. A scurrying sound.

Yet, every single time I stop, so does the sound.

I decide to perform a trick. I will pretend to hurry through the trees and then halt abruptly, fooling whomever this is into revealing themself.

I dash off through the trees, and then stop in a blink.

Scuttle scuttle.

Aha! I turn around and capture my hunter in the act!

But it is very much a relief.

As my stalker is merely a blackbird, staring at me from the branches above.

"Shoo. Shoo." I try to wave it off. "Go, get out of here! Begone!"

But the blackbird stares at me, calm as can be.

"Go on. I don't have all night to stand here being stared at. Shoo!" I wave it off again.

And now the blackbird flies off into the night sky.

I breathe a sigh of relief and chastise myself for being so paranoid. What on earth was I thinking?

It was only a blackbird.

But in a moment, the bird returns.

"Indeed. Why on earth are you pestering me with your presence?" I query the blackbird, who contemplates me from his perch.

And then another lands.

And another.

They gaze at each other, and then . . . look at me. At this moment I know I must be going mad. It appears as if these blackbirds are having some sort of symposium.

I stand, staring at them. They stare back at me, mute.

"Well, are you impressed?" I continue. "Perhaps you have never seen a princess before. My congratulations. Please, no need to curtsy or bow, as we happen to be in the forest and, quite frankly, you are birds."

And now the first blackbird crooks his neck. Quizzical. The other blackbirds chirp something and, as if in agreement, the blackbirds promptly fly away. Just like that. As if somehow, I have answered their question.

I look at the moon in the sky. "And you? What do you think? Are you going to begin following me, too?"

The moon does not respond.

It's very silly of me, I know, to be talking to celestial bodies and blackbirds. But the thicket is foreboding, lonely, and somehow the conversation with myself eases my fear, lifting me out of my dread and into a more contemplative existence.

An absurd little trifle. A game. A way of making light in the darkness.

Forward now, dear princess.

Except, not a moment later I seem to hear . . . a voice . . . coming from the direction the blackbirds flew. A sentiment whispered by the wind:

"I have dreamt you."

Nonsense. The wind could not have whispered an entire phrase!

I turn, petrified, trying to stay my nerves.

But there is no one in the darkness around me.

I imagine I must be hearing things. Yes, my mind is playing tricks on me, so tired am I from this journey.

It is only that, nothing more.

15

IT HAS BEEN exactly twenty-four hours since I made my decision and, in those hours, I have slunk out of the cliff village, scurried into the trees, and followed what appeared to be a trail, leading out from the other side of the clearing.

No, it's not the way Svan and I came. That is true. But there didn't seem to be much back that way except those belligerent painted creatures who trapped me (some of whose party the cliff dwellers beheaded), as well as that woeful panorama I first came to with the incessant blasting and the children wading up to their knees in muck.

So, this way it is. The road unknown. It behooves me not to think about the infinite dangers that may lie ahead. Of course, it's possible that whatever lies ahead is just fine. Wonderful, even. Gentler than the muddy forest at my back.

These are the kinds of things one tells oneself, you see, to keep going.

The forest does appear to be thinning out as the very first morning light blossoms into dawn, the birds serenading me through the canopy of leaves. Yes, the trees seem to be stepping away from me, stepping away from each other.

I'm tempted to hum a little tune, which is always a calming way to pass time, but who knows what such noise might attract. A dragon in waiting perhaps. Another cage falling from above.

So, silence then as I make my way through, the birds and the willows swaying their performance. And now the trees part completely, like two enormous green curtains, and present before me the most powerful sight yet from this mysterious realm.

A lake. Or a *former* lake. As far as the eye can see, an enormous white, glaring lake bed. But now there is no water, not a drop. Just a kind of chalky floor reaching out longingly into the horizon. As if the water has left it there, alone. Abandoned.

I, too, feel abandoned. There is nothing before me but wasteland!

I stand for a moment, not knowing whether to turn back, to traverse this white desert, or to simply surrender and return to whatever grim fate awaits me in the forest.

Yes, I do have water; I brought it with me in a kind of calfskin from my cave. But is it enough? How could there be a lake so dry? The wind whisks along, whipping up a bit of white dust, almost like talc, into the air.

I hold my breath against it. Oh dear.

The only way to get back home is to find somewhere, or someone, that can lead me back there . . . back to my parents, who are probably apoplectic about my disappearance by now. A wave of sadness washes over me as I think about the panic my poor mother must be going through. My father will attempt to be strong and conduct himself with some sort of decorum. But my mother, with her heart a hundred times the size of her body, is probably throwing plates across the dining hall by now.

I know. She seems demure. But did you know she once set fire to a highwayman? The rogue was attempting to rob her coach between kingdoms on the treacherous roads from Flivanci to Roix. She was accompanied only by the coachman and her maid-servant. The sun was setting and, as everyone knows, you simply cannot be on the roads after dark. She had the quick thought, she told me, almost an instinct, to throw one of the decorative torches at the blackguard. Apparently, the torch only grazed this rapscallion. However, he was so discombobulated by the sudden onset of the flames that he gave the driver enough opportunity to flee.

As you can imagine, my father always shakes his head at this story. I'm never certain whether it is in disbelief or pride . . . or something in between.

But my mother has always been passionate, especially where it concerns her only child. In fact, there was a time she told me, shockingly, I was *the only thing she really cared about*. Not gold, not the castle, not even my father, the king. She just said, "No, no . . . that is all poppycock and pomp. It's you. You are my heart. My very heart outside my body." She laughed then, and said, "It's not fair!" I laughed with her, and now, in the middle of this white arid lake, I find myself smiling simply thinking of her. Longing to be back home.

It is with that smile and that thought of the kindness of my mother, the light she emanates, that I continue. I have to make it back to her.

Back to our kingdom of pale pinks and baby blues.

Yes, I must make it back to Roix.

My mother awaits.

Once I find my way home, I will throw myself into her arms and I will feel that feeling, the feeling of being loved, cherished, as if nothing could ever go wrong and I am cradled, cared for, carried.

But a blackbird breaks my thought with its song. It occurs to me that perhaps this bird is mocking me.

Tears sting the corners of my eyes.

I am not cradled in this place as I have been before.

No, until I can find a way out, I must cradle myself. But I do not know if such a thing is even possible.

16

———————

THE SUN HAS wearily made an arc across the sky and, under that arc, I have made my way halfway across this dry bed. Each hour I think I am making progress, yet it feels almost like the arid lake bed is stretching itself out farther, an illusion, rendering my journey endless and infinite. Impossible to complete.

Before the sun decides to set itself to sleep, I will have to find a place, a kind of shelter, to sleep underneath the canopy of stars. But this is a bind I have gotten myself into; each direction as I look around—north, south, east, west—looks back at me, mocking me with the impossibility of finding protection from whatever or whomever goes bump in the night.

I am dizzy, dehydrated, desperate for sustenance. I should never have left the Cliff people. Yes, this was a terrible decision. Made in haste.

I count one, two, three steps forward into the nothingness when I hear it: a sound I would recognize anywhere. For unlike the strange language of the swamp creatures, and unlike the raucous merriment of the cavern dwellers, this is a familiar sound, a royal sound.

You see, this is the sound of horses. And not just horses. This is the sound of a horse and carriage.

As I turn in the direction of the sound behind me, I discover a sight startling in its beauty and artistry.

There, on the white salt sea, a tiny toy carriage in the distance, barreling toward me, the hooves of the horses shaking the dry salt bed. But not just any carriage. A white carriage, white as the salt sea itself. Camouflaged, almost, despite the galloping and the sound of the horses.

There it is, getting closer, and I notice that both stallions are white, too. And now I see, with an inaudible gasp, that even the carriage driver is dressed in white, from head to toe. A showy kind of white, adorned with lace and silk, baroque in its excess.

And, yes, his skin, too, is chalky—painted the color of the salt, the sea, and the carriage.

As the miraculous vision approaches, it dawns on me that I have been standing here gawking like a twit, when I best be preparing myself, or even protecting myself, from whatever it is that is coming toward me. Yet somehow, the flamboyance of the uninvited guest placates me. As if there is something in the silk and brocade that consoles.

I look down at my torn, sullied dress. Oh dear. This will not do. Whoever they are, they will not recognize me as one of their own. Not hardly.

This realization hits me just as the horses come to an abrupt halt.

The carriage sits there a moment, still, as I watch, frozen. The two of us in the middle of this white seabed, statues posed for a portrait.

Now the elaborately engraved door of the ivory carriage opens.

I wait in anticipation for what feels like an eternity when a white shoe dips itself out of the interior.

Now the ankle and then a leg, torso, and head. All adorned to such an extreme, it would make a countess blush. Silks, lace, brocade, toile. Fabrics I do not even recognize.

The passenger seems to be talking to himself on the way out the door as he dusts himself off, apparently not noticing me.

"By all the gods!" he barks. "Remind me never to hire a driver from Noove! Do you think there's a bump or gulley in the road you did *not* barrel into?!"

My language! He is speaking my language!

I let out a gasp, and this immediately draws his attention, his head popping up at high command. He also has a face painted white. His skin is ivory, yes, and his hair is a kind of white powder wig. Out of the corners of the wig, I detect the color of his actual hair. Ash. Somewhere between blond and brown, as if it can't decide quite what to do with itself.

"Well!" He sets his eyes on me, a kind of slate blue. "Well, well. What exactly do we have here . . . ?"

It's not the most comforting of tones. In fact, it's a bit like that of a wolf perusing a flock of sheep.

"Why, this is quite extraordinary!" he decrees. "A damsel in distress in the middle of the Blanche Sea? Is she really here? Or is she some sort of mirage? If I didn't know any better, I'd say I've drunk too much quine."

It's at this point I realize it would be pointless to run. A tardy realization.

He makes his way closer, vain in his gait. "Well, does the apparition speak? Is she a specter from the Wraithen? Or a lost jewel from the Sapphire? Or is she simply some kind of mute? Rejected from her kin? A dunce? A nitwit?"

Not sure how to reply, I suddenly hear my mother's voice: *You are a princess. That is something you carry in your bearing, in your grace, and in your voice. Most important, of course, in your heart. A princess must never be flustered. A princess makes others flustered.*

Now my spine arranges itself, straightening from the small of my back up to the tip of my head, as if held by a string.

"My name is Princess Elizabeth Clementine DeBoudas Roix of the Kingdom of Roix. House of LeBrazeiux. Second house of DeBoudas. My father is king and protector of the Roix Kingdom. My mother, erstwhile Countessa Alexandra DeBoudas, is queen."

A silence in the seabed, even the dust sets itself down.

"HAHAhahaha!" His laughter kicks the pale dust back up again. "My, oh my! Well, well." And now he bows an overly pompous bow, tipping his hat and placing it regally on his heart.

"So. This disheveled creature, found in the middle of the Blanche Sea, just north of the Kreff Forest, is a princess. Well, doesn't that make me the luckiest noble this side of the Wraithen?"

"*You* are a noble?" I ask, unconvinced. Although, to be true, he does have the unsullied features and delicate face one might associate with the class.

"But of course. I mean, I can't prove it. But now that I think of it, neither can you," he quips.

"I have nothing to prove to you, noble or not," I respond.

At this, he takes me in, from head to toe, marking each inch of my dress and my bearing.

"It's possible I have found a diamond in a dirt box." He squints at me. "Where are you heading, Princess, might I ask?"

"I need to get back to my kingdom of Roix. Do you know it? Do you know the way there?" I try not to sound too desperate.

He thinks for a moment. "My dearest princess, if I knew, I'm sure I wouldn't tell you. However, I do not know. So, happily, I do not have to lie. In any case, you can't stay here."

At this, he turns on a dime and heads back to the carriage. He nods at the driver and then hops back in.

I stand there a moment, in a kind of blind panic.

But now he dips his head out again. "Well . . . are you coming?"

"But . . . I don't know who you are or anything about you," I declare. "How could I possibly just—"

"My dear. In two hours, the sun will be completely gone from the sky and the moon will offer you little in the way of light, as it's just a sliver tonight, and in this darkness you will be plagued by dregs and cannibals, who roam these parts with a vengeance, looking for food. Not to mention the giant lizards. The odd enormous spider. You will be considered a feast by one and all."

I contemplate this with a shudder.

"So, if I were you, I would quickly pirouette over here and hop into this transport before the sun descends one more degree and the three of us are left to fend for ourselves against the barbarians." He smiles, gestures, and adds, "Unless, of course, you *wish* to sacrifice yourself to the gods this evening."

A flash of something between rage and annoyance runs through me and I quickly march toward the carriage.

"Well then, if I must," I add. "But I do insist you stay on the other side of the carriage."

"Of course, *Your Highness*. What kind of philistine do you think I am?" he asks. "Besides, I hate sharing a carriage bench, particularly with princesses."

I'm not entirely sure he's telling the truth about these dregs and cannibals. Or his distaste for princesses. And yet. If I am going to die, I'd prefer to die in this elegant ivory carriage than on a spit in the middle of this white salt sea.

I'm not sure what that says about me, but at this point, I am unsure that I care.

17

OF COURSE, I should be trembling in this situation, in a strange carriage in a foreign land with an unfamiliar person who may or may not have the best of intentions.

And, although there is nothing in him even pretending to sympathize with my situation, I find myself feeling oddly at home.

Maybe it's hearing my own language, or perhaps it's his haughty ways . . . a kind of soothing familiarity amidst the chaos. We have many cavalier nobles at home. Dandies in brocade and velvet. They are like castle wallpaper; ubiquitous and full of snark.

"So, pretend princess, tell me what brings a royal creature like you to these doldrums near the world's end?" He leans back in his seat, amused, on the opposite side of the carriage.

The interior of this carriage is certainly the most sumptuous thing I've seen in this alien place. The seat is finely cushioned and there are miniature paintings in oval molding, gold-gilded frames, tiny landscapes with little rosy-cheeked children posing in finery, proud and doughy, in the midst of some lush garden.

"Are we near the world's end?" I inquire.

"Certainly. Frankly, the only things beyond that barren salt sea are the Cliffs of Grey and the swamp, fetid and savage. God only knows what comes after that." He lifts a silver tin cup to his mouth, drinking in.

"Is that water?" I say, trying not to sound too desperate.

"Ah, yes. Where are my manners? Here you are, dear princess. A bit of liquid to sustain you for the journey." He hands me a small tin cup, pouring from a metal flask.

I look down at the cup, but now is not the time to be suspicious. I happen to be dying of thirst.

The taste is rose, water, and something sharp, like ginger.

"What is this liquid?" I ask.

"Oh, it's simple peasant water really. But never fear, there's enough quine in there to eat up anything that could make you ill. As you know, pure water can be poison if not treated in some manner. Also, ale. But you don't seem like the ale type, quite frankly."

"Well, I've never tried it, to be true." I think. "Tell me, what do you know of this 'fetid and savage' swamp and the Cliffs of Grey, as you call them?"

"Nothing, really. No one does. The Cliffs of Grey are filled with barbarians who will slit your throat for sport and the swamp is filled with flesh-eating cannibals, as discussed." He shrugs. "Of course, farther on are the Sapphire Mines, but no one ever goes there. Except the Azelle. Not a race, I'm told, but a religion. And an ancient one at that. People say they're mystical, but if they are, I'm not sure why they ended up being worked to death in the Sapphire."

"The Sapphire?" I sound it out. "What is that?"

"Well, you're far too pristine to need it. But you will one day. Believe me. You will cling to it as we all do. Mark my words," he informs me. "Tell me, have you at least tried quine, or am I going to have to explain that to you as well?"

"Of course; what do you take me for?" I answer, annoyed.

"I take you for a very befuddling character who I happened to find in a random place in the middle of nowhere," he replies. "Tell me. If you really are a princess . . . do you speak Fricella?"

"Of course. Not only do I speak Fricella, but I speak Gurbath, Lilcott, and High Rovelle," I answer, proud.

"You do?" He regards me anew. "Then tell me. What is a pompfe?"

"An apple. Don't insult me," I reply.

"And a manzine?" he asks.

"Also an apple." I roll my eyes.

"Ah! And what about a pompfe de thvierre?" he tests again.

"Again, an apple. But an apple of the earth. Also known as a potato."

I smile.

"I see." He seems rather pleased now. "And do you play the pianette?"

"Of course," I answer.

"Ah! But what about the flauth?" He thinks he's bested me.

"Better than you, I assure you," I reply.

Somehow this titillates him. He seems to like a little spar.

He reaches into the basket on the floor, pulling out a bottle. "Only the finest. I was actually saving this, but it's not every day one picks up a pretend princess."

I don't take the bait.

He fills our metal cups with the pale liquid and ceremoniously toasts. "Cheers—to damsels in distress and the ridiculously dashing men who save them."

"Are you meant to be the ridiculously dashing man in this scenario?" I quip.

"But of course!" He laughs, cheerily clinking tin cups and taking a sip.

It's not a bad quine actually. "Not horrible," I say, savoring. "Long on the tongue."

"Do you like your quines as such, fake princess? Or perhaps a dry Blueche from the Sauvage region?" He smiles, his nose just a little in the air.

As he revels in his own banter, I take him in anew. His jaw is sharp and his features seem in absolutely perfect alignment, as if placed in some ideal ratio in relation to one another. His lips are full, his eyes impeccably proportioned when seen in reference to his strong nose and prominent cheekbones. His smile displays a set of flawless teeth, nearly as white as the powder he wears on his skin. His hair, beneath the wig, appears luxurious in its volume and gleams as it catches the waning light. His eyes are an alarming shade of gray blue, made even more striking by their juxtaposition against his white powdered skin.

Without question, Prissy and Bolanda and the entire court

back in Roux would titter over him should he ever enter the palace. They would blush and giggle, whispering amongst themselves behind their exquisite fans.

And yet, there is something about him that is a bit rough around the edges. I find it hard to believe he is any sort of lord or count or other respectable being. I cannot quite put my finger on it . . . what he might be.

"Do not be intimidated by my vast knowledge of quine, dear possible royal. . . . It is a custom of the kingdom to know, and possess, quine from all regions of the realm. From the fruits of the Blanche, from the vast rolling fields of Sauvage, to the tawny bounty of the Danek hills, and, of course, one simply cannot count themselves a noble without a light, dry white from the farthest regions of Blissley—"

"Would it be terribly rude of me to ask where we are going?" I interrupt.

"Oh, no. Indeed. Not rude in the least." He turns the metal cup in his hands, in a manner not unlike the wheels in his head turning.

"Well, then. Where are we going?" I inquire.

"My darling pretend princess." He looks up from his cup. "I am taking you to the center of everything!"

18

THE ABRUPT HALT of the carriage awakens me from a slumber I don't quite remember entering. I spring up, confused, yet there is no one else here.

The carriage is empty.

Outside, I hear the sound of chattering and realize I don't even know the name of my dapper yet somehow irritating coach mate. But his voice, outside the carriage, seems to be giving orders to the driver.

I dust myself off, not wanting to look more of a fright than I already do in this new place. What did he call it, the center of everything? But before I can prepare myself fully, the door swings open.

There he is, my nameless companion.

"Ah, I see we've woken you. Please, go back to sleep, my dear. We won't be arriving until dawn," he informs me.

"But why are you—" I'm still in a daze, clearly.

"Out here? Well, because who knows who we might find on the road. There are sinister characters in these woods. And, you see, I have a princess to protect." He nods, about to close the door.

"What is your name?" I blurt out. "Sorry, you haven't told me, and as you have pointed out, you did save my life."

"All in good time, my pretty princess." He bows his head and shuts the carriage door.

Pretty. He called me pretty. A blatant lie. And with that one word, I find myself wondering if this all has been another grave miscalculation.

If once again I am to be eaten alive.

19

THE CENTER OF everything.

That is what I wake up to here in the dawn, in the amber glow of morning light. The carriage door is ceremoniously opened, revealing above me a city on the hill, a city, also, of white. White towers, white turrets, white steeples, an entire village in ivory going up up up the hills, culminating in the most beautiful crystal castle I have ever seen.

If I am honest, the *only* crystal castle I have ever seen.

The morning sun seems to be turning the entire village into a kind of peach: each wall, each path, each street a different shade, and changing instantly. Blink and you will miss it.

I stand there, gazing up, transfixed. My carriage mate steps down from the horses, landing next to his driver, who stands on ceremony, holding the door.

"Welcome to Alabastrine," he declares. "Well, what do you think, dear princess? Will this suffice?"

"I should say so," I utter, still stunned by the grandeur of this place.

"We must hurry before it gets too crowded, as it is wont to

do. We're early, luckily, and therefore no one will see you in your shabby attire," he informs me.

Yes, he's right. Everything here is so *clean*. I do not wish to be seen in my present state of dishevelment. That will not do.

Whomever I shall meet here, whatever royals there may be, they are my only hope of getting back to my kingdom. I am sure of it.

If they see me in my present state, they won't recognize me as one of their own. They'll be unlikely to help me in that case. Additionally, it would be mortifying.

"Wherever will I find the appropriate dress for this ivory kingdom?" I ask my carriage mate.

"Oh, don't you worry your pretty little head about that." He smiles, offering a nod to the driver. "See that you take us up the back route, so we might avoid any insipid interactions before we arrive."

The driver nods, leading us up a winding path, through what appear to be mostly side streets and alleys. At the end of a steep and very narrow staircase, we arrive at a mother-of-pearl inlaid, ivory-colored door.

The driver, or perhaps all-around manservant, fusses with a chain of keys, finally finding the right one and opening the door before us.

"After you, Your Pretend Majesty." He bows dramatically as I pass him by, going through the exquisite front entrance and down a long corridor.

He calls after me, "There's a door at the end there, just go through it."

And there is, indeed, a door.

I pause for a moment, not knowing what I will find on the other side.

"Don't be silly, dear girl. It's just my home. One of them, that is," he calls out to me, following now.

I open the door into what can only be described as the dwelling of a madman.

20

IT'S NOT THE layout. Or the lack of adornment. Quite the contrary, the adornment is what constitutes the madness!

Here a bear rug, there a gilded-frame oil painting of a pompous baron. Here a birdcage, there a life-sized statue of an ancient goddess. Although I know very little of this realm and what they may or may not prize, it's obvious to me that this particular collection of curiosities must be worth a small fortune. There is even a bronze treasure chest near the marble fireplace, filled with gold and silver coins.

My stride slows, taking in each infinitesimal detail, until I come to rest facing him. He appears to be enjoying this.

"I know it's not much. But it is, as I said, only a pied-à-terre. If you are nice to me, one day you may see my palace." He takes a seat in an embroidered wingback chair. "Although *I'm sure* it pales in comparison to the castle you call home."

"Why do you have all these peculiar things?" I ask.

"Well, I fancy myself a bit of a collector. I have items here from across each of the seven realms. Why? Do you not like them?" he asks.

"No, it's just a bit odd . . . ," I muse, continuing to look around the cavernous, overflowing room.

His manservant stands at the door, awaiting instruction.

"You may go now. I shall expect you at tea." He waves him off.

Ah. So, now it is just the two of us in this place.

"Don't you think it's high time you tell me your name?" I ask him.

"Ah, yes. My name. Very important." He smiles. "My name is Count Peregrine. Although no one calls me that. Count, that is. Simply Peregrine will do. Of course, Mum used to call me Perry, but you're not allowed, because you're not my mum."

"Very well, I shall call you Peregrine," I reply. "Tell me, where am I to sleep in this higgledy-piggledy place?"

"Don't worry, dear. You have an entire wing to yourself." He gestures. "See, just behind that stuffed giraffe there. You see the door. All for you. There is a bath there and I shall call my housemaid to come and wait on you. That is, if you so desire."

"Oh, no, please don't. I should like to sleep," I demure. "If that's possible."

"Not only is it possible, Your Eminence, it is preferable. Go then. I shall send her in at teatime to prepare you."

"Prepare me," I reply. "Prepare me for what?"

"Well, dinner of course. You can't exactly enter Alabastrine without at least trying a bit of our famous cuisine. Renowned not only for its sherry but also for its superior class of fois grachiere," he says with pride.

"Ah, yes. And shall I go in tatters?" I look down pointedly at my rumpled dress.

"Oh, no. You shall not," he assures me, refusing to reveal anything further.

"Well, this is all very mysterious. But I am tired. Perhaps when I awake you can tell me what I shall be wearing tonight."

I turn and make my way past the enormous taxidermy giraffe.

I cannot see him now, but I feel his eyes on me. And I don't quite know if this fills me with disgust or something else entirely.

I don't think I've ever been quite so bothered by anyone before.

21

***

OUT TO DINNER. Out to dine! I know I should be unhappy, nervous, and wishing to be returned to my world abruptly. But that does not seem to be what is happening, judging by the flutter of my heart and how quickly I jump out of bed at teatime.

Instead, I seem to have the energy of a child the night before Noel.

Anticipation. Perhaps it's just the idea of a fine dinner, which I have not had for days, and the possibility of scintillating conversation. Back in that dreadful swamp, I was the dinner! And then, too, at the Cliffs of Grey, the image of the two disembodied heads staring up at me from the dirt . . .

No, I think. Put it out of your mind.

But here, now, in this place of refinement, I will be doing what I know exactly how to do. I shall be dressing up in fine clothing, at a fine table, as I smile and nod through dinner. Every once in a while, I will be required to say something pithy, and that, too, I know how to do. It is what I have been trained for my entire life.

As if on cue, there is a knock on the door and a polite female voice behind it.

"May I please come in, miss? Do you mind? Are you awake?"

"Yes, do! Come in, come in!" I reply.

The door opens and reveals a pale, petite young lady in white livery. A humble servant's costume, meant to leave all the adornment to the one she is serving.

She glides in silently, deferentially, and leaves what looks to be a dress and cape on the ottoman. She then backs up, standing next to the door, awaiting instruction.

"A dress? And a cape, I see," I say, mostly to myself.

She nods and I walk over to inspect the finery.

Dearest readers, how can I describe this to you?

Imagine you took the clouds out of the sky and placed them ever so delicately in the form of a pearl dress, brocade and lace, with the silver lining of each cloud embroidered into the dress.

I gasp as a hold it up. Even in my kingdom, a kingdom of pale pinks and baby blues, this dress would be the most exquisite piece of artistry in the land.

"Tell me. Do all the ladies of this kingdom dress in such resplendent fashion?" I ask the chambermaid.

"Some do." She keeps her glance downward, then adds, "A very few. The count, to be true, is very influential. All these curiosities you see here are gifts from all the kingdoms."

I contemplate this. So he is actually a count. And this place, Alabastrine, it is not so different from our realm, where the very few waltz about whilst the rest scurry behind picking up crumbs left in their wake. Not a fair arrangement, to be sure. But one my father, the king, tells me can't be helped. One that if abolished would lead to absolute disorder and chaos. Anarchy.

Cats marrying dogs. Trees spontaneously combusting.

I can hear his voice in my head now. *A strong hand, my sweet princess. That is what a kingdom needs. What a king must provide. A strong hand! That is how order is maintained.*

My questioning this system is often met with scoffs or sarcasm.

My mother seems sometimes to nearly agree with me, although she is clearly resigned to the structure in place. After all, she is queen.

"Tell me, do you know where we will be going tonight?" I query.

The maid looks up. She seems caught.

"What? What is the matter?" I ask her. "Did I say something inappropriate?"

"Oh, nothing. Just . . . may I be honest?" she asks, eyes still to the ground.

"But of course; what is it?" I reply.

"I suppose . . . well . . . um." She seems to be reaching for something. "Well, I just, for a moment, I was . . . a bit jealous."

"Oh. Oh, yes. I'm—I'm so sorry. I shouldn't have mentioned it," I console her.

Yes, it is a bit of an odd thing to apologize to a servant in this way. But then again, most everything in this realm is a bit odd. I suppose I should have thought about it. The fact that I, who know nothing of this kingdom, am treated so luxuriously in this place . . . when she, who is actually from here, is confined to serve me. No, it is not fair.

"I'm so sorry. I didn't mean to offend," I tell her.

"No, miss. You make no offense." She changes the subject. "I will draw your bath presently." She nods.

A bath! I can't believe it! The most delicious luxury imaginable. After the noxious swamp, the cliff dwellings, and the brutal, never-ending march across the salt sea, this bath will feel like being positively reborn.

It seems impossible that I find myself so contented in this place. There are marzipan candies on the credenza in shapes like miniature fruit. An apple, an orange, a strawberry. The bright, happy colors make it impossible to be anything other than blissful. Yes, this is a whimsical place. A place of eccentricities and trifles.

It is too lovely to be believed. I should be wanting to get back to my kingdom of pale pinks and baby blues, but in this moment I am in no hurry.

Suddenly, I have a thought. Gratitude! I should be grateful for the gifts of this fine dress and this fine place of rest, this delicate, lovely chambermaid and this blissful ability to actually bathe. This Count Peregrine must think me an ingrate! Rude and spoiled, as if this is all my due. My mother always taught me to be thankful for whatever gifts life or anyone else has given me. She would not approve of my current behavior. I can hear her voice: *Gratitude, my darling, gratitude is the key to life. For the grateful pauper who enjoys his gifts, the sun above him, the moon in the night sky, the beauty of the day . . . that pauper is much wealthier than an ingrateful noble who wallows in misery.*

It is with this thought that I run out of the room in the

direction of the entry. Yes, I will tell Peregrine how very appreciative I am. I will apologize for my petulant manners. I will tell him that my head is reeling from the whirlwind of this unfamiliar place. He will forgive me.

As the chambermaid sees me, she makes a mad dash in my direction, calling out, "No, no. You mustn't!"

Continuing on, I reply, "What? No, you see, I must. It's the only polite thing to do, you understand."

She continues to rush in my direction and I find myself getting slightly perturbed. "It's truly fine. Please, don't bother."

"No, miss, but I'm drawing a bath for you!" she cries out. "Stop, please!"

But it's too late. Before she can actually tackle me, I swing open the door to the sleeping quarters and there . . .

. . . standing in front of the looking glass . . .

. . . is what looks like my companion, Count Peregrine, if Count Peregrine were much less handsome. He stands there, caught, his jaw less square, his face now taking on a kind of asymmetric quality it did not before possess. One eye slightly droopy and more almond shaped than the other, and both a swampy sort of brown color, not the piercing blue gray I first saw. And his hair . . . not the full mane I spied in the carriage, but duller, more unruly, his hairline uneven. His skin is mottled with sun spots. He gives me a sheepish grin, and then ceremoniously raises the glass he's holding in his hand, bringing it to his now-thin lips, and imbibes a blue liquid.

At this, an impossible thing occurs.

At once, the liquid seems to perform some kind of enchantment.

Now the skin's speckles erase themselves and the hair thickens. His jaw sharpens and his irises swirl in color until they glow blue gray once again. And there he is in the looking glass, now looking devastatingly handsome once more.

Peregrine's physical transformation has left me speechless. I stand there in the doorway, befuddled and a bit terrified.

He turns to me and shrugs, guilty. "You were going to find out sooner or later. Now is as good a time as ever, I suppose."

"But—what—" I stammer. "How—"

"Indeed. The answer to 'what' is 'the Sapphire.' The answer to 'how' . . . well, that is a bit more complicated." He contemplates. "You see, my esteemed princess, we are all . . . all of us here, enslaved by this blue concoction. In love with it, you might say. It is a blissful journey, especially at first. But then the concoction becomes necessary. No longer blissful but essential."

"I'm not sure I understand. How can this—"

"Of course you must never try it." He frowns. "I forbid it. No, we shall keep you free of this curse."

"Curse? How is it a curse?" These thoughts swim in my head.

"Some believe the curse is growing ugly. But truly, the curse is in not *wanting* to grow ugly. The desperation is really the jinx. The constant need for beauty. We all have it."

"Who are 'we all'?" I ask.

"Everyone," he huffs. "The entire kingdom of Alabastrine! We are all beholden to the Sapphire."

He fixes his hair in the looking glass, unbothered, as if this isn't some type of insanity. "To grow ugly in these kingdoms? Well, that is a crime. It means certain death."

"Simply to be unsightly?" I scoff. "This can't be true."

"Ah, but it is. You see . . . it's a bit of a vicious cycle really." He takes a seat in a powder-blue velvet chaise longue, pondering how to parse it out. "The Sapphire keeps a person, a man or a woman, beautiful. Gorgeous, dashing, what have you. The Sapphire costs money. If a person has no money, then a person has no Sapphire. If a person has no Sapphire to keep themselves beautiful . . . their face eventually turns sallow, or pale, or old, or pockmarked, or simply not pleasing to behold. So if you're ugly, you must be poor. And if you're poor, you end up being ugly. And, to wit, both are deemed unworthy. If found on the street, you would be shipped off."

"Shipped off?"

"Yes. To the place where the Sapphire is mined. A fate *worse* than death." He lounges there on the chaise longue, vaguely bored.

"I'm sorry. I am having a difficult time understanding this . . . ludicrous system," I say. "You are saying that being ugly here is actually not allowed."

"Correct." He nods. "Being ugly or poor. Or both. The two go hand in hand, really."

"And everyone, everyone we see, simply . . . must imbibe this blue liquid—"

"The Sapphire," he corrects me. "It comes from the Sapphire Mines. It's a bit confusing, now that I think of it."

"So everyone must drink this Sapphire concoction, not just

out of vanity . . . but out of sheer survival?" The pieces are falling into place.

"Exactly. The princess understands." He raises a glass of quine. "Huzzah."

"But this is horrifying," I reply, astonished. "What an atrocious fate. To be trapped. By this . . . drink. By this . . . absurd obsession."

"Don't blame me, I didn't invent it." He gulps his quine.

"But whoever did? Whoever should invent such a cruel fate?"

"The Veist, of course." He squints. "All cruel things come from the Veist, even these kingdoms, built out of spite."

"The Veist? But what is that?" I ask.

"The Veist is not a *that* but a *she*. And she is everything and nothing at all." He sips his quine, nonchalant. "A mystery like the great obelisk of Chakuk, or the caves of Flyth . . . something one can never know, really. No one has ever seen her. Or seen her and lived to tell about it."

"How can you be so . . . indifferent? This is diabolical. What happens to the ones unable to get this . . . enchanted concoction?" I continue. "What becomes of them?"

"I told you, my dear obstinate princess, they are shipped off in droves. To the Sapphire Mines. There, I imagine they are worked to the bone, until they keel over into the abyss." He contemplates this. "Yes, that sounds about right."

"Well . . . ," I ponder. "Why wouldn't they use the Sapphire they find in the mines?"

"Ha! They'd be murdered on sight." He shakes his head. "Really, Princess, don't be so very daft. It doesn't suit you."

"And this Veist?" I continue, perplexed. "Where is she?"

"Again, she is nowhere, and she is everywhere." He pours himself yet another glass of quine. "However, since you are so very curious, I will tell you. It is rumored that she has sometime been sighted, in a kind of physical form, far beyond the Wraithen Kingdom."

"And where is that?"

"Oh, that is where you must never, ever go, my alluringly inquisitive yet slightly annoying friend. You see, here in Alabastrine, things are warm. Fuzzy. Happy. Frivolous. The people are young, glittering, carefree, and unconcerned, the nights filled with dancing, song, quine, and general revelry. As you can see, I'm quite fond of it." He smiles, genuine.

"So?" I shrug. "What does that have to do with anything?"

"The Wraithen is quite different." He exhales. "It's full of bitter, vile miscreants. They are cruel, unhappy, greedy, and vicious. They kill slaves for sport. They kill each other on a whim. Also, they seem to make a habit of insulting the Alabastrine, which is really quite irksome. They're just jealous. Obviously."

"And are they, too, shackled by this Sapphire concoction?" I ask.

"Yes, of course. It is the way of the kingdoms. Can't be changed." He drinks his quine, and makes it into a kind of jingle. "But don't worry, fake princess, you will not have to imbibe for years, maybe twenty. As it is, you are quite pretty the way you are. Not that I have noticed. Because I haven't."

Twenty years? Is it possible I will have to stay in this accursed place that long? Will I never find my way home? Suddenly, the thought of being so abandoned, so lost, overwhelms me. And I find myself crumpled up, taking a small seat by the door. Before I know it, my face is in my hands and I am in tears. For the very first time, my situation comes barreling down upon me and I am no longer equipped, either with my wits or wonder or humor, to endure it. No, I am lost here. Desperate, abandoned . . . hopeless.

Silence in the room now, beyond my quiet sobbing.

I had thought, in my naive way, that I could handle any situation I was given. That, as a princess I would be able to rise to whatever occasion and contend with any outcome with both gravitas and grace. This is what I was taught; this is what I was educated to do. Everything with aplomb. A bon mot here, a pithy remark there. But here I am in the presence of some unknown count, who may or may not be dastardly, crying my eyes out in a room full of stuffed leopards and giant birds.

"Princess?" His voice interrupts my weeping. "Oh, Princess."

I can hear him coming over to me, the parquet floor creaking.

"Don't cry. Honestly, it's not that bad. You are in a safe place here. With me. To be frank, Alabastrine is the kindest of the kingdoms. And even though my devilish looks can be quite distracting, they do not make me stupid. I am actually quite savvy in the ways of this place. Indeed, you could not have stumbled upon a better, more capable companion." He lifts my chin, gentle. "You see, there is no need to cry. Here."

He hands me his silk handkerchief, ivory engraved in white.

He thinks for a moment, walking back over to his pale blue chaise longue. Now he exhales and sits, a look of consternation on his face.

The chambermaid interrupts. "Shall I . . . attend to the princess. For . . . dinner."

He looks up at her, as if from a stupor.

"No . . . actually. I don't think that will be necessary." He waves her off.

"I suppose I must look a fright," I admit. "Not quite dinner material, I suppose."

"Hmm," he acknowledges under his breath.

I expect him to continue, to say something witty, as is his wont. But he just stays there, staring at the design in the parquet floor.

"Should I . . . I suppose I'll go back to my chamber, then," I say, interrupting his thoughts.

"Yes . . ." He stirs. "Yes, indeed. . . . I'll have the chambermaid make you something. She's quite a commendable cook, actually."

"Well then, good night." I duck out, a bit befuddled.

"Yes, good night, Princess." He adds . . .

"Sweet dreams."

22

DESPITE THE CHAMBERMAID'S suggestion, wanting a nice night's sleep and actually experiencing one are two very different things.

As the moon, now just a sliver, now just the idea of a sliver, raises itself up to meet the stars, I find myself tossing and turning and then tossing again.

This pillow, too warm. This other pillow, too cold. This, that, and the other thing . . . until finally I decide to bin the whole idea of sleep and take a midnight visit with the moon.

The balcony here is a modest thing, but the cool night air rushes in as I open the diamond-paned windows and hear, outside, to my bewilderment . . . the sound of countless celebrations. Or festivals. Or weddings? It's as if the entire village, spread out like a white sea of towers and turrets, is celebrating its birthday or the fall harvest or Noel. All at once. To one side, up the hill, I can make out about twenty different glimmering facades, each with brightly lit colors of blue, green, and red. In some places, the blue seems to be a reflection of water, or even fire on water. And down the hill the cobblestone streets winding down to the ivory city walls . . . over thirty lit-up tents and enclaves, each offering their own rhythm. An aria here, some kind of drumming there, overtaken now, over there, by the sound of a snare.

Goodness. Is it like this here every night?

The sound of this drifting music wafts through the air, not the dulcet tones of the pianette or the flauth; the sound is rather an unfamiliar percussion, a kind of beating heart, an excited tempo. An impending something. Something sensuous and enthralling. It's going to happen soon! The drums . . . is that what they are? The drums beating and the rhythm seeming to go faster, to crescendo. The sound now, too, of a million heads thrown back in merriment. Ladies delighted. Men laughing.

It's really not like anything I've ever heard from an entire kingdom. Alabastrine. But it's inescapable in its seduction.

I decide: if I am stuck in this place, I must know more about it. I must discover some things for myself. I must, as my tutor would encourage, *explore*.

Surely my mother and the ladies of the court would disapprove, but there is no one here to chide or clutch their pearls or determine, with scorn, that *this is just not done*. I am on my own. I can avail myself of whatever I wish.

I notice a couple walking by, giggling to each other. The man is in white, just as the count and his driver were. The woman, too, is in a white dress. Both of them whispering, their faces painted ivory, as is the custom.

The couple continues on their way, down the white-stoned

narrow street, into some sort of establishment below. I hear the escalation of music as the door opens, the music floating out into the night air, past me, and then gone up to the stars.

I'm going to join them.

As I'm looking for a way to escape my perch, a strange thing happens.

Do you remember that little blackbird, the one who startled me during my daring albeit clumsy escape from the Cliffs of Grey? Well, a similar sleek and beautiful bird now lands spritely on the side of the stone alcove, and as I notice it . . . I also notice, just below it, exactly what I was looking for. A way to get down.

There's a wooden trellis painted white covered with climbing roses. Not as safe as a staircase, mind you, but the closest thing to a ladder a thing could be without actually being a ladder.

The little blackbird now flies away, the night awaiting him. And I find myself looking after him, watching him fly into that sliver of a moon. Odd.

Don't be silly, Bitsy. It's just a little blackbird and, truly, you haven't had any sleep. It's nothing more.

And yet.

Still.

It is . . .

Curious.

And there's something now, a voice drifting over the music in the distance . . . whispering just as the mysterious voice in the forest:

"I dream you."

I turn to search for the source of the voice . . . but there is only more percussion, now seeming to rise in volume, in intensity.

Perhaps it was just part of the song.

Off I go, into the night!

23

LUCKILY, I HAVE my dress! Oh, happy day! Or happy night, as it were.

The ivory makeup left by the chambermaid sits on the desk, in front of a small looking glass. I quickly approximate the ivory visage, hurrying before I lose my nerve. I throw on the dress, in a race between my reason and my will.

Before I know it, before I can stop myself, I'm descending the white rose trellis, hoping my exquisite dress isn't getting too rumpled. I don't want to look a fright for my Alabastrine debut!

I follow the path of that whispering couple, down to the doorway of the soiree below.

And here it is that I stop.

This is madness. What if I get caught? What if I am somehow offensive, or brash, or wrong?

No royals will see me, let alone help me get back to my kingdom. But I must see for myself about this place. I cannot rely on Peregrine, whose very appearance is a lie! I must know all I can firsthand if I am to have any hope of escape.

I am screwing up my courage when two white-dressed,

white-faced girls my age come barreling down the pathway and grab me playfully by the arm.

"Come, come! Eat, drink, and be merry, for tomorrow you shall . . . you shall . . . ?" one girl says.

The other girl finishes her thought. "Die! Or is it cry? That is the question."

"The question is . . . who cares?!" The other girl laughs, dragging me with them as if we've been best friends forever.

"Come, pretty girl. You'll make us look good. That dress will stop the men in their tracks!" the first girl declares.

"Wherever did you get it?" the other chimes in. "Never mind, never mind. I'm bored already waiting for the answer!"

I don't quite know what to say as I'm being dragged into this revelry. I don't know what to do or be. I feel as though I could be anyone or anything I choose. . . .

And I quite like it.

24

THE INTERIOR OF this rather loud and raucous establishment is bursting at the seams with all kinds, every different shade of skin, of language, of bearing as anything I have ever seen. Of course, the skin color cannot be determined from the face, as everyone seems to have painted themselves a mask of white. The dress of the people, every last one, all in ivory. And, of course, each face here a visage of porcelain perfection . . . sparkling eyes, silken skin, chiseled cheekbones. I find myself wondering whether everyone here uses the Sapphire or if there are actually some natural beauties. It's impossible to tell, really.

The sound of the percussion is louder, yet here I realize it was drowning out the pianette and the flauth the whole time. They are a part of the music as well. The lilting sounds of the classical instruments, a kind of minuet, somehow intertwined with the captivating sounds of the drums. The entire musical affair combined to give a sense of excitement, of a rush, of something about to happen, something either terrifying or transcendent.

And, of course, the dance. The men and the women, and even

many in between, are jangling about, some with such absurd movements it causes one to stifle a laugh. One particular dance, seeming more popular with the ladies, involves slapping the ground and then raising one arm high up to the ceiling.

But it's a glorious party. And even at the grandest of galas in my kingdom, no one ever, ever had this much fun.

My two giggling companions drag me in.

"What's your name, beauty? Or should we just call you that? Yes, I like that. It's settled. We'll call you Beauty," the first one says, and I realize she has hair the color of a red apple.

"My name is Apple. You see, because of my hair," she says, as if reading my mind. "And this, of course, is my very best friend since we were babies crawling around in nappies. In fact we used to get in trouble in the sandbox for talking too much. In baby language, can you imagine?! Her name is Ducky."

Ducky nods. "It's because of my lips. Everyone says I look like a duck. Quack."

I curtsy. "It's a pleasure to meet you both, Apple and Ducky. I am Princess Elizabeth Clementine DeBoudas Roix from the kingdom of Roix."

The two look at each other as I curtsy and they both BURST out laughing.

"Oh my God, do it again, do it again!" they demand.

"Um, okaaaay . . . it's a pleasure to meet you both, Apple and Ducky. I am Princess Elizabeth Clementine DeBoudas Roix, from the kingdom of Roix." I curtsy again.

Again, the two squeal with delight.

"Okay, now I'll do it. Now I'll do it. . . ." Ducky curtsies, and repeats in a mock formal voice, "It's a pleasure to meet you, Apple and Ducky, I am the grand whatever from the kingdom of something something and such."

"And I am the Contessa Lobstara, from the Undersea Kingdom of Enchanted Crustaceans." Apple curtsies with her.

Even though they are putting me on, it's difficult not to join in with their laughter. It's infectious.

"Oh, don't be mad, Beauty. We love you! Don't we, Ducky?"

Ducky nods. "Are you a princess? Really? I don't doubt it with that dress and those manners. Princess Beauty. Yes, that's what we'll call you. From the kingdom of . . . what was it?"

"Roix," I answer.

"Ladies, ladies, there is no dawdling on the dance floor . . . come, come!" A rather large man in a fine white wig, topcoat, and knickers interjects himself into our discussion.

"Demetrious! How dare you look so dashing without us?!" Ducky grabs him and they immediately head for the middle of the sea of hands and writhing bodies.

Apple leads me with them, whispering, "Demetrious is the son of the Knightbridge Azucar dynasty. The only heir. One day he'll be so rich he'll take baths in money!"

And there are two things I notice before we are swallowed up into the melee: One, Demetrious has skin the color of rich mahogany, underneath all that ivory makeup. And two, Ducky is truly stunning, cut from the same mold, it seems, as my mother. Wheat-colored hair, with sparkling eyes and sweetheart lips.

The way Demetrious is staring at her, I believe he thinks so, too.

"Oh, yes. He's in love with her." Apple reads my thoughts. "Isn't it grand?! She'll have her own castle one day! And we shall visit her! Let's get a drink. I'm too self-conscious to dance yet."

She drags me to the other side of the dance floor, where there's a line for service. I dutifully step in line behind all the others.

Apple looks at me and laughs. "Oh, no, dear. Heaven forbid . . . You're so cute."

She pulls me with her and before I know it, we are in a sparsely populated back room, with just a few people lounging about. There is only one man, behind a much smaller bar, standing there, seeming rather bored, drying glasses with a cloth napkin.

He looks up and, upon seeing us, his demeanor instantly changes. "Apple, what in all the gods—?"

"Now is that any way to greet a friend?" she teases. "This is my new best friend, Beauty. Well, my second-best friend. Ducky's in there dancing with Demetrious. And this is Billy."

"You didn't even say goodbye last night, or this morning or whenever. It was rude. You hurt my feelings," Billy chides her.

"Oh, come on, Billy. You know I'm not one for these so-called emotions," she replies. "If you're in love with me, that's your fault."

Yes, this is all quite overwhelming. There is an entirely different set of rules and morals to this place. Everyone seems quite open about absolutely everything. A far cry from the decorum of my kingdom.

"Come now, don't brood. If there's anything I can't stand it's a brooding bartender. And yet you all seem to be so fond of it!" Apple exclaims, handing me a bright-green drink with a bit of lavender foam on the top. "Here, try this. It's delicious. Billy invented it." She clinks glasses with me. "Schauff!"

Billy lifts his glass. "Schauff!"

"Schauff!" I raise my glass, taking a sip of the green drink.

"Do you like it? I think he should name it 'The Peacock' because of the gorgeous green. But he thinks he should name it 'Nights on the Sea.' Terrible name."

"'Dancers in the Night'?" he suggests.

"Even worse." She goes on, "You really don't have a knack for this, do you—"

And this banter continues, leaving me with a kind of empty numbness. All that is happening here is witty banter and gossip. Kisses in the air but nothing genuine. I suddenly have the feeling of being back at a gala in my kingdom, or at tea with my cousins, counting the moments until I can get back to whatever novel I happen to be obsessed with at the moment.

Certainly, there is merriment here. But I will learn nothing about my predicament in this place. I should leave.

It's within these thoughts that I begin to feel a sudden rush to the head, a bit like the music, overpowering . . . all the excitement, heading for something, something grand and breathtaking.

"Fantastic, yes? Just you wait," Apple exclaims, then she catches herself in the looking glass on the wall. "Oh, goodness, I look a fright. Hang on, hang on then."

Now she pulls out a tiny vial from her bodice, quickly imbibing it. And as we both watch her reflection in the mirror, her beauty is ever so slightly replenished . . . her skin just a little bit more effervescent, her eyes just a little more brilliant.

As her transformation is complete . . . the room now seems to fold itself in blurry waves, undulating. She murmurs something to Billy.

I'm not sure, but I think she whispers, "Now. Before she wakes up."

25

DO SOMETHING, BITSY. You've made a terrible mistake!

My inner voice is yelling out as I try to move my arms and legs, discovering to my horror that I can move neither.

"Get her in the back!"

"Here, we can wheel her out to the carriage house."

These words are floating through the billowing air, weaving in and out.

"Shh. Shh!"

"Is there anyone in the alley . . . ? Now go go go go!"

My head feels heavy—like it's dangling from my neck. But my consciousness is still there, begging me to do something.

I notice that my two kidnappers seem to be Apple and Billy. My newfound friends Ducky and Demetrious are nowhere to be seen. Is it possible they have no idea this is happening? If I had more time to think, the betrayal of my supposed new friend Apple would sting me. Friend?! More like fiend!

What have I done? My mother has only told me a thousand times not to stray by myself anywhere, not even in the light of day, beyond the castle walls. Yet here I am, venturing out into the mysterious streets of the Alabastrine. I'm a fool. How could I ever be so stupid? I would kick myself. If it were possible to move my legs.

But as my limbs are of no use to me, there will be no self-flagellation. I am simply consigned to watch as the scenery around me changes to some sort of dark alley . . . and then, much to my horror, to the back of a carriage.

The percussion and minuet rhythms fade out from my hearing as the sounds of night take over. I look up and glance at that sliver of moon once again, this time my enemy. The air has turned itself into some kind of wavering soup.

"Now, now. Before anyone notices she's gone!" I hear Apple barking in a whisper.

Lolling my head over to one side, I see her ivory-painted face looking furtively around and then the slam of the carriage door and pure darkness.

All is black.

26

A KING'S JOURNAL

Oh, this is simply too much to be tolerated! The insolence around me, the ignorance!

No one, not one person in the entire kingdom, seems to be able to make sense of what has happened to our dearest sleeping princess. No one can wake her with any tincture, ointment, incense, or any other preposterous thing.

What's worse is . . . my poor queen refuses to sleep anywhere but where the princess lies, paranoid the princess may wake in the middle of the night. Thank goodness we moved our darling Bitsy from that terrible tower. My queen would catch her death from the damp rather than leave our daughter.

And, of course, I shall have to have a proper room somehow made up for my queen, there in the garden, a royal tent. There she may sleep under the moon with our slumbering Bitsy.

To make matters even more unbearable, my nieces, Prissy and Bolanda, came this morning . . . in an effort to cheer everyone up. They managed to bring an entire acrobatic group from God knows where, flinging themselves around the kingdom like witless fleas. Then Prissy and Bolanda insisted on having their portraits painted, sitting next to the princess in her slumber. They then had reproductions immediately commissioned, with a few daft words at the bottom. A ghastly expression written by Prissy. Something like "Sleep, dream, live." They plan to have these aforementioned reproductions distributed all throughout the kingdoms, saying this will inevitably lead to the cure. Balderdash! Those two want all in the kingdoms to look at their portraits and comment on their beauty. The vanity!

I am being punished.

Yes, there is a part of me that believes I have brought this on myself . . . that it is, in some way, related to my great secret.

No, I cannot tell the queen.

To tell her would be to break her heart.

And, you see, her heart is already so terribly broken.

27

I MUST AWAKEN. I must!

I am now in a stupefied daze with a view merely of darkness. It is confusion upon confusion. The only sense that cares to function is that of sound. My ears discern the vibrations of the music fading quieter and quieter into the background, then just the clickety-clack of the horse hooves upon the cobblestone. Every once in a while, the sound of another soiree bursts into the perimeter, to just as quickly pop out again. It's as if I'm being absconded away through a thousand parties; the laughter a cruel joke at my expense.

Suddenly, the carriage stops, the blackness continues, but there is some commotion, the sound of a fight, the sound of a skirmish.

I hear the thud of something hitting the ground. Then the sound of some kind of fumbling on metal . . . the latching of a lock?

Within milliseconds the night air comes rushing in.

My senses a myriad of disorientation, I am suddenly slapped across the face with what seems like a wave of ice-cold water.

And now the sound of a voice.

"My dear fake princess! What have you gotten yourself into?!"

28

"DON'T YOU EVER do that again. Wandering around by yourself. I'm surprised at you. A princess! I'd have thought you'd know better." He continues to scold me. "You have no idea who and what is out there! Let me tell you, mon ami, it's not pretty."

Peregrine goes on lecturing me in innumerable ways, but it is the most beautiful sound I have ever heard. Somehow we have made it back to his entryway, although I have no idea quite how.

"You could've been killed. You WOULD'VE been killed. Predators out here. Everywhere! And you wander about without a guard! You're quite mad! What did they give you? Somak? Klaycko? Maybe a combination of both?"

"Uifowjfvooiua" is my answer. Although I meant to say I didn't quite know.

"Never mind. You're in no condition to answer. And your dress?! We'll have to send it out first thing in the morning."

Again the disapproving shake of the head.

The chambermaid breaks his admonishment, entering and rushing over.

"Oh dear God," she exclaims. "Wherever did you find her?"

"Kidnapped by some hooligans! Good thing I know every nook and crevice of the kingdom, as if I'd invented them," he answers, proud of himself. "You know, I've lived here my whole life. I could walk the streets blindfolded."

The two of them manage to carry me on both sides, hoisting me on their shoulders, past the stuffed giraffe, to my quarters.

As the chambermaid puts me back on the bed, taking off my shoes and fetching some water, he continues to berate me from the corner.

"Oh, pretend princess. You half scared me to death." He puts his head in his hands. "You simply cannot understand the derelicts that dwell in this place."

My words stumble out. "I thought you said . . . here . . . was the best of all the kingdoms?"

"It *is*!" he exclaims.

As he goes, trying to talk himself down from a great height, the sound of his voice wafts past me. There are a million thoughts I could have or may even be having, but because of the strange potion they simply tumble forward and then spin away, as if on a carousel. Spinning round and round until there's nothing to see but lights and colors, dazzling, and music as distorted as a funhouse looking glass.

29

IT'S DUSK BY the time I wake, or am awakened, by the chambermaid, costume in hand.

"Here, you must put this on. Luckily, I didn't have to wash it. There were just a few stains, which I covered with chalk. An old family secret, passed down from my granny."

I rub my eyes, the feeling in my head as if I'd been clubbed with a cudgel.

"Ah, you've a headache. Well, that's to be expected. That will require another family secret, if you'll just hold on a moment. But please, do get up as we are running late. Also, there are a few biscuits here, sweet things, you might like to nibble on before dinner. First dinner. My mother used to call it lady dinner, so you wouldn't end up wolfing down food in front of any potential suitors."

"Yes, I am familiar with this concept. My mother used to call this dressing dinner."

"Excellent!" She rushes out and returns in a few moments with a concoction that looks a bit unappetizing, a slug-colored drink.

"You can't possibly want me to drink that." I peer down at the muck.

"Do you want to lose your headache?" she asks, then hands me the drink.

I hesitate.

"Come, come. You mustn't tarry," she chides. "We don't have all night."

"Fine." I gulp down the globby drink, choking a bit on its general globbiness.

But, yes, it does work. Like a charm, actually.

"And now for the dress. Don't worry about the face, I can do that. I've been painting faces here in the Alabastrine since I was a girl of ten winters," she says with pride.

"Why *are* all the faces painted white?" I ask, finally having the opportunity to satisfy my curiosity.

"It's a tradition in these parts. Something having to do with the salt sea and purity." She thinks. "But you mustn't be seen for miles around without it. It's just not done. Not in this society, that is."

"But it's not worn in others?" I ask.

"Oh, no. Heavens no. It's just the custom of this kingdom," she replies.

"This kingdom? And how many kingdoms are there?" I ask.

"Well, five, of course. Six if you count the Cliffs of Grey, but nobody really counts that. There's no society there and they're all savages." She helps me into my dress. "Hands up in the air, there you go."

The dress falls around me and she inspects it, looking for any remaining stains to chalk. Every once in a while, she goes in for a correction.

"And what do these *savages* dress like?" I continue.

"Well, they hardly dress at all, I've heard. But I've never seen them. No one who has ever seen them comes back to tell the tale." She chalks a spot near the hem.

"I've seen them," I blurt out.

She drops her chalk to the floor. "What?! No. Impossible."

"Yes, I have. I've seen the Cliffs of Grey, and even ridden on horseback with one of them," I inform her, suddenly quite proud of myself.

"No." The disbelief on her face is as if I'd roped the moon and ridden it to the sun. "And you were not killed?"

"Apparently not," I reply.

"And they did not eat you?" she asks.

"Well, if they did, I didn't notice," I chirp. "They even wanted me to stay."

"Wanted you to stay?" At this point she has to sit down. "Blimey."

"Yes, and fight. They kept saying that," I confide. "It was quite odd, really."

"You do know that none of them live past twenty winters. And that they all go mad," she informs me.

"Go mad?" I repeat.

"Yes. Every single one of them. And I don't know why any of them would ask you to fight. Fight who? Whoever it is, they'd most certainly lose. They've lost already!" she replies.

"Hmm." I think about it. The violence of the Cliff people certainly shook me. But they didn't seem mad. Despite my fear, there was also beauty in their society.

"Well, whatever it was, be glad you got out of there alive." She shakes her head again. "And now, dear brave princess, it's time you let me paint your face; you have a big night ahead of you."

I sit dutifully on the threadbare wingback chair, pondering all of this.

She chuckles to herself.

"Truly, you should be dead."

30

———— ◆ ————

THE CARRIAGE RIDE on the way to this promised dinner is a bumpy one, through narrow, winding streets. Having taken advantage of dressing dinner, I'm a bit worried I might be nauseous all over my newly restored dress.

"You look lovely, fake princess." Peregrine nods to me.

Across from me, he sits on his pillowed bench in the carriage, wearing a white topcoat, white knickers, white wig. He must have taken his fair share of Sapphire before this outing. His features are in complete alignment, his jaw bold and square. And though he is covered in chalky paint, there is no denying the magnetism of his visage.

"I suppose I never thanked you for getting me out of that deplorable situation last night." I add, "So, thank you."

He dips his hat. "I was excruciatingly worried. I'm sure I went a bit overboard in my chastisement. I do apologize."

"Who were those women, those people?" I ask.

"Oh, dregs. Louts. Blackguards. Rogues. Rascals. Rapscallions." He adds, "Alabastrine is full of them. If they were not such before landing here, the city makes it so. A decadent place, really. Some even call it depraved. Any vice one has, it will be amplified in the Alabastrine."

"But they couldn't all be dregs," I muse. "At the soiree, at least."

"That's the fun thing about our dear Alabastrine. The thing that draws people from all the other kingdoms. Here you may find a prince amongst thieves, a count amongst sinners . . . and even the odd princess." He emphasizes the last word, indicating he's referring to me.

The carriage pulls to a stop.

"Ah, here we are. Wonderful." He disembarks, ushering me out of the carriage.

"Now, Princess, this is an Epicuriana, with a long tradition, over one hundred winters," he explains. "It is very difficult, if not impossible, to gain access to this very exclusive club. And its location, because of this, is hidden. Yes, it's a secret, as all good things are. A way to keep out the hoi polloi, you see."

"Oh, I see."

"Yes, and part of the tradition is that all new honored guests must first be received with their eyes shuttered," he informs me.

"What?" I ask.

"Blindfolded, my dear. It's the tradition." And before I can protest, he proffers an ivory-colored silk blindfold and covers my eyes.

"This seems a bit odd," I tell him.

He pats me on the shoulder. "Don't worry, our beloved Alabastrine is full of strange traditions. But you won't have to worry yourself about them much longer."

31

ONCE AGAIN MY ears become the prime registry of my senses, as there is a distant sound of voices, chattering, merriment . . . the usual sounds of a fine establishment.

I cannot deny the excitement I feel to see this elegant place, the Epicuriana my new companion has been going on about.

I am just about to have a thought, something about the lack of the sound of cutlery, when the laughter and voices cease and now there is a silence so empty I can hear my heartbeat.

But it's not a peaceful silence. No, no, it's thick. A thick, foreboding silence, a silence with a charge . . . like lightning deciding where to strike.

"Ladies and gentlemen, may I present to you, Princess Elizabeth Clementine DeBoudas Roix of the House of Roix." And with that, the blindfold comes off.

There is an audible gasp.

I see this Epicuriana is not a restaurant at all . . . but a kind of amphitheater, similar to the ones in the history books about the ancients. And I am in the middle, there with Count Peregrine. Center stage, as it were.

There are, clearly, more gentlemen here than ladies, less than a handful of those. And the gentlemen can hardly be called gentlemen, for despite their white-painted faces, their vulgarity betrays them . . . in burps, gulps, and salivating lips. They sway and gulp down their goblets, teetering out of their seats.

"Well then, shall we start the bidding?" Peregrine begins, turning to me.

Seeing my look of astonishment, he whispers, "Don't look so disappointed, my dear. I said Alabastrine was full of rogues. . . . I never said I wasn't one of them."

32

"TELL ME! WHO here wouldn't want to own their very own princess?" Peregrine seduces the crowd.

"Miscreant! There is no such kingdom and, therefore, there is no such princess! You've made it up! She is an impostor!" a voice yells out from the audience.

Peregrine searches the crowd for the voice. "Ah! Our friend Fleck from debtor's prison is the expert!"

This draws a hearty guffaw from the crowd.

"My loyal patrons, I have exhibited for you a host of things from lands near and far. And now, I bring you *this*!" He gestures toward me with a flourish.

"This is a novel offering from the likes of you, Peregrine!" a heckler calls from the audience. "Branching out into new markets?"

"Inflation! Taxes!" Peregrine contends. "We do what we must to get by."

Now Peregrine surveys the audience further, walking around me as if showing livestock.

"Have you ever seen such gorgeous flowing hair, lips like Cupid's bow." Now he turns to the audience, a quick pivot. "Not only fluent in Fricella and Gurbath but also Lilcott and High Rovelle. She plays both the pianette and the flauth."

A general murmur through the crowd.

"It is obvious she's a product of only the highest breeding; her carriage, manners, voice, demeanor are a light in the darkness. And curious! She is curious, too . . . in the most amusing way. You see, a conversationalist! A sparring partner! For what man wouldn't want to have such wit in his life, by his side. . . ."

"Are you selling her or writing a love poem?!" A wisecrack from the audience.

Peregrine stands still now, somehow caught. For a moment he is silent.

"Don't be silly!" he recovers. "I mean only to enumerate the advantages of purchasing a bona fide princess!"

Purchasing. So this *is* exactly what it seems. Peregrine means to sell me to the highest bidder.

"Well, no one's ever sold a princess. Is it against the law?" a voice calls out.

"My friend, we are in Alabastrine. There is no law." Again, he draws a laugh.

Now the general response from the throng varies from vague curiosity to feverish note-taking. Some of the handful of women whisper into the ears of their companions. Some of the men leer and continue stuffing their faces with plates of figs and olives. Some of these men recline leisurely in their seats, as if lounging in their own personal bedchamber. Others can barely hold still, giddy, as if they are ready to jettison from their seats.

"I ask you, nobles, and I do use the term loosely . . ." The crowd responds with a knowing chuckle. Yes, they are in the palm of his hand. He is a showman. "I ask you, truly, who wouldn't want to wake up to such a portrait of beauty, the very picture of elegance, of innocence?" His blue-gray eyes lock on mine. His voice lowers and he nearly whispers the next part. "Why, she is a doe."

My face reddens, inflamed with what can only be anger. *"Tenderness?"* I hiss. "How dare you?"

"I *doe* wish you would get on with it!" one of the men yells out, causing the others to spit up with laughter.

"So *doe* we all!" More raucous cackling.

Peregrine blinks. Then he steers himself back to the bidding. "Shall we begin? Who wants to start? For, again, who wouldn't want to own their very own princess?"

I look out over the sea of scoundrels. A pinched, somehow sinister man calls out from the audience, "I would. Give her to me."

Peregrine turns, finding him in the audience. "Oh, no. I'm not selling her to you. She'll be dead by midnight."

The gallery erupts in laughter.

Who are these horrible people?

Peregrine interrupts their glee. "This is not some guttersnipe from the Sapphire or some beast from the Cliffs of Grey! This is an exquisite jewel . . . possibly the most beautiful in all the kingdoms, worth as much as a kingdom herself."

I can hardly believe my ears. Bidding? For me? None of this can be real. I feel ashamed of every moment I have spent with this foul salt sea thief, this unabashed Count Peregrine, and his grand charade.

And what of the chambermaid? Did she know what was to be my fate? Somehow a betrayal from the same sex is a thousandfold worse.

"One hundred coin!" a voice blurts out from the crowd.

"An insult. I won't even consider it." Peregrine scoffs.

"One fifty!" A different voice from the crowd.

"Two hundred!" Now the first voice.

"Half what the starting bid should be," Peregrine elaborates. "Are you blind? Do you not see the effervescent beauty that stands before you?"

I finally snap out of my bewilderment, trying to recover. "Actually, in my own kingdom, I'm considered quite plain! Really, ask anyone—"

"Hush!" Peregrine shushes me, then turns immediately back to the stands. "As you can see, she is as humble as she is royal. Another enchanting trait—"

"Five hundred!" a deeper voice rings out.

Peregrine peers up to see where that voice came from. "A start."

"Five fifty!" The original bidder again.

Now an extremely large man with an unnaturally smooth face chimes in. "Six hundred! Take it or leave it."

"Take it or leave it?" Peregrine mocks him. "My dear friend, one does not take or leave such a dazzling treasure. A once-in-a-lifetime acquisition."

"Six fifty!" Another.

"Six seventy-five!" Yet another.

"You see, my princess," Peregrine addresses me, "there are many parties who wish to lay claim to you. They struggle against each other to possess—"

"Ten thousand!" A hush falls over the amphitheater.

All attendees seem to lean in at once, trying to determine the source of the bid.

Peregrine's eyes go wide. "I'm sorry. What was that you said?"

"Ten thousand coin. It is my final offer." The voice comes from high above, somewhere in the back.

"I see. Yes, well . . . if there are no more bids, then—" Peregrine is interrupted.

"Ten thousand coin and my country estate!" the smooth-faced man blurts out. "On Lake Thebes. Worth twenty thousand coin last it was taxed. Take it now or it's off the table."

Peregrine doesn't hesitate. "Sold! Sold to the handsome man for, you heard it, ten thousand coin and one country estate on Lake Thebes!"

The crowd erupts into applause. Some laughing, some whistling, some standing and cheering. "Huzzah!"

"A new record, I believe. Let it be written in the books!" Count Peregrine relishes his moment of triumph.

But the smooth-faced man comes barreling down, interrupting his moment. "Come, come, lout. Let's draw up the papers and be done with it."

He grabs me by my wrists, bullish, leading me back with him.

"No! This cannot— I do not consent to this!" I protest.

Peregrine follows quickly, not wanting to risk his treasure.

"Careful, careful, friend. You do not want to destroy the

merchandise," he chides the smooth-faced man.

"What do you care, imbecile? She's mine now. I can destroy her however I want." He scoffs.

I look at my betrayer, Peregrine, who cannot bring his eyes to meet mine.

"What a coward you are," I say, taking him in. "How could you?"

He doesn't answer me, choosing to focus on the rich bully and the transaction at hand. "Only in coin, you see. Only in coin and key. Nothing less."

"Yes, yes." The bloated sandpaper man waves him off. "Gold, silver, and a key to the happy home by the lake!"

The man in rags next to him, his servant, loads more than a few burlap sacks onto the table next to Peregrine.

"You cannot leave until I count it. My prerogative by law," Peregrine informs him.

"Yes, yes. Fine." My taut-faced owner reaches into his topcoat, grasping here and then there, and then here again, fumbling for something. Finally, he takes out a metal key, leaving it on the table. "Here, peasant. And a map to find it. It's not difficult. There are only three estates on the lake. Mine is the grandest, of course."

"Mine now," Peregrine retorts, snatching the key off the table.

As the money is counted, I stand there, held now by the strange-faced man, who is inspecting me close, the ale on his breath palpable as he invades the space around me, inspecting every hair on my head, every curve of my form.

I stare straight at Peregrine, who continues to avoid my gaze.

I do not know who I hate more. . . . Him for his betrayal? Or me for my stupidity?

"You cannot do this!" I spit the words.

The tight-faced man laughs. "And yet we just have. Now be silent, wench, or I shall silence you."

Finally, when the coins, gold and silver, are counted, my new owner begins collecting his many belongings and barking orders at his servants.

Peregrine takes this moment to whisper into my ear, "After three bridges, there's a pub. He will stop. Because he's a foul, disgusting creature. They serve him all he could ever eat and more. He prides himself on this, thinking that they actually like him. That is your moment. If you do not escape then . . . you never will."

Tears of frustration sting my eyes. "I trusted you," I reply.

"I'm sorry, Princess." And now he kisses me on the top of my head. "Whatever you do, don't stray to the Wraithen. And do NOT come back here."

I stare through him.

He explains himself: "I can't sell you again. And besides . . . I wouldn't be able to part with you twice."

At this confession, something changes in him. He looks up, shamefaced.

"What is all this?! Give me my girl!" Now the bloated hand of the man grabs me by the arm, leading me out.

I look back at Peregrine, who meets my look. And for a moment, I think he will change his mind.

But that moment comes and goes.

He does nothing.

I am betrayed.

Part II

1

A KING'S JOURNAL

I am at the end of my wits. Were it not for my beautiful wife, the queen, I should have chucked myself off the south tower by now.

Thus far, we have been visited by exactly fifteen healers, five soothsayers, and a funny little man from the outer territories who smelled as if his last bath was ten winters ago.

Each time, my advisers assure me that whomever I am about to meet is a genius of some sort and that they will surely be the one to wake my daughter out of her slumber.

Then each of the men proceeds to subject the sleeping princess to a series of ointments, spells, tinctures, leeches, and bloodletting.

After each one inevitably fails, they apologize profusely and pronounce that the princess is beyond repair.

The soothsayer even went so far as to suggest I put my darling princess out of her misery. This was met, obviously, with a quick and painful ride down the north turret staircase.

The queen is, of course, out of her mind with grief. It pains me to no end to see her sink deeper and deeper into despair. A king is not meant to feel helpless, or, at least, to show it. A king is meant to be strong for his queen, and his kingdom.

Then, yesterday, an absurd thing happened.

The queen and I were startled by a hideous old hag, wrinkled and misshapen, who insisted on telling us her ludicrous solution.

I was just about to have her removed from the castle when, to my surprise, my unpredictable queen decided to, indeed, give her an audience.

What followed, from the hideous mouth of the unfortunate old hag, was a theory that the sleeping princess must be kissed to awaken. Kissed! As if that ever helped anything.

Nevertheless, she continued to warble on about some sinister spell that could be altered only by the mere kiss of some predestined prince, who would then forevermore be known as "Prince Charming."

Honestly, I had to stifle a laugh.

But to my great horror, my wife seems to think this is a perfectly acceptable plan of action. A desperate attempt, rife with superstition and folly. Yet I must try to be understanding. I do not wish my darling queen to spend the rest of her life in tears.

Nevertheless, it's pure poppycock.

I await this plan's utter failure. This crone cannot be gone from our palace too soon.

2

―――――◆―――――

THE CARRIAGE OF my new vulgar, taut-faced companion is much more elaborate than even the carriage of that reprobate Count Peregrine. Both the exterior and interior are gold-gilded, pastoral scenes painted within the miniature gold frames. Even the ceiling is painted with a heavenly scene involving clouds and angels. Magnificent, albeit a bit over the top. The cushions on the sides are burgundy velvet, and if it weren't for the amber glob sitting directly across from me, snoring away, the entire thing would be the very picture of elegance.

As he snores away, I contemplate him. The very first thing he did, upon the carriage doors closing, was wipe the white paint off his face with a vengeance. As if the paint itself were a kind of insult.

Now his quine-stained lips are held open, his jaw slack, as the spittle collects in the side of his mouth, glistening, only to be brought in or rearranged at his stirring after a bump in the road.

It's a curious thing, his skin. How unnatural it looks, pulled tight . . . as if he has the impression of constant surprise. Is this, perhaps, the result of too much Sapphire? Too much wealth? Decadence?

How grateful I am that he's asleep. For I cannot imagine what horrors may come when he wakes.

The advice of Peregrine rings in my head. *Escape then . . . or you never will.*

A shudder runs through me.

I've discerned that his name is Gork. For that is what his servant calls him. Master Gork.

Thus far, he has seemed uninterested in me and much more interested in the copious amounts of ale available in this painted carriage. A supply for an entire village to make it through winter.

I noticed he didn't offer me any ale, although I wouldn't have taken it. This, in combination with the condition of the ragged clothes on his servant, leads me to believe this is not a munificent man. His unlucky manservant serves in tatters; even his shoes have holes in them, his big toe peeking out the front.

This is a man who clutches everything to him and won't let go. Stingy. Despite his wealth.

There is a miniature window behind the little velvet curtains that keep the light out. I peek through, not wanting to wake the sleeping Master Gork.

Peering out, there is no landscape to see. Only tree after tree, forests thick with green, as if this path is the tiniest possible path through a great expanse of leaves.

But then a strange thing happens upon us on the road. At first, I hear only the sound of the horses, then the wheels, the squeaking of what must be a very old cart, and what sounds like hushed, furtive tones.

I peek out the window, searching for the source of the noise, and see, ever so briefly, a cart passing by. A cart with a cage sitting atop it. Perhaps it is some sort of animal, I think. It is only upon the moment of the cart's passing close that I realize the horrifying truth. No. It's not an animal. No, not at all. It's a cage filled with people. And a very specific kind of people . . . wretched, unfortunate, sullied people. These castaways are packed in like sausages, their wrists and ankles tied, their bodies gaunt, their eyes saucers, their mouths parched, with cracking lips, some of them hunched over into what I pray is sleep. I cover my mouth in horror, still unsure my eyes are not deceiving me. And as the terrible sight passes, I see the eyes of one of the captives glance up. And for a moment, I think he sees me. But it is too quick to say anything, to do anything, and even if I could, this snoring, greedy Master Gork would surely do not a thing.

The last thing, the petrifying thing . . . as the cart retreats in the distance, I see one body, the hands and neck limp, and it's clear: this is the corpse of one of these unfortunates, having died upon the journey, being simply carted along with the others, as if nothing has happened. The shock of this, the callousness and inhumanity, sends a chill down my spine. So, that diabolical Peregrine was at least telling the truth about this. Here it is the gravest crime to be wretched, to be poor, to be unsightly.

How far I am now from my fairy kingdom. From my life of pale pinks and baby blues. Here, in this cruel place. An unforgiving realm where the sullied are tied up like chattel, taken to who knows where and for what purpose, left to die on the way.

What other devastating sights in this landscape await me? What other merciless crimes and victims does it hide?

Round and round the wheels of the carriage go through the barricade of leaves. The carriage wobbles from side to side, despite its pomp. A cumbersome thing dolled up to look regal.

The snoring of the ruddy Gork is now coming out in fitful snorts. I peer out the window, wanting to fly up through these leaves like one of the blackbirds that has accompanied me on my journey. Away from this dreadful place!

The rhythm of these carriage wheels continues, monotonous and endless. So far I have counted two bridges. I am waiting for the third. And then I shall fly far from here, or die in the effort.

3

THE SKY IS pitch-black as we pull up to a gray-stone structure, complete with sign, beneath a single lantern. "Gray Horse Tavern," it reads, with the silhouette of a horse on a black background.

I counted a third bridge just moments before.

So, Peregrine was right. There it is, the pub where Master Gork will gorge himself silly.

My smooth-faced companion jolts up as we come to a stop. He rubs his weary eyes as the carriage door opens and the driver lends him a much-needed hand to balance his lumbering body out of the carriage.

Master Gork takes no notice. Instead he stays, eyes on me. "It's not far now, little dear. We'll be home for good."

He licks his foul lips.

This would be the perfect time to panic, except the gears in my head are spinning too quickly, trying to plan my escape.

"But first, I cannot bear to miss my beloved friends of the Gray Horse Tavern! You will wait here, of course, as you are my possession. No longer a princess, I'm afraid . . . if you ever were one. That Count Peregrine is renowned for deception."

"Is he really a count?" I ask him.

"He claims to be . . . but, as I said, the man is a known liar. I will leave my guard here to watch over you. We don't want our precious cargo getting any funny ideas. . . ."

He reaches into his topcoat, fumbles, and pulls out a long pipe. Now he searches hopelessly for a match. He throws up his hands and reaches into the side pocket of the coach, finding a small metal tinderbox. He lights his pipe and blue smoke emerges. The Sapphire. A slight smile creeps onto his too-taut face.

His head bobs forward with a sloppy grin. "Not for you, dear, not for you."

The vulgar oaf waddles out, over the dirt clearing and into the warm laughter of the pub. The driver now slams the carriage door, standing in front of it, officious.

Well, according to Peregrine, this is my only hope, this chance here. But chance for what? What can I possibly do with the driver standing right there, staring at me, like he is guarding the gold of ten kingdoms?

I wish to creep away. But it seems impossible. Still, there must be something I can do. Some way I can grasp the reins of my fate.

I have been trained to offer the pithiest bon mot, steer any conversation away from conflict, politely avoid an invitation . . . but this? There was certainly no instruction on what to do if sold to a smooth-faced stranger with foul breath and even fouler intent. My mother must not have seen reason to include this in the lesson plan.

But now a thought begins to form . . . now somewhere in the ether.

My mother . . .

As if mocking such concentration, a peal of laughter spills from the tavern, gray tobacco smoke billowing out from the windows.

Smoke.

Smoke . . .

Yes, that's it.

The thought now coalescing . . .

Remember what Mother did in the forest when faced with a marauding highwayman!

I see my hands reaching out before me, grabbing the metal tinderbox from the opposite side of the carriage.

I stop myself a moment. Will this work? If I'm caught, what will they do to me?

And if I don't act? Then what will they do to me still?

Peregrine did warn me. This is my only chance.

I see my fingers grabbing a match from within the tinderbox and striking it. The match erupts in flame. I reach for velvet curtains, ripping one off its bearing and lighting it on fire.

Any hesitation I may have is driven out by the picture of my mother, hurling that torch at that bandit. She was brave. I can be brave, too.

The velvet curtain erupts and before I know not to stop myself, I hurl it out the carriage door, onto the back of the driver.

"AhhhhHHH!" His topcoat catches flame, his pants quickly follow, and now his wig.

I catapult myself out of the carriage, just as I used to catapult myself from under the moat to the portcullis . . . past the flame-engulfed driver, presently dancing a fire-laden jig, and now, dear friends, I begin creeping fast, into the woods, away, away from the dancing flame.

"Heeelp! Heeeeelp!" the flame-engulfed driver screams out.

Feeling a bit guilty, I look back to see the driver throw off his wig and his topcoat. They land inside the carriage. The poor driver doesn't seem too hurt, I assure myself. Now the tavern empties itself out to the dirt clearing, to witness the carriage, engulfed in flames.

I turn and hurl myself forward, running through the brambles and branches, each one like a switch to the face . . . but this is it, this is my only escape; there is no choice in the matter. And this is no time for creeping. I can't remember the last time I wasn't forbidden from doing so, for a princess never does, but this is a time to run.

Behind me, the commotion grows, the sound of the taut-faced oaf calling out, "Where is she?! What have you done, you imbecile?! Find her! I have paid a king's treasure for her—find her!"

The sound of laughter soon follows. What a dastardly place. Who would laugh at such a moment?

But contemplation must come later. I fly through the forest, trying to avoid detection. If I can stay under cover of the forest, yet still close enough to count the bridges, I might make my way back. Back to Alabastrine, back over the salt sea, maybe even back to the Cliffs of Grey. Perhaps the cliff dwellers will forgive me. Perhaps they will help me back to my home.

This is a vicious, unfeeling place. An underbelly, a kingdom of never-ending hells.

The sound of the drunk patrons and the screaming and the laughter begin to dull, and for a minute, I almost believe I am safe.

But that is before I hear the sound of the dogs.

4

THE BARKING OF the hounds in the distance shakes me to my core, spurring my feet faster than I ever remember them going before. The sound cleaves the night air, biting it off in canine jaws.

If I can just make it back to the third bridge, I can cross the river. If I can cross the river, the dogs will be thrown off the scent and unable to follow. I've seen this a hundred times with my father on the hunt. The hounds abruptly stopping on one side of the river, barking helplessly as the fox gleefully crosses and skitters into the forest.

The barks chop through the air, gaining on me. If they find me, in their excitement, they will rip me to shreds, a pack like a mob. I've seen this, too.

The third bridge. It seemed closer before. Now the length between the river and myself seems to stretch itself out in terror.

Now I hear the sound of carriage wheels squeaking over wooden planks. That's it. That's the bridge!

I throw myself forward toward the bridge, hearing the hounds closing in behind. It's a stone's throw now, if only the dogs don't catch me.

The air is a cacophony of excited barks; they know they're about to pounce. Tonight they'll have a princess for dinner.

But here it is!

The river.

It's wider than I had imagined, the bridge not seeming quite that long before. But, of course, then I wasn't running for my life. And how deep is the water? How deep could it be? There's a current to it, though it is difficult in the dark to determine its strength. If there are rapids I would practically be signing my own death warrant, jumping in, in the dark.

RUFFRUFFruffRUFF RUFF!

The hounds are upon me now, so close they're deafening.

No time for contemplation.

SPLASH!

The cold water slaps me. I'm in the river now, brocade dress and all, hurling myself forward. The current is, indeed, stronger than I had imagined. More violent. And now I hear the sound of the dogs fading as the rushing water replaces it.

Downriver now, I can picture exactly what they're doing, barking helplessly, hopelessly, a pack of affronted beasts. One on top of the other, each one barking, dashing hurry-scurry.

Outfoxed.

But there's no time to celebrate, as the rapids rush deeper and faster, tossing me to and fro. There is a lucky thing. Unlike my vain fairyland cousins, Prissy and Bolanda, I've always loved the water. Thrown myself happily into every swimming hole, lake, river, or sea. Prissy and Bolanda used to tease me and tell me I looked like a wet rat. My father, on the other hand, would smile and say I must have been a dolphin in another life.

But still, this godforsaken dress is hitching on every branch, every rock, every bramble, so that my balance is turned not only by that of the current but by this ludicrous frock.

Down, down farther, and now, a great rushing rapid before me. I hear it before I see it, filling me with dread and then . . . under.

Under the water I go, my entire body struggling for breath.

5

———— ❖ ————

THIS COULD BE it.

The moment.

I give up.

Let the water rush over me and sink me down down until all my trials and tribulations cease. Never to struggle. Never to worry. Never again to bear the slings and arrows of outrageous fortune.

How easy it would be. To give in. To slip quietly under this cascading sea, down down to the bottom, where there is no such thing as greed and betrayal.

Yes. A sweet embrace. A watery grave in a foreign land.

And just as I am about to open my mouth, let the river water pour in and seal my fate, there's a picture placed in my head.

Not a thought.

Something placed.

And there it is, in front of me.

All around it is lit up as if by candlelight, and the face in the middle is gentle, kind.

It's my mother's face.

Shimmering.

Tranquil.

Kind.

And even though she doesn't speak, she doesn't need to. I know what she's thinking, as that, too, seems to be placed in my head.

Come home.

Come home to me.

I will wait for you.

And with this thought, this thought like an embrace, I am suddenly shooting up through the rapids, up now, gasping for air with my head above the water and the current batting me this way and that.

I will wait for you.

And now the forest turns itself to me and reaches its arms out. A branch catches me out of the rapids. The branch now cradling me gently, guiding me to the riverbank.

Thud.

It forces me into an eddy, shielded by the branch between the rapids and the shore. Protected.

Gasping still, barely able to hold on, I inch my way sideways along the branch to the river's edge, the mud and the muck now sticking to me, gluing me to the riverbank.

I pause for a moment to catch my breath, then fling myself up onto the edge of the river. Covered in mud. Soaking wet. Spitting up water into the mud.

And yet, somehow, in this moment of muck and choking and shivering to the bone . . . I feel for the first time something I'm not sure I've ever felt.

Elation. A kind of relief. But not just relief, as if my whole body has come forward from the dead, a rebirth in the river, and now my heart is beating a thousand times a minute and I feel like I, I by myself, could lift all the trees in the forest with a single hand. Like I'm not someone who withers in silence, always waiting . . . waiting for someone else to do something, to say something. Waiting for permission.

No.

I was a princess in peril.

And I saved myself.

I *am* the permission.

6

━━━◆━━━

SOAKING WET BY the side of the river, I realize I must find shelter. Shelter and a hearth, a fire. A place to hang up this cumbersome dress, now soaked to the stitching.

If I attempt to trace my steps by the riverbed, upriver, perhaps I can find the third bridge, and stay parallel to the road. The forest will hide me, yet I may find some establishment.

Not a surety, but it's truly my only hope at this point—to make it somewhere dry and warm. This soaking dress could actually be the death of me.

I head upriver, keeping the river's edge directly to my right, not wanting to lose my bearings. The sound of the rapids is deafening and offers a shield for my clumsy footwork through the brambles. My brain keeps within it only one thought: make it to the bridge.

But that thought gets broken in two when I see what appears to be a tiny square of light in the distance, through the forest, up ahead.

I look closer and realize I am looking through the branches at a very small window, lit up from within, about two lengths ahead.

Home and hearth.

Except . . . I look like a soaking-wet wench from the river bottom! I cannot simply walk up and say, "Greetings, strangers! Please let me in!"

Yet the window is not grand; perhaps this is a kind, humble home. Mayhap they will pay no mind to my bedraggled appearance.

I head toward the square piece of light in the darkness, until my eyes can finally make out the outline of a stone dwelling. Inside, there is what sounds to be an old man talking to himself.

I inch closer, his words still muddled, until I reach the opening of the window. I stand there beside it, hidden and eavesdropping.

"Well, what do you expect? Nothing good can come of this place. No. Nothing good at all," the old man goes on. "Alabastrine has always been a den of mischief."

"But Grandfather, this was not just mere mischief. This was . . . why I've never heard anything like it! The stories they tell! About what they saw!" The voice is that of a young lass, perhaps no more than fifteen winters.

"Ah, yes, and tell me? What did they see? Or, more likely, what did they *say* they saw?" the old man asks.

"They say they were all there in the baths—"

"The baths of Alabastrine? A decadent place," the elderly man jeers.

"Yes, and the men, most of the men from the auctions were there," the girl goes on. "The ghastly human auctions."

"Yes, I know. A terrible thing that. To sell a soul like a bale of wheat," the old man replies.

"Yes, well, the men were there. Then, I am told, suddenly the baths turned dark, as if the sun itself had been blocked out of the sky, and there were a thousand blackbirds, suddenly all there, circling, in the midst of all the steam of the baths. And no one knew were they came from," the girl recounts.

"Yes, that is peculiar," the old man acquiesces.

"But that's not all, Grandfather. They said there was a man there, one of the auction traders, lying facedown on a slab, waiting for his massage. And they say that all of a sudden, just before him, the blackbirds had a kind of metamorphosis. That they turned into the shape of a woman, a tall woman with raven-black hair, and they say she held the poor man down! Then she whispered into his ear some kind of foreign words." The girl is almost hysterical now.

"A woman made of blackbirds? What nonsense!"

But the girl insists, "Yes, they all saw it! All of the girls there, the ones that survived."

"Survived?" the old man asks.

"Yes, because you see, I'm told, when the words had been uttered, the devil words, the woman, the raven-haired woman . . . turned BACK into blackbirds and flew up, back out. *Whoosh* and then vanished. And then, this is the worst part . . . they said the steam was suddenly gone and all that was left was the white marble of the baths and the men, the men—" She stops herself.

"Well, go on, dear," he says, impatient.

"The men . . . all lay strewn on the marble floor of the baths. Dead," she finishes.

There is a silence in the little room.

"The man on the slab and the girls were the only ones who did survive."

"And what did the men supposedly die of?" the old man asks.

"That's the issue, Grandfather. No one really knows," she goes on. "But dead they are. It's magic. It must be! It's something dark from the Wraithen—"

"Don't ever speak of the Wraithen!" The old man whips around. "Keep that word out of your mouth, dear girl!"

Having lost myself to this macabre story, I almost forgot my purpose here. Quite simply, that I am freezing to death here in the forest.

Could I approach them? Would they cast me out? Or would they be kind?

The sound of a woman breaks the air.

"Can you discuss this tomorrow? It's late." The voice comes from the bed.

The old man gets up slowly, making his way over to the corner. I peek in and see that there are three frail bodies there. Three feeble souls.

I remember the words of Count Peregrine. How, here, to be wretched is a crime.

Whatever could they be doing here? These three brittle souls, this grandfather and this girl. Are they hiding?

A million questions muddle my head.

"Who goes there?!" The old man barks toward the window.

I freeze against the wall.

"Who is it?! I know you're there," he commands. "Show yourself, trespasser!"

7

"SPEAK! I SAY, speak!" the old man goes on, inching closer to the window.

I take a deep breath.

"Please, sir. It's just me here." I gulp. "Out in the cold. Soaking wet, to be true."

"Who is it? Who dares to stand there eavesdropping like a common criminal?!" he snaps back.

"Sir. It's only me. I am alone, here in this forest. Lost and alone," I reply.

And now I hear the voice of the girl. "Grandfather, let me see. Prithee, move out of the way."

Before he can stop her, the girl has poked her head out of the window, directly beside me.

"Blimey!" she exclaims, seeing me there, shivering in my sullied dress.

"Hello," I whisper, my mouth in a squiggle.

"Come in, come in! You mustn't tarry out in the cold. Come, stand here by the fire. By the gods! You could catch your death."

She rushes out through the doorway, grabbing me and dragging me inside.

There I am met by a roomful of stares. The first stare is that of the old man. But there are three other stares, three sets of suspicious eyes, peering out at me from the corner.

"No need to hide further. She has seen you!" the old man proclaims.

And with that, the three sickly souls begin shuffling out of the shadows.

"Grandfather, find some more blankets!" the girl tells the old man.

"Well, is she a ghost?" one of the wretches asks.

"Not possible," replies Grandfather. "Dear child, your lips are blue. Where have you come from?"

"I fell in the river," I answer, the young girl leading me over to the fire. She covers me with a blanket.

"We must get you out of these clothes," she says. "You can borrow my sleep dress, at least while your dress is drying. I know it seems forward, but . . . you could honestly catch your death! Here, come with me. Behind this table here; I'll hold up this blanket while you change. Here. Here's my sleep dress. It doesn't look like much but it is quite cozy."

I follow her orders as she bosses me about, grateful to have someone here who can think straight. Someone in charge. And most of all . . . someone kind.

Grandfather keeps his eyes on me, suspicious. "The dress is white. Or it was once. Did you come from Alabastrine?"

"No! I mean, yes," I say, seeing his shocked reaction. "I was taken there. By a man. Who lied to me. And then . . . tried to sell me."

At this last part I look down at the floor . . . dirt with a worn thatch rug over it.

A hush falls over the room.

"And did he?" Grandfather asks.

"I escaped. That's why I fell in the river," I explain, now changed into the sleep dress, indeed soft. Warm.

"I see." He seems pensive. "Would you like some tea? Some bread?"

"Oh, please. I cannot tell you how much I would!" I blurt out. "Thank you. You are very kind."

The three fragile beings are now sitting at table; they look at me as if I am the most perplexing creature in all the kingdoms.

"Are you a witch?" one of them asks, tilting his spotted face.

"Most definitely not," I answer.

"A pauper?" the second one asks.

"No," I reply.

"Well, are you a woodsprite, then?" the third one chimes in.

"No. Not a woodsprite," I reply. "At least, not that I know of."

Grandfather gestures to the fire. "Here. You must sit until you are warmed again. You must be chilled to the bone. And some soup; you must have a bit of broth to warm you from the inside."

And now the girl wraps another two blankets around me, one on top of the other. She gives my shoulder a gentle tap of assurance. "I'll just put the kettle on."

"You are such kind people. I cannot thank you enough. If we

were nearer to my home, I could offer you—"

"No need to repay us, dear girl," Grandfather interrupts. "If you don't mind my asking, who is it you were auctioned off to?"

I hesitate, hating the sound of the words. "Well, he had a very smooth face, oddly tight, shiny skin, and he was quite vulgar. I believe his name was . . . Master Gork."

A hush falls over the room.

"I take it . . . you've heard of him," I surmise.

"Yes. Well, to be true, it's a good thing you managed to find your way out of that one." Grandfather replies.

"Oh? Do you mind my asking . . . why, exactly?" I inquire.

"Well, dear girl, that . . . person . . . is renowned for his cruelty. It is said he's keen on humiliating his serfs . . ." He trails off.

Now the girl leans in and whispers to me. "In a rather public fashion. He tortures them. Then leaves their heads on spikes in the village square. It's quite awful really."

Stunned, I close my eyes and shudder, wanting to put this thought out of my mind the moment I hear it.

"Ah, there's the tea!" she chirps, her disposition changing completely at the whistle of the kettle.

Grandfather tries to change the subject. "So, child. Where is home, then?"

"The Roix Kingdom," I reply.

Their faces answer me in a blank, and I continue, "Somehow I fell down a deep, deep chasm and ended up here . . . in your kingdom. I know it sounds strange. But one moment, I was at home in my castle, and the next I landed in a swamp near the Cliffs of Grey."

At this, the three anemic souls begin to whisper among themselves.

"Of all the places on God's green earth! And yet here you are to tell the tale!" Grandfather exclaims.

But the three sorry beings continue to murmur among them.

"Good Lord, what are you three going on about?" Grandfather turns to them.

They go silent, sharing looks. Then one of them, hesitant, delicate, leans in to whisper into his ear.

Grandfather listens, his expression changing. And then lets out a large scoff.

"HA!" He shakes his head. "What nonsense!"

"Grandfather . . . what were they saying? You know, it is rude to keep secrets," the girl chides.

Grandfather hesitates, then exhales. "They think— And again, this is fiddle-faddle. However, they think she might be . . . *The One Who Fell from the Sky.*"

I have heard this phrase before, in the Cliffs. But what does it mean?

The girl gasps and immediately Grandfather checks her. "But these are the fanciful tales of a bygone era. Nothing more."

The girl withdraws, chastened. "Yes, I suppose."

Nevertheless, she peeks up to share a look with the three thin souls. A secret look, seeming to mean they know better.

"Dear girl, you must tell us how you came to be here, in our humble little corner of the forest." Grandfather pivots, wishing to change the subject.

"Grandfather, don't meddle. She's obviously been through something horrible. Why, look at those scratches on her face. Poor girl."

And now the girl hands me a tin mug, with hot tea. The best tea I have ever imbibed.

"There. That should do the trick. We've some bread here, too. I am sorry to say we are out of butter," the girl apologizes.

"Oh, please, don't apologize on my account. I should be on my knees thanking you right now, for your hospitality," I tell her.

"Indeed," Grandfather responds. "Well, the Cliffs of Grey are a place of great peril. Just as the Sapphire Mines are known to kill hundreds each winter."

"Sapphire Mines?" the girl asks.

"Yes, oh yes," he adds. "The Azelle are soon to be extinct, I predict. Persecuted for their ancient beliefs, you know. Quite a thing, quite a thing. All to collect the Sapphire, of course. All for men, and women, to stay pretty and vain in this godforsaken land," he answers. "Where to be wretched is a crime. The bastards."

A shudder runs through me as I think of the cage full of unfortunates, the cart passing by me in the middle of the night, their drawn faces, the corpse.

"Grandfather, please try to control yourself. Is that any way to speak in front of company?"

I think on it. "But why do they actually do it? The Azelle?"

"Do what?" he replies.

"The work in the mines," I answer.

He tilts his head and looks at me, as if stymied by such a question.

"My dear girl, they do it because they have no choice," he declares. "Because otherwise they'll simply kill them."

"But who will kill them?" I ask.

"The Wraithen, of course," he answers. "If they don't work in the mines, the Wraithen will slaughter their children and their friends and anyone else they might hold dear. They've done it before. An entire Azelle settlement was wiped out two winters back. A terrible thing."

"The Wraithen. I thought the Wraithen was a place. A kingdom?" I sip my tea.

"It is a place. And it is also a thing. A system. An order, I suppose," he informs me.

"But who is giving these orders? Who makes this disgraceful law?" I ask.

Grandfather whispers to me. "The queen of the Wraithen. She is the one who has set it all in stone. If it is a law, it is an order, and if it is an order, it comes from her."

I contemplate this in silence. "What is her name?"

"Do not even ask such a thing." He looks into my eyes, dead serious. "Now, it is time we all, finally, rest."

"But I don't want to rest!" one of the three wisps interrupts. "I want to stay up and look at this strange lady!"

"Come now." The granddaughter begins to tuck the delicate woman in as if she's a child. "It is late. The sun has gone to sleep and now so must we."

A sweet, warm, tender sight. It grips me, reminding me of home. Of family. Of my mother. The delightful pleasure of being tucked into bed. How I long to be home! To be tucked into bed.

"Yes, let us all retire." Grandfather turns back to me. "There is a mat there. Bring it here by the fire, so to keep warm. In the morning we shall take you back. Back to . . . where is it you would like to go?"

"If it's possible, if it's not too much of a journey . . . I'd like you to drop me off at the salt sea."

"Dear girl, you're mad!" He scoffs.

"I know where to go from there. I'll be fine. I just need some water, perhaps. And bread for the journey—" I assure him.

"My dear girl, this is an absurd request," he replies. "Why, you might as well ask to be taken to the jaws of hell."

"Please, sir, it's the only way I know to possibly return to my home. If I can just find the place where I came into your world, I might return to mine."

Grandfather looks at me, hesitates. "Well, I have a few small errands that direction. It will add half a day's drive, I suppose, if we cut through the forest, which we must."

"We won't come anywhere near to Alabastrine, would we?"

"No, my dear child," he answers.

I nod. "Good. I would not want to return to that place." I stare into the fire, the flames dancing, the picture of Peregrine betraying me seared in my head. I could kill him. I know these are not thoughts for a lady, but I cannot stop seeing his face as he threw me to the wolves.

"A despicable place, this land. It is cursed, did you know? They say it were created out of spite." And now he contemplates the flames, as well.

"Oh, Grandfather," the girl chides. "You should not poison the mind of this sweet girl. For she is clearly from another land. One that is innocent."

And that thought sticks through me like a knife. The thought of my home. A home that is innocent. Without these terrible sights and crimes. A longing forms inside me like I've never known. My heart wishes to jump out of my body and find its way home.

8

GRANDFATHER IS AS diligent as he is humble, preparing the horse and cart for the journey through the forest.

The sun has risen to the tops of the trees now, the morning dew on the grass caught by the sunlight, turned into crystals.

The granddaughter does all she can to help, bringing forward bread wrapped in burlap and blankets for the cart. "I'm sorry I can't go with you. It's all so . . . adventurous."

There's something so cheerful about this girl, even in the face of this dreary place. I find myself wondering if that's just the way it is, if some people, no matter the circumstances, are happy, and take life lightly, and others, no matter their circumstances, are brooding and filled with bile. As if all of that is decided the moment one is born. Could that be? Or does one have a choice?

"Oh, leave that here. We shan't take the whole house now!" Grandfather hands back a few things to the girl.

"It's just, I want to make sure she has everything. For the journey. It's not exactly a safe one." She looks at me. "I mean, I'm sure you'll be fine but it's best to be prepared, I always say."

Grandfather gives her a look and she winks at me. "Never mind him, he's had too many winters. But he's a good man. Just old."

I stifle a laugh.

"Well, this OLD GRUMPY MAN is ready to go. Dear girl, are you ready?" He turns to me.

"Oh yes, thank you," I reply.

The granddaughter throws her arms around me in a bear hug.

"Be safe, be strong, be hidden, and drink much ale," she directs me.

"Ha! Thank you so much, for taking me in and for doing all of these kind things for me. I am so very grateful."

"Oh, fiddlesticks!" she teases. "It's not every day we find a drenched wench in the woods!"

"Goodbye, then." I smile.

"Cheerio, then." She thinks, adding, "Be sure you don't die."

9

A KING'S JOURNAL

I am near my wit's end. The hideous old woman has been set here the past fortnight. Now she has convinced my wife of this ludicrous plan to have every prince from here to the sea come round and lay their lips on the mouth of my dear slumbering daughter. Disgusting!

And yet, our dear queen has fallen for it.

By the gods, if this works I'll eat my minstrel's fiddle.

Tomorrow is the first day, the first "trial," if you will.

A young prince named Gilgamorte, from the dark kingdom to the east, is set to arrive sometime between midday and evening. My wife is, of course, all in a tizzy about what is to be served, what is most certainly not to be served, what tapestries are to be hung on the wall, what tapestries are to be taken off the wall, etcetera, etcetera, etcetera.

Of course, when I asked her "Why on earth does it matter?" she replied:

"But obviously it matters; what if Prince Gilgamorte is, indeed, this Prince Charming? Can't you see how important it is to make the right impression?"

"With a name like Prince Gilgamorte, I'm sure we should serve him bats for dinner."

"Oh, that's just like you. Our daughter's fate hangs in the balance and you are cracking jokes. Very fine, indeed," she scolded me.

"Yes, indeed," the old crow chimed in from the corner. A crow indeed, as there are blackbirds hanging about, cawing infernally, since she arrived.

"Why is SHE still here?" I asked my wife.

"Because she is our most trusted adviser on the matter, as you know. As I've told you a thousand times."

"Yes, but darling." And at this, I leaned in, lowering my voice to a whisper. "Must she always be about? Look at her, she's a fright."

"I heard that!" the old crone interjected from the corner.

"How could she possibly hear me? I can hardly even hear myself," I added.

"HOW CAN YOU POSSIBLY HEAR ME? I CAN HARDLY HEAR MYSELF." The old crow mimicked me now, parroting my words.

"Insolence!" I turned to the old bat. "How dare you speak to your king in that—!"

The queen attempted to settle me down. "Now, now, dear. Remember, we have but one purpose here, and that is to get our daughter back."

Well, dear journal, I suppose she is right. But this old crone, she is unbearable. I cannot stand to look at her. And yet, she seems to always be looking at me. Peering through me. As though she knows my deepest secret.

Could she?

No, that is impossible. The only other involved was banished long ago.

Still, I am as desperate to get this old hag out of the castle as my wife is desperate to find this alleged charming prince.

I'm not sure how much further I should allow it.

10

THE JOURNEY GOES much more quickly than I'd expected, owing most certainly to the old man's wisdom about these country roads, which I am informed follow the same routes as the ancients', built centuries before the kingdoms. It's a funny thing; we pass not a single soul.

This entire excursion, I've once again had the feeling that I must be in a dream. The tiny roads through the forest are so empty.

I am grateful for the secrecy, however, and grateful to be in the hands of such a kind man.

He hums merrily to himself the entire way. I find myself left to my own inner thoughts and musings. Something about the hooves of the horse on the path, the repetition of the wheels of the cart, circling on the ground . . . a hypnotic thing. Almost a meditation.

I had thought we would spend the night somewhere, but Grandfather insists on continuing on through the night, so certain is he of the route. He doesn't spell it out, but it's clear he is whisking me through the forest as quickly as possible for safety's sake.

For though we are alone, peril lurks and we both know it . . . too well. This unsaid thing lies somewhere between us.

Smoldering.

By dawn, I can see the barren salt sea in the distance, a white mirage lit up by the glare of the morning sun.

I had thought the old man was to leave me here, at the edge, but he continues farther, over the ivory expanse. A gesture of kindness, I suppose. By the time we reach the other side of the dried white sea, the sun is high up and the sky is a kind of blaring gray, as if the sun refuses to come out from the clouds.

"I will leave you here, young lass. I cannot go any farther." Grandfather helps me to my feet, out of the cart. "You must be careful. Stay under cover of the trees, and if you hear someone, do not make yourself known. Hide in the brush. Do you understand?"

"Yes. I am, actually, an excellent hider. In my kingdom I made sort of an art of going undetected," I assure him, not elaborating further on my creeping.

He smiles and looks directly into my eyes. "Please be safe, dear girl."

"Yes, sir. And you, as well. I should not forget your kindness. . . . Thank you." I nod, solemn.

He nods with a paternal smile. Then he makes his way back to the horse and cart. "Goodbye, dear lassie. Be safe!"

I continue to watch him, the familiar sound of the cart and the hooves of the horse on the dirt. Now dimmer, now dimmer still. Watching him dwindle in the horizon, there is a part of me that wishes to run after him. But the part of me that is desperate for home is ten times greater.

Home.

The thought of it fills me with longing.

Yes, yes, I am on my way back home.

That is how I shall think of it. Every step takes me closer to the palace and my mother and father.

The squawk of a blackbird—there seems to be no other type of avian creature in this realm—wakes me up from my momentary trance.

I must make it to the Cliffs of Grey before nightfall. There, if I beg, perhaps the cliff dwellers will help me find my way back to the place where I fell from my kingdom.

But this thought is halted by the sound of a rustle through the leaves near me. Startled, I duck down behind a shrub, holding my breath.

No need, though. A sprightly, chipper squirrel makes its way out of the brush. How silly I am, scared of my own shadow! I cannot allow myself to be overtaken with fear. *Fear leads to misgivings, misgivings to confusion . . . confusion to madness.* The words of my father, ringing in my ears: *Fear is a poisoned chalice; do not drink of it.*

I take a deep breath, finding my courage, and begin my journey back to the Cliffs of Grey. I have always, strangely, had a keen sense of direction and, much to my surprise, the way seems to beckon me. Yes, I remember this giant rock, and that mountain range there, to the left. It is all coming back now and I am confident of myself, confident I can make it.

Fear leads to madness. Do not drink of it.

Yes, I will make it back soon.

More, this will all make an excellent story at a feast one day. We will laugh and toast to my adventures and my daring escape!

Yes, we will do exactly that . . . just as soon as I (if I ever) get home.

11

THE SUN IS dipping down now in the sky, turning the forest amber and gold, before I make it back to the Cliffs of Grey. Giddy, I am, to see the children, running about the caverns by candle-light, giggling to themselves, the universe in their eyes, shining bright.

But there is no one frolicking in the waning day.

Not now.

When I was a little girl my mother would read me stories at night, just before bed, about dragons and faraway kingdoms and ships of gold. Every once in a while, she would pause, make a decision, and then skip ahead, turning the pages in silence, omitting something too dark or too scary or too cruel. I would ask her, always, "Mother, why did you skip over that part?" And she would kindly whisper, "Nothing, darling, just monsters from the deep." And then I, of course, would ask, "Mother, is there really such a thing . . . as monsters from the deep?" And she would laugh, kiss me on the forehead, and say, "No. No, darling, of course not."

And as I stand in the blinding golden light, burning sideways from the sun, and peer out at what is left of the Cliffs of Grey . . .

I know that was a lie. Clearly, my mother was protecting me. There are, indeed, monsters.

The sour scent of smoke meets my nose. The scene sets itself . . . the blood on the ground painted a bright orange by the sun. Yet the whole settlement is some shade of gray. The tables and chairs. The rugs and blankets. The clothes have all been burned.

And the people . . .

Their bodies lie about, turned black as stone. The ground is seared ebony beneath them.

I cover my mouth as I realize what exactly I am looking at.

An enormous fire. A mass death.

I have never seen such a gruesome thing.

I have heard, here in this place, of unspeakable things. Listened to stories of the Azelle being worked to their graves in the Sapphire Mines, understood that people are killed for sport in the Wraithen, heard of the wretched, cast out and enslaved for their unsightliness.

But those were words. Abstractions.

This is real. This, this is a cruelty a thousandfold.

As I manage to make out the figures, the outlines, amongst the wreckage, I begin to recognize a few faces from my brief time spent here. The laughing face of a stranger at table, now frozen in a rictus of pain. The full head of red hair of a woman, reaching down to her waist. Now partially destroyed by flame.

My head now swims with rage and helplessness. The bile in my throat mixes with my tears, everything salt and ash.

I close my eyes, collapsing inside, the breath knocked out of me. Hoping, perhaps, that when I open my eyes, this will all just be a kind of macabre nightmare.

But there again is a sound in the brush, the snap of a twig, and I open my eyes, aware now I may be in danger. That a terrible thing may happen to me.

Well, let it.

What do I care?

Why should I survive when this entire village is perished before me? By the looks of it, as if they never even had a chance. As if some diabolical force simply wiped them from the face of the earth.

No, I do not care what that might be in the woods.

What does it matter now?

12

ABOVE ME NOW, there is the first star in the sky to the west. The moon deciding to be late.

A voice comes out of the forest.

"So . . . the princess decided to return?" It's a woman's voice, deep, not seeking approval or permission.

"Who is there?" I say. "Show yourself. Do not hide like a common thief."

"Ah, I am a thief now, am I?" the voice replies. "And yet I am not the one who snuck out like a bandit in the dead of night."

"Show yourself. I refuse to be insulted by one I cannot see," I answer.

And with that the trees make way and the branches bow; the leaves stand at attention. She makes her way through them, imposing, and the secret is revealed.

It is the pewter-gold woman from the Cliffs of Grey.

Keela.

"Are you surprised?" she asks. "Do you remember me? Do you remember me from the caverns?"

"Yes, of course I remember you—"

"Then you remember that you left us?" she interrupts.

"I watched a barbarian behead two men before my very eyes for no reason," I reply.

"And how do you know it was for no reason?" She bristles.

"I— What?" I stop, confused.

"I suppose you didn't recognize those two men from the swamp. The ones who captured you," she continues. "And I suppose you didn't realize they were there only for you. To bring you back as their captive, as their catch, and to kill you, to sling you alive on a spit?"

I stand, silenced.

She shakes her head. "Svan was kind enough to save you. You, who know nothing of our ways, and did not think to even ask. You simply judged us and left like a prowler in the night."

"But—their decapitated heads were left on the ground to rot," I answer.

"That was a tribute. To you. A pledge. For your safety. And a warning to their kind."

My face burns with shame. Could I have misjudged so easily?

Keela wastes no time sizing me up. "You are a fool. A frivolous little princess from an imaginary land. No stronger or more purposeful than a leaf in the wind."

My next words fly from my mouth before I have the chance to think about them. "You do not know the things I have survived since we last met! You have no idea what I have done to assure my survival! And speaking of which, why have *you* survived? Why are *you* not dead like all the others? Why were *you* not here to protect them? Are you not the *guardian* of these cliffs?"

I contend. "Quite the guardian you are! Look at them! Look at these poor souls, slain. Are you not ashamed?"

A silence stretches between us. I blink. Such terrible, pointed, *unpleasant* words. Words that I would be scolded for using in my kingdom.

I thought such words had been scrubbed from my mind. Trained out of me. And yet, they have emerged from some deep corner of my soul.

My mother would have me apologize for them.

I shall not apologize.

"Yes. And I am ashamed," Keela answers. "I have spent the night here in tears, having returned to this."

"Returned? Why had you left in the first place?" I ask.

"It was a trap," she confesses, defeated. "They lured us out and then slaughtered everyone left behind in the village."

I ask, "And what of Svan? And the girls, the two sweet little girls who were so kind to me, and Wyeth, your son?"

"Happily, none of them are here amongst the embers." She closes her eyes, as if to banish the thought.

I breathe a sigh of relief. A small glimmer of hope.

"But who has done this?" I turn to her. "Who could commit such an unspeakable act?"

She looks at me now, shaking her head. "Poor *princess*. So ignorant."

"Please." I try a different tack. "You are right. I know nothing of this place. That is why I am asking these questions. Who burned this village?"

"The soulless. The cruel. The murderers. Possibly sent by order of the Wraithen." She exhales. "Perhaps the Veist herself."

"The Veist?"

"Yes," she continues. "Creator of the sun, the moon, and the stars. Creator of this dark, hateful world. Created out of spite."

"Out of spite. Out of spite! It isn't the first time I've heard this! Worlds cannot be created by ill feelings. And whose spite could even achieve such a thing? It's preposterous. You are all under some sort of delusion. Some collective hallucination," I tell her.

"Does this seem like a hallucination to you? These bones marred by fire?!"

I stand silenced.

"There is only one law of this land. It is the rule of the Wraithen. Both the people and its kingdom. Because of it, we are all at the whim of the one known as the Veist," she adds. "And there is no court or office or kindly authority to plead your case to or from whom to seek justice."

"And where is this supposed all-powerful Veist? This supernatural phantom?"

"Choose your words wisely. The Veist is an omniscient, unstoppable force," she answers. "It is rumored she lies somewhere deep beyond the walls of the Wraithen, beyond its people and its towers . . . in a place some say doesn't exist."

"But what would such a being have to do with this place? This place here, on the edge reality?" I ask her. "Why toy with the unfortunate creatures of this village? Why the Cliffs of Grey?"

She pauses. "That *is* a mystery. We had been forgotten, it seemed, for a great many moons. Until you."

An idea begins forming now. Swirling in the depths of my mind, not quite taking shape. "You are not alone in your tragedy. I heard a story. I overheard it, to be true. About another mass slaughter in the baths of Alabastrine . . ."

I trail off, blind in my own ignorance. Why should this be related? I'm like a child grasping around in the dark.

She looks at me, curious. "Tell me this story."

"It was said that there was a form . . . in the baths. A form of blackbirds, hundreds of them. And somehow . . . this form . . . turned into a woman."

"Blackbirds." She ponders.

"And then the woman bowed over and whispered some words to a man. A man who was simply lying there on a slab. And some-how when the steam cleared . . . the entire baths, everyone inside, was dead, with only a handful of survivors to tell the tale."

"And the man? The one whispered to," she asks. "Did he survive?"

"I don't know. I don't know what any of it means . . . or even if it's all just rumors and conjecture."

Keela pauses, turning this over. "Alabastrine is known for many things . . . revelry, decadence, depravity . . . but slaughter is not one of them."

"What could it possibly mean?" I ask.

"It means something exceptional is happening in the kingdoms, something unprecedented." She contemplates. "Something singular."

"But what could it be?" I ask.

She looks at me, still turning it over in her mind. "This slaughter. It happened here; it happened in Alabastrine. Both places you had . . . recently left."

I frown. "But what does that—"

She interrupts me. "Perhaps the subject of the slaughter, the target, has eluded the assassins. Perhaps the target . . . is you."

13

———◆———

THE MOON IS high in the sky now, congregating with the stars. Here, in the Cliffs of Grey, the stars shine brighter, a canopy of candles, a kind of blessing, so bright you feel you could reach out and touch them. There, Orion's Belt. There the seven sisters of the Pleiades. There Ursa Major, pointing to Polaris and Ursa Minor. These stars, these constellations, one of the few things my father taught me. It was clear, his love of the heavens. How he wanted to pass it on to his daughter. Staring at them now, it's a wonder that they are the same stars. Curious, yes? That in this terrifying dark world, the stars are just the same.

"They will be buried at morning. It shall be hallowed ground." Keela interrupts my train of thought. "Or will you run out in the night again so you do not have to witness our pain?"

Ashamed, I can only answer, "No, I will stay to see them ushered on to heaven. I would never absent myself from such eulogy."

"Do you see behind me?" she asks.

"I'm not sure—"

"Behind me. Look closer." She lifts her chin in a kind of dare.

And then I do see it: one by one, the trees and branches come to life, and I realize that there must be a hundred men and women, camouflaged in the trees and rocks, in shades of rust and brown and gray, just as the foliage and the mud and the cliffs. I remember now the nearly invisible painted barbarians in the swamps.

"How long have they been there?" I ask.

"Since you've been counting stars," she replies. "A little trick we learned from the swamp people."

The men and women stand now, in our midst, warriors each. Painted to look like the forest but equipped with bows and arrows strapped to their backs. A menacing yet astounding sight. They move so quietly; you cannot even hear one footstep.

"They are ever so stealthy," I marvel.

"They are trained. They are fighters. If you choose to stay, you also will be a fighter. If you choose to, you will avenge these deaths by our side." She gestures to the destruction all around us.

An owl trills in the forest, adding his counsel to the discussion.

"But I—" I start. Keela raises a hand to cut me off.

"*You* do not believe you could be a warrior," she continues. "You think of yourself as weak. That is not your fault. It is what you have been taught. To be silent. To ease the path of those above you."

Stunned, I feel the eyes of the warriors on me.

"But look around you. Look at these faces." She nods toward the warriors, who stand upright, imposing, as if ready to spring at any moment. "They, too, had been taught lies. Different lies, but lies nonetheless. Every one of them. The men, taught they are born to be worked to death in the mines, or used as pawns in someone else's war. Cannon fodder. The women, taught to be used and discarded. Both expendable. We created our own way here, long ago. We formed a society in which these lies had no meaning."

The night is still now, as if the moon itself is leaning in, listening, the stars on the tips of their toes, Orion eavesdropping.

"We do not believe in these myths used to control us," she declares. "Why should you?"

There is a part of me, not a small part, that is whispering, Whatever is happening here is not your problem. Your job is to find your way back to where you are from. Back to your family in Roix.

Yet my eyes range over the corpses on the ground. So many of them. Innocent lives lost.

And what if Keela is right? What if they are lost *because* of me?

The wind howls around us. A mournful sound.

Keela continues, "It would seem that you have a stake in our plight as well. *You* are connected to our pain in ways we have yet to understand. The malevolence follows you. I wonder if you are the one who will finally defeat it, as was prophesied."

I turn back to Keela. "What do you mean?"

"It has been said that the only one who can cure the spite that created this world is . . . The One Who Fell from the Sky."

My head spins. "You said that was a silly myth."

Keela nods. "And yet . . ."

And yet . . .

This is impossible. These people—this place. They did not exist. And yet, somehow I have tumbled into this strange world. I have fallen to it. I am here.

"You are correct. All of my life I've been taught to not make a fuss. To smile and nod. But there is a point when a fuss must definitely be made. In the face of such horror, I cannot turn a blind eye. I will stay. And fight. And when the enemy is defeated, I will find my way home."

14

A KING'S JOURNAL

Ha! I am vindicated.

Two moons ago, our much-anticipated guest, Prince Gilga-morte, arrived to our much-decorated castle.

Of course, at the behest of my wife, the entire affair was the very picture of pomp and ceremony. The only thing unpleasant about it was that skittering old woman, our own personal sage, tucked in the corner like a sinister, greedy spider.

I'll have you know, Prince Gilgamorte did not disappoint.

No, no! All the luxurious splendor of our kingdom was met, stone for stone, with his own pretension. Indeed, his nose did not seem to falter below the height of the tapestries, hung high on the castle walls.

A dark sort of dandy, this one. As full of himself as the peacock, parading its dazzling feathers for all to see. His sartorial flare, in deep plum, purple, and black . . . in velvet, silk, and brocade, as if at any moment, he might turn into a gorgeous bat and fly straight out the turret whence he came.

The court gasped mightily as he waltzed into our presence, seemingly doing us a favor. Thin as a rail he was, with a gait smooth as glass. He seemed to glide across the hall. And there, both the queen and I sat in our thrones, to welcome him. She more than I, of course.

"Prince Gilgamorte. We welcome you to the kingdom of Roix," my wife greeted him.

At this, the spindly prince set his eyes on his poor underling, who dutifully came forward.

"Prince Gilgamorte, of the Kingdom of Rumin, House of Vlindall, Second Son of Estonvilla . . . is his full title." At which point, the underling bowed humbly, making his way back to his place behind the prince . . . having, essentially, corrected my queen. In her own castle.

Ah! So the prince is as proud as he is vain.

"Yes, yes," I interceded. "We all have titles, and if we should list them all we shall be here till dawn. Tell me, Prince Gilgamorte, have you been informed as to why, exactly, you've been summoned?"

"But of course. To marry your daughter, the princess," he deigned to answer.

The queen and I shared a look.

"Yes, well," I added. "It's not quite that simple."

The prince frowned, his worm-thin mustache bending downward.

"You see, as strange as it may sound . . ." I searched for the words. "At first, there must be a kiss."

The court gasped in astonishment.

"But this is very forward, Your Majesty," the prince replied. "I have never heard such a thing."

The queen interceded then. "Yes, well, it is a bit of a strange time, here at our kingdom. You see, the princess is actually . . . asleep."

Again, the court responded in inhales, exhales, and general sighing.

"Asleep, you say?" The prince seemed genuinely intrigued. "How so?"

"It is a kind of enchantment," the queen informed him. "A strange sort of slumber that can only be removed by the kiss of a prince—"

"A worthy prince," I elaborated.

"Yes. That too," my wife admitted, with a pinched smile.

"Ah!" Prince Gilgamorte exclaimed. "Well, of course. For who, other than me, should be worthy of such an honor? It is quite logical you came to me. And I compliment you on your good taste."

I tried to catch the queen's eye but she deliberately ignored me. Once she sets her mind on something, there's no undoing it.

"Yes, well, shall we to the garden, then?" The queen dismissed any further discussion, eager to accomplish the task at hand. "We can dine after. We have a lovely banquet prepared."

"Ah! Wonderful. I am quite famished," Prince Gilgamorte confessed.

And then the three of us made our royal way out of the grand hall, down the promenade to the garden. The old woman scuttled behind us, like a little mouse after some cheese.

At one point, the prince noticed her, turning around. "Excuse me, Your Majesty, but might I ask . . . who is this . . . woman following us? Is she meant to be here, or shall I call my guards?"

"Yes, yes," I answered. "Unfortunately, she is part of this whole—"

"Ceremony!" the queen interrupted. "Yes, it may seem odd. But she is an essential part of this royal tradition. You know these traditions, always a bit strange. No one ever seems to know the origin, the rhyme, or the reason."

"Ah, yes," the prince conceded. "In my kingdom of Rumin, there is an odd tradition involving a magic scarf and an old sow. The handkerchief must be burned from the northern edge, lest we all die of scurvy."

"Yes. Exactly." The queen smiled.

At this point, the figure of the princess, asleep on the slab in the midst of the garden, became clear ... the vines and flowers serving as a kind of verdant proscenium. The prince drew breath at the sight, clearly impressed.

"What a beautiful yet melancholy sight," he exclaimed. "I shall be happy to rid your poor daughter of this terrible curse."

"Ah, yes. We shall be very grateful," smiled the queen. "Well, let us not tarry."

"Yes, let's get this over with," I said under my breath, the queen elbowing me ever so subtly.

"Well, then." The prince came around to the other side of the slab, gently above our dear princess Bitsy. "Say goodbye to all these tribulations, my dear."

At this, Prince Gilgamorte leaned down, in all his glory, and gave the princess a kiss.

At which point the princess remained in her slumber.

And Prince Gilgamorte transformed into a frog.

15

THROUGH THE THICKET of trees we emerge. This is a place of secrets, hidden deep within the forest. Keela leads us through the dense branches and brambles until we reach a kind of hidden camp.

At first, it's difficult to discern what is before me. Underneath tents made of burlap, held together with weathered rope, arms are being readied, archery: arrows and bows. Underneath others, the preparation of more sinister-looking swords, the sound of metal and sparks from iron weapons being forged. The hustle and bustle of this place . . . a kind of organized chaos. Keela is clearly building an army to be reckoned with. My plan, which she has so graciously adopted, will benefit greatly from this feral army. They certainly do not look like shrinking violets.

There is one thing that stands out to me amidst the hurly-burly, partly due to its incongruous nature. There, on the edge of the camp, is the little ash-haired boy I met . . . Keela's son, Wyeth, the one obsessed with collecting buckets. And now, to my amusement, he seems to be peering intensely into a bucket of water, this one with a metal tool of some kind poking out. He squints intensely at his experiment.

Drawn to him, I saunter over to ask him exactly what he is doing.

"Hello there. Do you remember me? You once asked me for a bucket. Now I see you've found one. What is it in that pail of such concern?" Despite my kind tone, he doesn't seem to notice me. "By your look, it might be the universe."

Then, in a kind of confounded daze, he looks up at me, trying to figure out what exactly is interrupting his thought process.

"It's a frog," he answers.

"Oh, only a frog, well . . . it must be quite a fascinating one, to garner your attention so," I chide.

"It's a dead frog," he replies, matter-of-fact.

"Ah. And is that why it's so fascinating?" I ask.

"No, not really. The question is . . . what killed it?" he confides. "You see, I had captured this frog just last night, alive and well."

"Oh, well, I am sorry."

"I do have a theory." He thinks. "But it will take a bit of experimentation."

"Do you mind my asking . . . how old are you?"

"I am ten winters. Why do you ask?" He squints up at me, the sun in his pale blue eyes.

"Oh, no matter. I suppose I'm just a bit impressed," I say, giving a warm smile.

"Well, don't be," he replies. "Until I figure it out. Otherwise, I've nothing but a dead frog in a bucket."

I chuckle a bit and return to Keela's side as she observes a young woman in training.

She turns to me. "Well, it's now or never, Princess. You see that tent there? They will train you. I shall have my hands full training this army. I trust you will be in good hands with them." She turns to leave.

"Wait? You're leaving? B-But—" I stammer.

"You will be better off without me there to distract you. You've much to learn," she clarifies.

Before I can protest, she turns and leaves me alone to contemplate the little ash-haired boy, who is now setting out a series of buckets with the intensity of a mad scientist.

16

THE SUN BEAMS down, my bare arms warming in the heat. The great stallion gallops beneath me. There! In the distance! The target. Now, to reach back for my quiver and nock the arrow. Muscles straining as I pull the bow string, Keela's lessons ringing in my ear. *Focus, breathe.* I steady my upper body against the thundering strides of the horse. I take a deep breath. Now! I loose the arrow. It strikes. A little to the right, but I've done it! My heart beams. I hear the rumble of hooves behind me. I turn to see Keela not astride but standing atop her horse, effortlessly balanced. She pulls her bow. FSHEW! She has hit the target dead center.

I am learning.

It's been over forty moons, from sunup to sundown, and I don't quite recognize myself anymore. It's as if another person has crawled completely under my skin. Or, perhaps, that person was there all along. Just waiting to surface.

Despite my previous ignorance of agile horseback archery, I am not completely useless here, you'll be happy to note. Point of fact: my favorite accomplishment is being able to teach my long-held knowledge of creeping, hiding, and generally being able to blend into the shadows. It requires dexterity, stealth. And, to the shock of my peers, I have actually been able to teach scaling up steep walls in an impossible-to-detect manner. This seems to be a favorite of the assembled troops. In fact, just last night, I noticed a group scaling the walls for fun, teasing each other. I'm bursting with pride to report I have turned the entire group into expert creepers.

There really is something to it, something to all this training, activity, and exhaustion. Something about losing oneself to the moment. No time to overthink it; the arrow either hits the target or it doesn't. You either scale the wall or you fall. There's no pretense, a kind of beauty to the simplicity of it.

Last night, however, there was an eerie moment I've kept to myself. Just as I closed my eyes to sleep, I heard that voice . . . the same whispery voice in the wind I heard in the forest and then, later, in the Alabastrine. This time, however, it felt like the voice was whispered directly into my ear:

"I will dream you."

I started from my pillow then, looking around for the source of the voice . . . and, again, nothing but the wind, howling outside my tent. I stood up, dashing outside to find the culprit. But, no, still no one out there but a handful of stragglers, far on the other side of the camp. After a few confounded moments, I decided I was dreaming. That I had to be dreaming.

Then, awakening this sunrise, all thought of it was erased by Keela at the foot of my bed, informing me that we have a long journey ahead, to the Sapphire Mines. She intends to build as large an army as possible, including integrating the freed miners from the Sapphire. I had not known this was part of her strategy, but Keela isn't the most communicative of sorts.

At this moment, now, I am packed and ready to depart, wondering what awaits us in the Sapphire. Stories have been told around the fire about what goes on at the mines, but they seem a bit fanciful. The kind of thing that gets passed down, exaggerated more and more each time in the telling.

On my way to the very edge of camp, I happen once again on Keela's little ash-haired son, Wyeth, conducting another experiment. This time, he has set out row upon row of his many pails of water. I notice each bucket now has a frog at the bottom.

"What is this interesting project?" I inquire.

"It's to see what will happen to each frog if there is a lightning storm. You see, some buckets have a metal rod poking out and some do not. It has something to do with the metal, I think." He adds, "Now I just have to wait for a lightning storm."

"And what are you expecting to happen?" I query. "If there is indeed a lightning storm?"

"Well, you see, a frog in a bucket during a lightning storm is no issue. But . . . if there is a rod in the bucket, particularly a metal rod . . . it seems the frog will die."

"Really?" I ask. "How do you know?"

"Because it happened by accident, last spring. This made me curious. So I have now reconstructed the experiment, with limited success." He continues, "The question is . . . will a wooden rod in the bucket achieve the same result? And if so, why? And if not . . . why not?"

"Fascinating." I admire the boy, who still continues the precise placement of each individual bucket. "I shall be intrigued to revisit your findings."

"Will you really or are you just having me on?" He looks at me, curious.

"No, I'm quite interested, my dear boy. In my kingdom there is a man my father commissioned to do such intriguing experiments all day. He's quite clever." I elaborate: "In fact, he even invented a system of gears and pulleys to draw up the gate beyond the moat from afar."

"Interesting." He asks, "Do you miss your home?"

"Yes. Quite. I miss my mother. And even my father these days. Surprising, that, as we never seem to see eye to eye," I confide.

"Perhaps one day you'll return," he replies.

"Mayhap. Who knows if it's even possible? But I cannot give up hope." I nod, a quick smile. Somehow the smile protects me.

"Mayhap I could help you." He thinks. "I'm not sure how. . . ."

"You just worry about your magnificent experiment," I tell him. "Young man, I'm sure one day your name will be known in all the kingdoms."

"Oh, I don't care tuppence about that." He squints into the distance. "I just care about the confounded rain."

"Hm." I grin. "Spoken like a true scientist."

"Come on then! We don't have time to sit around all day squawking!" Keela is at the edge of the camp, impatient. She waves at her son with a smile.

"Don't you wish to say goodbye to your mother?" I ask the boy.

"She already said goodbye. And kissed me. And hugged me. Six times," he replies.

"Ah, well, I am very jealous of your kisses and hugs from your mother," I confess to him.

He takes the point and I nod, turning now to Keela and the long journey ahead.

It's two moons to the Sapphire Mines, over an arid and barren terrain. A kind of thirsty landscape, parched by the sun. We've doubled our supply of water because, apparently, if we run out, we'll die. And that just won't do.

There are meant to be creatures from vipers to buzzards to a kind of beige, ravenous dire hound that only stalks in the night. There are meant to be prickly plants that can cut you and tear at your clothes and a cat, smaller than a lion, that can nevertheless chase you and kill you by leaping upon the back of the neck and mauling you to death.

We shall see.

17

KEELA AND I are accompanied by twenty to thirty warriors on horseback, some young men, some young women, and some something in between. We have not encountered any of these supposed night-ravaging dire hounds or devilish felines, but we've been privy to the company of more than enough lizards and the odd snake. Perhaps the magnitude of our warrior battalion has discouraged such dangerous creatures, who choose instead to bathe in the sun or spy behind the nearest rock.

Before we even begin to reach the Sapphire Mines, we encounter an endless array of wooden structures, tiny shacks, on the horizon, hundreds of them.

The lot of us halt as we try to gauge this strange panorama.

"What do you suppose they are?" Keela asks. "Do you think this is where the Azelle live?"

"Is it only the Azelle who live here?" I ponder.

"Mostly the Azelle. The wretches of the Sapphire have been taken from all throughout the kingdoms. Some are infirm, feeble; some are simply unlucky," she informs me. "Those who come here are from every corner of the kingdoms. They are originally

Alabast, Cliff, or Jopi, but those in the mines become the Azelle, believing in the ancient superstitions. I suppose it is the only belief they can cling to. . . ."

"Well, perhaps these shacks are their dwellings," I answer. "Although it's difficult to tell the size, they do look rather small."

"Do you see anyone? I don't see a soul," Keela states, grabbing the reins and heading us toward the sight. Closer and closer we go, until we hear the unmistakable sound of crying—a baby crying—coming from one of the myriad huts.

Keela and I share a look and begin leading the horses toward the noise, trying to discern its location.

Still no one around as far as the eye can see through this barren landscape. We dismount and walk, the wind whipping the dust around us, as we follow the sound of the unhappy infant.

Upon closer inspection, these little box huts look terribly uncomfortable: haphazardly nailed pieces of wood, many cracks within, flies buzzing around. Despite the fact that each shack is no bigger than a small carriage, there are bunks in each. I count ten in one shack. That's ten people meant to sleep in this tiny space. Unfathomable.

Finally, we reach the source of the crying and find a little baby, wrapped in a threadbare blanket, wailing his little lungs out. Normally, the sight of a newborn is a kind of blessing but, in this case, it is a horror. For the baby is extremely skinny, with dirt and grime on his face, covered in his own filth.

CRASH.

Suddenly, we hear this from the other side of the bunk; turning around, we see the arm of a girl of about thirteen winters.

"Please! Please don't tell on me," she pleads. "I promise I will get back to work tomorrow. It's just that I—"

"No one is going to tell anyone anything, dear girl," Keela interrupts her. "We are not your masters, nor do we desire to be."

"Oh. Well, then who are you?" the girl asks. Her face, too, is covered in dirt, with a little blue dust seemingly rubbed into her worn clothing. No shoes on her feet. Her eyes, enormous, a kind of deep brown that seems to dominate her entire countenance, made bigger, most likely, due to her dwindling frame.

"Why is this infant here alone?" Keela asks.

"Because all infants here are left alone," she replies.

"But he could perish," I add.

"Yes, many do," the girl answers, matter-of-fact. "I wanted to stay behind today to take care of him. But it's against the law and if I'm found out, I could be thrown in the mine."

Keela and I share a look.

"No matter; here's some food and water for you. Is there milk for the baby?" I ask.

"Only a little. His mother works in the mine," she answers.

"Why don't you come with us? We have business there and we cannot leave you to this place," Keela explains. "There will be no one here by nightfall."

I hand the bread and water to the girl. She hesitates, then consumes them as if they were her first meal for many a fortnight. "Tell me, how far is it to the mines from here?" I ask.

"It's just a short ride. A longer walk for us, of course," the girl says between bites and gulps.

"How many guards? At the mine?" Keela prods her.

"Guards? You mean the guardians?" she replies. "Yes, on most days there are about twenty guardians. And they are well and good. They are not to be questioned."

This last part is spoken like a kind of chant, a mantra.

"And how many workers at the mine? Is your mother there?" I query.

"Oh, no. My mother was injured in the mine," she says to the dirt floor.

"Ah, so where is the doctor?" I ask.

"If you are injured in the mine, it means you are chosen by the mine. To be thrown in," she states. "A sacrifice to the Sapphire."

I find myself having to keep my expression blank and my demeanor calm as I hear this hideous practice.

"And how many workers are there?" Keela repeats.

"I'd say hundreds; who knows, it's difficult to tell. There are so many that are sacrificed to the Sapphire each day. That is an honor, they say," she adds.

"And do you believe it? That it's an honor?" I ask.

"Are you trying to get me in trouble?" she replies, a hint of fear in her voice.

"Certainly not. That's the furthest thing from my mind." I smile, offering her my flask of water.

"Tell me, girl," Keela asks, "could you lead us to the mines?"

She swallows down a large piece of bread. "Do you promise not to turn me in?"

"More than promise," I assure her. "You have my word."

Keela grows impatient. "Ride with me. You will lead us. But we must be very quiet, remember."

"And what of the baby?" the girl inquires.

"We shall bundle him up here and bind him to my friend," Keela informs her. "It will be better for him to be wrapped next to a warm body than all alone in this cold."

The girl thinks about it for a second, then gives a nod of consent.

Before I know it, the infant is wrapped in a kind of cloth lump tied to my chest. A funny thing: the moment we pick him up and put his head upright, bound in the cloth, he stops crying immediately. And then, with the movement of the horse, the gentle rocking, he falls promptly to sleep.

It's distracting, while we ride toward the mines, this little precious bundle snoozing away in such peace. Blissfully unaware that in just a few moments, his entire destiny may be changed.

Whether it is for good or ill, I cannot say.

18

WE SMELL THE Sapphire Mines before we see them. It's the stench of rotten eggs and something a bit tinny. There is bluish smoke billowing up from the large hole in the earth and the sound of orders being barked. Through the numerous rock formations, I cannot help but peek through the tiny crack between the stones. Although, now that I have, I will forever wish I hadn't. My eyes cannot erase this sight, no matter how I may try in the winters to come.

Imagine if you will an enormous pit filled with gray and blue smoke, billowing up from what seems like the center of the earth. Around the pit, in lines, there are hundreds of these so-called Azelle, shackled around the neck, marching into the sinister pit, one by one. Some are wheezing, coughing, hacking away, but forced to labor nonetheless. Behind each line, standing almost bored, are guards, or perhaps "guardians," who every so often use long batons to poke at the wretches to keep them in order. The Azelle are every age, from four to eighty winters, girls and boys, men and elders, their faces long and filled with resignation.

Every once in a while, one falls to their knees and is ushered unceremoniously to the deepest, blackest part of the abyss . . . and thrown in. The first time I see it, I cover my gasp with my hand, silencing myself. But it makes my stomach turn and head swim, the cruelty of it. My eyes are now burning with the smoke of the mine, and it's impossible not to feel an overwhelming hatred of these guards and pity for the unlucky souls who have been forced into such a miserable fate.

In the chapel, back in my kingdom, there are oil paintings in blacks and crimson, portraying the seven circles of hell. This pit, crowded with these unfortunate wraiths, looks exactly like these works of art. Diabolical, swarming, desperate.

Keela stops ahead, shielded by the rock formations, and sends the girl to me. I nod, indicating I will stay back with her and the infant. Keela and a rather numerous group of warriors begin to creep into the mines, seamless and stealthy.

SMACK!

The sound of a baton against skin and bone.

CRACK!

Each sound beckons us to end this madness.

The girl sees me peering in at this wretched sight.

"My two brothers are down there, in the mine. And my cousins. My aunt was there just until a fortnight ago . . . then she became one with the mine."

The nonchalant way this "becoming one with the mine" is posed boggles the mind. But it's clear there has been a kind of lifelong indoctrination here. An acceptance of this abysmal life as completely normal, as there is perhaps nothing to compare it to.

It's impossible to see any kind of movement from Keela or the rest, but that is the point of creeping. You cannot see it or hear it until it is too late.

I continue observing the appalling scene, butterflies in my stomach. What if this plan doesn't actually work? What will become of us? Will we end up skeletons in the mines? A chill goes through my veins. A fate worse than death. One would be tempted to slip into the black pit on purpose, just to end the torture. Although in shackles, you would take the entire line with you. Perhaps that is the reason for the shackles in the first place.

It seems like an eternity as I stand there, peering through the rocks, not knowing the outcome of our attack. The nausea in my stomach persists and it's possible I might even be trembling. In fact, it seems to take so long that I am beginning to wonder if perhaps they gave up and decided to strategize further. I look back to the spot where they descended . . . no, not there either.

And then it happens so quick, at such lightning speed, I scarcely believe it's happened at all. If you blinked, you would miss it.

I shall try my best to describe it to you, as the description will take longer than the actual event.

The guards, or "guardians," stand with their batons, perhaps lulled into a sense of complacency, perhaps drifting off on the noxious fumes of the mine. Keela and the other warriors, without sound or extravagance, at the same exact moment, as if one cohesive being, come up from behind every guard, every last one of them, and immediately, on cue, cover their mouths and pull their weapons across their throats. The myriad guards grab their necks, some stumbling, some collapsing completely, and the rocks are immediately painted a deep shade of crimson.

It is a synchronized event, and not one of the so-called guard-ians is spared. Now only the slaves are left, unheeding, still continuing to march forth, sans guards. As if they are captives now of only habit.

"HALT!" Keela calls out over the mine, her voice echoing off the rocks.

The wretched come to a complete stop, having been indoctri-nated to follow orders without question.

Most continue to look at the ground, waiting for the next command.

"I am Keela, guardian and steward of the Cliffs of Grey. We have slayed your oppressors," she pronounces. "You are now free."

Now a handful of the destitute look up, squinting, in confusion.

"You no longer have to toil in this horrific place. We shall undo your chains and release you," she states, nodding to the other warriors.

Some of the younger ones, the children, begin to smile . . . as if they knew someone would save them all along. That it was inevitable. Some of the older ones stand perplexed, having borne years of torment.

Now Keela and the others begin methodically removing the shackles, stealing the iron keys from the grisly corpses of the guards.

I cannot help but wonder if they are so hypnotized by the "guardians" that they might protest. But little by little, they begin to grasp the situation . . . and little by little the life seems to come back to them.

As if understanding somehow, the baby begins to gurgle.

We both have a little laugh. "Yes, and you are free, too, little one."

As Keela returns to the top of the mountain, we meet her there. "Congratulations," I say. "You have done the unthinkable."

Keela deliberates. "Yes, but it was a bit too easy."

"What do you mean?" I ask.

"There's something strange about it," she adds. "How could this terror last so long if it was so easily thwarted?"

"Perhaps it was the idea of it, the thought of it, that seemed so insurmountable. Or the audacity of it." I consider. "Perhaps that is why no one has ever tried."

"That may be." She ponders. "Still, there's something to it. There's some sense in me, an instinct, that doesn't trust it."

"Keela, look around you. Have you not seen a more rapturous sight?" I gesture toward the celebrations now springing up around us. "Take a moment, just this once, to be happy."

"Yes, I suppose," she acquiesces. "But, truly, I fear I've made a miscalculation. I'd hoped some of them would be able, and willing, to join our army. Now that I see their woeful state, through no fault of their own, this cannot be. What kind of an army could they possibly make? Some of them can barely walk."

"Perhaps they have skills we cannot discern," I suggest.

"Perhaps." She thinks.

"Well, at least they no longer have to toil in the mines. How unspeakable a life they have lived!"

"Yes, they've suffered enough," she says, watching their newfound revelry. "Perhaps it's for the better that we face our enemies without them."

"What will happen to them?" I ask.

"It's up to them now, isn't it?" she adds. "They are many different people. Some may return to their homelands. Others may pilgrimage to the place where their Azelle superstitions were born."

We begin to make our way out over the barren landscape, our horses now moving along at a leisurely pace. I look back and see the smoldering Sapphire Mines, the smoke coming up gray and blue. How many bodies are buried there? How many ghosts will haunt this place? What will happen now, with no Sapphire to quench the obsession with beauty throughout the kingdoms?

What will happen to Alabastrine? I shudder to think of it.

The baby boy looks up at me, his eyes sparkling in the sun. No matter. We did the right thing.

19

A KING'S JOURNAL

Well, now we've done it.

The queen is in a frenzy after the great transformation of Prince Gilgamorte.

First, there was the issue of his clothes, fallen around him like a discarded cocoon.

The old crone, now suddenly lively and full of advice, hurriedly gathered them all and hung them God knows where, probably in her old shoe house somewhere under a bridge.

If you can believe it, it was me, ME, who had to run around, dashing about, this way and that, to catch the startled frog—I mean, prince—as he hopped all about in despair. Undoubtedly mad with confusion. And who could blame him? For this was, indeed, a proud prince to be handed such an unfortunate fate.

And yet, I can't help but see a kind of cruel justice in it.

Nevertheless, the poor frog—I mean, prince—was finally captured, by yours truly, in a mighty, heroic, and bold way . . . and deposited quickly into a dainty little cage, meant for the queen's lovebirds, which she never quite got around to acquiring. The queen is like that, you know, frivolous, always up to something and then, the next second, up to another. Like a butterfly she flits around. If I wasn't in love with her, I'm sure it would test my patience.

So, the prince now lives in a prissy white cage, with intricate lattice, in the form of a frog.

Between the princess's sudden slumber and the prince being turned into a frog, I'm beginning to watch my back, keenly aware that perhaps I may swiftly be turned into a bunny rabbit! Or a gargoyle. Or maybe something humiliating, like a squid.

And yet, if you can believe it, the queen has planned for not one but two additional princes to attend our little charade here this evening. I'm assuming she wants to rule out as many princes as possible, and hasten the discovery of our elusive Prince Charming. I'm also assuming she won't be allowing the second prince to see what happened to the first prince.

The entire escapade is quite a comedy of errors, and I find myself feeling as if we are somehow trapped in a nightmare. But the queen manages, as always, to coax me through this trial with a few light words and assurances. She's quite a lovely queen, I must say, despite the many oddities of her character. The other day she told me she detested wearing a corset!

Madness!

But my nights are spent tossing and turning, bewildered by this confounding slumber of my daughter, distraught by the time . . . ticking away . . . before the child's eighteenth birthday. Before the curse, if it truly exists, takes hold.

I cannot take the chance. She must wake soon.

20

THE CLOSEST PLACE to seek shelter on our route is the Danek Forest, which seems to be one of the few places in this land not fraught with warning and sinister tales of woe. It's quite different from the swamp near the Cliffs of Grey. This forest seems to mostly consist of slender, spiky pine trees in a shade of dark green, almost black, in the mist. It's much colder here, due possibly to being on higher ground or perhaps the winds rushing through the trees.

There was a small village the first night where all of our rather large and cumbersome caravan, which includes our warriors and a number of the freed Azelle, stopped for shelter. In fact, it was a bit strange how the Azelle insisted upon this *specific* village.

Keela gave everyone in our group coins, mostly taken off the bodies of the now-deceased guards, to provide them with food and shelter—if not in that particular village, there was a string of villages across the way. This way everyone could at least begin to build their lives back.

Yet, I notice that the Azelle people seem to have stayed in the vicinity. What's more, they seem now like a much livelier bunch. Somehow fortified, bold.

Keela, a bit flummoxed by their strange behavior, finally chooses to address them. "Esteemed people of the Azelle! Pray, why do you tarry here? You are free to go. You are saved."

"Yes, but you are not saved," a woman replies, coming forward. She seems like an elder compared to the rest. Upon closer inspection, she's truly not that old, perhaps my mother's age, but worked into old age, stooped over with burden. Her skin is beginning to lose the patina of the Sapphire soot from the mines, now just a kind of pale gray dust. She turns to me. "You have come sooner than I thought, dear child."

"Pardon me?" I reply.

Keela interrupts. "What are you called, elder of the Azelle?"

"Ah! I am called many names. Not all of them good." A twinkle in her eye. "But for this moment, in this time, you may call me Shakvi."

Keela tries not to grow impatient. "Yes, Shakvi. Well, consider that you have *saved us* . . . and feel free to go on your merry way."

But the elder, Shakvi, pays her no attention, keeping her attention only on me. "I had thought it would take you longer," she says, her eyes piercing.

"I'm sorry—"

"Never mind, sweet girl," Shakvi interrupts me. "So our quest begins. We have saved you."

"Wait, I apologize . . . ," I say, thinking I must have heard her wrong, or that her language is somehow confused. "How exactly have you saved me? I've only just met you."

"Ah, yes! Time. A funny concept really." And now she smiles, a light in her. "I say this just as I've said it in the past. Just as the stars above shine from long ago. Time is an idea. Something to mark. Nothing more, nothing less. We have always saved you. You have always come to us. In the pastfuture. In the futurepast. In the present, and always."

Keela has had enough of this bewildering conversation. "Come, we must rest. No more time for . . . *stimulating* conversation."

She quickly steers me away from Shakvi, who seems somehow amused by this action.

"I'm not sure I understand," I whisper to Keela.

"Come on. This way." Keela leads me off.

The elder, Shakvi, turns away lightly and saunters back toward the makeshift camp of the Azelle.

Keela gives me a look. "Don't worry. They're all quite mad from inhaling all that Sapphire in the mine."

"Really?" I ask. "Is that the general consensus?"

"Oh, yes," she insists. "I've heard stories since childhood of the madness of the Sapphire wretches."

"Oh," I reply, still a bit stymied. But this discussion of time is stirring something within me . . . something just under the surface, my mind unable to grab the thought.

"They're extremists. Zealots. Best not to get pulled into their madness." Keela nods, confident, and leaves me to my musing.

Yet as I look out at the impromptu camp of the Azelle, I can't help but feel a sense that they are privy to some unknown language one must never learn, or dare to speak. I notice, too, in the light of the campfire, the elder there, Shakvi, with a group gathered round her. She whispers something, catching the eyes of the circle before her. I peer farther into the light and see her holding something. A tiny wooden box, nondescript and inelegant. Now she holds up the minuscule box ceremoniously, a kind of proclamation:

"Now that we have been reunited with our ancestors, with our ancient wisdom, with the great spirit . . . we shall nevermore be vanquished! So it is written! So it shall be!"

Yes, Keela must be right. The Sapphire dust must have gone to their heads.

21

THE SUN HAS set itself to sleep now and the entirety of our group seems to follow suit. Keela and I sit by the campfire, strategizing on our imminent, and potentially fatally flawed, attack. The rest of what is left of the Cliffs of Grey and Keela's army are meant to rendezvous with us tomorrow, at the edge of the Danek Forest.

"Don't you find it strange, what she said?" I ask, still unable to shake the words of the Azelle woman.

"Who?"

"The Azelle elder? The bit about having already saved us," I reply. "Doesn't it strike you as odd?"

"Oh, that again. Don't waste one more thought on it." She smiles. "As a princess, you should be able to recognize fairy tales."

"Yes, of course," I continue. "I suppose my imagination might have been running away with me."

"Right, well, we've no time to waste on such nonsense. We must focus on getting into the Wraithen Kingdom." She ponders. "It is the only way to the Veist."

"How do we know the slaughter is of the Veist?" I ponder. "Isn't there a poss—"

She cuts me off. "The Veist is the source of all horror and pain. Nothing in the kingdoms happens without the direction of the Veist. The cooperation of the Wraithen. The armies of the Wraithen Kingdom. The entire realm quakes in fear at every mood of the Veist. You must know this. . . . All is for naught if she is not defeated."

"Yet no one knows exactly how to find her," I argue.

"The Wraithen is the only way. There, there is a gateway. We just need to find a way in."

Suddenly, I have a recollection of Peregrine's annoying diatribe in the carriage . . . the idea burbling to the surface.

"Ah!" My mind whirs. "There are nobles there, yes? In the Wraithen Kingdom?"

"There certainly are," Keela affirms.

"Nobles love nothing more than their quine," I tell her.

"And . . . ?" Keela asks. "What are you getting at?"

"Their quine must come from all regions of the kingdoms, various grapes and vineyards. A source of vanity and boasting, prestige. And this prestige, this desire to have the finest quine, the finest everything from all of the kingdoms . . . that is the fulcrum. The soft underbelly."

Keela looks at me, intrigued. "How so?"

I let the wheels in my mind complete their rotation.

"I know how to do it!" I tell her, suddenly giddy. "I know how to get into the Wraithen."

22

IN THE MORNING, we are met at the edge of the Danek Forest by Keela's blossoming army. Some of them are familiar faces from my many moons of training, but there are some new and unfamiliar. The grace and maneuverability of warfare comes easily to them. Like dancers, they are as comfortable on the back of a horse as a player on a stage. To wit: if an arrow is shot from one of their bows, five more will be shot immediately, before the first arrow lands.

My diabolical plan will require our entire group to be cleaved in two, with Keela staying back with the army while I make my way to Alabastrine. I will be accompanied by twenty warriors from the Cliffs of Grey. These warrior women are lithe and sinewy, many with hair shorn, some with hair sticking straight up the middle. Many have painted skin, the significance of which eludes me.

As we prepare ourselves for the journey, back over the salt sea and over the fields to Alabastrine, Keela comes to greet me while I pack my horse.

"You have come a long way from your simpering royal customs," she gibes. "Even your sickeningly pale skin now has some color to it."

"Sickeningly pale!" I protest.

"Pasty," she teases. "Disgusting. Unhealthy really."

I can't help but chuckle. "Not all of us can be gorgeous gold."

But now she turns more serious.

"Are you sure? About this strategy?" she asks. "I would hate to lose you."

"You mean after my many moons of training?" I grin.

"Well, that too," she replies.

I finish up fastening my pack and buckle it, eager to make it to Alabastrine within a fortnight.

"It may be more perilous than you think." She leans in, warning, "This could lead to death, you understand?"

"I am aware," I tell her. "But if we do not at the very least try . . . then are we not dead already?"

She lets that percolate.

"And what about your former home?" she continues. "Do you not miss it?"

This stops me. "More than I can put into words. But if there is a way back for me, I don't yet know it. So there is only one direction—forward. And of course, one has to be able . . . to live with oneself."

"And could you not live with yourself?" she asks. "If you didn't join us?"

I ponder. "After what I saw . . . no. No, I could not. And . . . let's say I did. Then I would be changed anyway. Because I would not be the person I thought myself to be."

She takes this in. "You are braver than I had thought."

"Or possibly more stupid," I reply.

At this she lets out a laugh. "Perhaps."

What a difference this is from the catty insults and tittering gossip of my cousins, Prissy and Bolanda, back in Fairyland. To be able to draw strength from each other instead of tearing one another down in derision.

"Well." Keela nods. "Goodbye, then."

"Yes. Goodbye. We will meet again," I tell her, taking on her usual confidence in this moment.

"Yes, of course," she responds.

A moment of silence as we both imagine the possibility of this not happening. Of this being the last time we see each other alive. Of what darkness might await us.

"I will see you soon, sister," she tells me. I'm brought up short. *Sister.* I have never been called that—by anyone. It is an honor.

"Yes . . . sister. I will see you then."

23

A KING'S JOURNAL

As one might imagine, none of these aspiring "Prince Charmings" have made the grade. Indeed, we now have a kind of menagerie of frogs in the garden. They are all well-fed and cared for attentively. All of them there, in their individual cages, ribbiting away, particularly in the evening, so that one can hardly sleep. A cacophony of frogs.

Clearly, there is a great sense of urgency, as now it is only a matter of time until all the queens and kings in the land come wandering over, demanding the return of their sons. We've been able to keep this inevitable circumstance at bay, thankfully, by sending out word that a kind of tournament of wits and fortitude is in order. Jousting, fencing, chess, that sort of thing. But it won't be long until, I fear, all our heads will be on a platter, encircled by a very angry group of frogs and their royal parents.

Yet, despite all of this, two nights ago a strange thing transpired, which I found even more disquieting. I have no intention of sharing it with the queen, so as not to alarm her.

I was quietly standing alone in the corridor after dinner, minding my own business, when the hideous old woman approached *me and began speaking to me with the familiarity of one at court. It was quite astonishing and, frankly, I was appalled.*

To wit, she had a hideous, sinister grin on her wrinkled old face.

"Your wife, the queen, is ever so lovely." She continued to stare at me, unnerving me to the core.

"Yes, certainly she is," I replied, attempting to hurry off.

Then she had the audacity to put her common, shriveled hand on my royal arm and whisper, "A queen must be beautiful, yes? Above all else."

At this, I drew my arm away from her, repulsed.

"Old woman, I am a benevolent ruler, but remember your place! You are here only at the whim of the queen and I should hazard you not overstep your bounds. You've managed to turn every prince in the land into a frog. Clearly, you do not understand the danger you've brought upon the queen and I."

"Oh, ever so sorry, Your Highness." She bowed then, an amused sort of grin on her countenance. She then backed off, snickering, and immediately scurried down the corridor. Stranger indeed, she seemed to be whispering a little tune to herself: "There are stars in the sky, there are mountains so high, there are dreams, there are dreams . . . I have dreamt you, I dream you, I will dream you."

Then she turned to me with a mischievous grin, putting her finger to her mouth in a shushing gesture. Then back to her whispering song: "I have dreamt you. I dream you. I will dream you."

I stood there, astounded and befuddled by her leering and insolence. Before I knew it, she had disappeared down the long passage.

Yet, even to this moment, her words and frightful visage haunt me. What does this strange song mean? Does she mean the queen some ill will? Or, perhaps, both the queen and I.

There's no use telling the queen about this disturbing incident, anyway, as my wife truly has bought into the old hag's ridiculous, ever-so-sage advice.

Nevertheless, I have ordered the royal guards to double their presence outside the bedchamber doors.

One can never be too careful.

24

MY STRATEGY THUS far is commencing as planned. Now for the essential step:

On the approach to Alabastrine, I'm shocked to see, outside the main gate, my two erstwhile female companions. What were their names? Apple and Ducky, I recall. There they are, the two frivolous girls who took me into that bawdy establishment, giggling and gossiping all the way. And then the one, Apple, betraying me. Only this time neither of them is laughing and dancing, or if they are it is a terrible pantomime of a jig, with the wind moving their limbs only slightly.

The two young women are, instead, on display at the enormous ivory city gates, impaled for all to see. Their white dresses are stained in deep crimson blood, now dried out in the sun, flies buzzing around them. It's a ghastly sight. And I cannot imagine what law they must have violated to be consigned to such an ungodly fate.

I turn my head away, only to notice the looks on the faces of my fellow warriors.

"Try not to look at them," I deflect. "Follow me."

On my way to find Peregrine, I attempt not to think about the harrowing sight, now seared in my brain, but the more I try not to think about it, the more ferociously it returns. Like trying not to think of a white horse.

Upon reaching the doorway of Chez Peregrine, I whisper to my companions to dismount and wait for my signal.

I do not even have to knock, as the sweet chambermaid comes rushing in from the market, her basket full of fruit and bread.

"You there! Remember me?" I call out to her.

She looks back at me, her discomfiture apparent.

"No, don't be scared. I mean you no harm. Nor your master," I assure her.

She remains frozen, unable to speak or calculate what the right thing is to do at the present moment.

I clarify, "Do not despair. I have only come to have a few words with Peregrine. Nothing more."

She nods, still hesitant, and I utilize her uncertainty to brush past her into the eclectic home of our dear count. True, this was once a bohemian paradise to me, but now it seems a seedy, dishonorable place, a thieves' den. I bristle remembering the deplorable fate this rapscallion left me to. Reprobate!

Before the chambermaid can stop me, I march right down the corridor, past the stuffed giraffe, the candelabra, the hanging rugs and hundreds of trinkets, to the door of the master's chamber, which happens to be open.

Inside, conked out from whatever debauchery occurred the night before, lies our beloved Count Peregrine, napping away.

"Well, well. It appears your betrayal has done nothing to

increase your station. Quite the opposite," I declare loudly, attempting to wake him. "What a pity."

He wakes up in a stupor, squints, and upon seeing me, recognizing me, his face suddenly seems to brighten, a smile like a child on the morning of Noel . . . but then he covers this, proud, calm, collected, and proceeds to make his way to his feet.

"You." There's something in the way he says it. As if holding it in the palm of his hand, gently, like a rare butterfly.

"Yes, me." I stand, a bit confounded.

He fumbles then but catches himself on the wall. "I believe I told you . . . yes, I think I did . . . never to come back here."

He finally manages his effort to stand there before me.

I pull my hand back. *SLAP!*

No, I have never slapped anyone before.

Yes, that did satisfy.

Truly, I realize it is wrong to strike another.

But you must admit, he deserved it.

"You! You miscreant! You flea! You flea upon the ugliest toad! You told me a lot of things, none of which were true." I stand there, defiant. "You are the lowest, most vile, deceitful reprobate to ever grace the face of the earth!"

He recovers, tending to his cheek with his hand.

"Ow! That hurt. Princesses aren't meant to slap people. It's beneath them. Also, I am certainly not the most deceitful in all the kingdoms. I would recommend me as being one of the cleverest, but that's debatable seeing that you are now here, in my—"

"Why did you smile just then?!" I blurt out.

"When?" he asks, rubbing his cheek.

"Just then, when you first saw me?"

"I didn't." He scoffs.

"Yes, you did," I insist.

"No, I didn't!" he avers. "I assure you, Princess, I know my face. The one you just slapped in a very un-princess-like manner, I must say. And my face . . . my face that I know so well, that you just attacked like a deranged goblin, did not smile. I assure you."

"Yes, it did."

"It did not. Because you, YOU! Are a murderer."

"A murderer?" I scoff. "Whatever do you mean, scoundrel?"

"How horrible it is, that wicked sight . . . those two beautiful girls strung up like pirates, impaled for all to see. You are *ruthless*. I hadn't realized it. And now, of course, you have come for your revenge on me. Well, go ahead. String me up as well! What does it matter . . . ?" At which point he stumbles into a crystal carafe, knocking it over.

"I must admit, I have no idea what you are talking about," I reply.

"Oh, don't you? So, it's just a coincidence, then, that the two very girls who betrayed you are now the two very girls hanging up outside the city gates, strewn in blood? Their flesh pecked away by blackbirds? No, Princess. Sorry, I am not that stupid." A bitter laugh, which then turns into a cough.

"Absurd! That is a ridiculous thing to say! I have no more to do with that than I do the sun coming up or the moon waxing and waning. You're a fool if you think so," I protest.

"HA! Well, if you didn't do it, then who did, fake princess?" he queries. "Answer me that."

"I've no idea. And frankly, I'm tired of defending myself from such ludicrous accusations. As if I could ever do something so cruel and vicious. You do not know me at all, I'm afraid," I pronounce.

"Well then, if not to string me up in revenge, why *are* you here? And how are you here, by the way? The last I saw you, you were the prisoner of Gork," he reflects.

"Luckily for you, I am not here to take my revenge. I did however, take your advice, and managed to escape at the Gray Horse Tavern after the third bridge, if you recall telling me."

"Ah! So it did work. . . . Surprising, that. I had not thought you could possibly make it. No one ever has escaped Gork's sweaty clutch. The forest around there is quite extensive and full of derelicts, to be honest," he confides.

"Yes, well, I was lucky enough to find the only kind beings left in the kingdom, it seems," I inform him.

"Ah, well. A bit of luck. How nice for you." He looks me over, seeming to sober up a bit. "You've changed somehow. What is this you're wearing? Are you going to a costume ball of some kind? Dressed as a potato? I have heard there is one in a fortnight but I haven't heard anything about one this evening. How depressing! Am I not invited? I should certainly have been invited—"

"I can assure you there is no such event," I reply.

"Are you quite sure?" he inquires. "Because I cannot bear the thought of being rejected. No, I must have been invited! Perhaps you are hiding it? To spare my feelings. Well, don't bother! Tell me. Go ahead. Tell me. I can take it. Who is throwing a costume ball without me? I must know!"

"You can stop making a fool of yourself," I tell him. "There is no such ball. Anyway, not to worry. I am simply here to ask you a favor."

"A favor?" he contemplates. "Hm, I am curious. Prithee, what could this favor be? It's not money, is it?"

"No, of course not. I would not stoop to such a level," I reply.

"Good," he snaps. "I should not stoop to the level of giving it."

"Fine."

"Fine, indeed," he replies.

Unbidden, a growl of sorts escapes my throat. "A more impudent man I have never known."

"So impudent you have returned to me." He grins. "Tell me then; I can bear the mystery no longer. What is this *favor* you ask?"

"I want you to sell me," I state. "Again."

He turns his head to one side, amused. "Sell you? Why . . . this is quite a surprise. What a novel idea. To sell a princess twice."

"Will you do it or not?" I ask, becoming impatient.

"Well, dear fake princess, as much as I would love to, I cannot," he answers.

"And why not?"

"Because it is impossible for me to sell the same girl—princess, I mean—twice," he informs me.

"But it would not be here, my deceitful friend." I smile.

"Oh? Prithee tell, where would it be, then?" he queries.

"The Wraithen," I reply.

A moment of silence now.

"The Wraithen? My dear, you are quite off your rocker," he responds. "Do you know what they do to serfs in the Wraithen? You'll be dead by midnight."

"That is for me to contend with," I answer.

"No, no. Listen to me. The nobles of the Wraithen are not like us here in Alabastrine. They're not . . . fun. They have no glee, no whimsy, no love. Their only joy is cruelty," he continues. "They tear men up for sport. Let alone what they do to women. I've never even set foot in the region, let alone within the gates, so vile a place it is."

"Can you do it or not?" I ask again.

"My dear, it's not that simple. First, there is the Murder of Shadows to contend with. Yes, you heard me. The *Murder* of *Shadows*. Sounds fun, doesn't it? Well, dear princess, there is no way into the Wraithen without facing it. Many men have tried. All have died," he informs me. "And even if we did, somehow, miraculously cross the Murder of Shadows and reach the gate—which we will not because we will obviously perish first—they would never let us in."

"Even to sell a princess?" I continue. "You yourself have the greatest collection of curiosities, and quine, from all over the kingdoms. You said one cannot even consider themselves to be noble without the finest quine from every corner of the region. Well, the same must be true for all goods. All curiosities. And especially . . . the curiosity of owning a princess."

He thinks. "It might raise an eyebrow."

"And what if it weren't just me?" I bait him. "What if it was a sale that could make you a rich man forevermore, one of the richest in all the kingdoms? With lands and treasure beyond anything you've ever dreamt of?"

"Well, now you have my interest, of course," he admits. "I do love my gold. But to trade in the Wraithen Kingdom! Do you know they file their teeth into fangs there? Yes, actual fangs. No, dear princess, you have no reason, no reason on earth to risk such a thing."

"Oh, but I do. You see, the things they are doing. The deaths all around the kingdoms, the slayings, the servitude, the lives of only labor until the grave . . . I cannot just sit and watch as villages are burned to the ground. This injustice, the terrors of the Veist. We can't just allow it. Or ignore it."

"Why not?" He shakes his head. "Princess, it's . . . moving that you care so very much. But this is the way it's always been . . . and this is the way it will always be."

"Why?" I counter.

"Because we don't want to die or be shipped off as well."

"And have you no bravery, then, Count Peregrine?"

"I have enough," he replies.

"Well, I already know what you're made of," I add. "I'm only asking you to help me and become the richest man in all the kingdoms."

"Ah, yes, back to the gold." He reaches for the bottle, pouring himself more quine.

"One moment, dear annoying Peregrine," I tell him, popping out the door and marching back down the corridor.

In a moment, I return and greet him through the doorway,

where he stands, looking vaguely suspicious.

"You will not just be selling a princess, you see." I wave my arms in a grand gesture. "You will be selling all of us. Every last one."

And now I let in my troupe of women warriors.

Peregrine looks up, taking in the dazzling sight.

"Oh. Oh my." His jaw must now officially be lifted off the ground.

He looks at me as I await his answer.

"Well, dear princess. I'm sure we can work something out."

25

"TELL ME, HOW is it you come to know about the Murder of Shadows?" I ask Peregrine.

Our entourage has now traveled overnight, over the two bridges, en route to the Wraithen. Surrounding our carriage are the warrior women on horseback. Impressing the Wraithen is necessary to gain entry to their kingdom, which made it compulsory to bring along this absurd ivory carriage of Peregrine's. He has even fastened a prisoner cart to the back of the carriage, a grisly sight with its bars and hanging shackles.

Peregrine insists upon riding in his ostentatious white carriage, and he has even insisted I ride with him, declaring that he cannot have his prime object of sale getting sullied and muddied up on horseback. Fastened to the back of the carriage is a rather large trunk, full of brocade and silk dresses for the lot of us. The warrior women, still on horseback, will surely scoff at such vanities.

"Everyone knows about the Murder of Shadows," Peregrine finally answers, pouring himself yet another tin of quine. "How do you think the Wraithen exists? No one in their right mind would attempt to cross it. Which is why I am quite certain we will die. Which is why I am quite certain I must drink all of this quine."

"Indeed," I prod him further. "But what do you know about it? What have you been told?"

"Oh, nothing, nothing to worry about really, just that it finds your weakness and sets it against you, that any encounter with it means certain death. Hence the name. Murder of Shadows." He gulps down his quine, reaching for the bottle to refill it once again.

"But what else?" I ask. "What does it look like?"

"Um . . . let's see. I've heard everything from a black shadow with no dimension to a dark mist that somehow can enter inside a man's soul. I've even heard it can disguise itself. The stories are endless; who knows which of them are true," he continues. "You see, it's difficult to understand such a thing when there are no people alive to tell the tale of their encounters. So that is something to look forward to."

"Very amusing," I reply.

"Cheers." He raises his tin in a mock toast. "Shall we toast the fact that, due to your escapades, there is a Sapphire shortage . . . and I am getting uglier by the day?"

"You're not getting uglier," I confess. "You're getting more . . . yourself."

And this is true; Count Peregrine's face may not be quite as smooth and perfect . . . but there's a ruggedness to it now, without the Sapphire.

"It's as if you're a real person," I add. "An actual person."

"I don't want to be an actual person," he replies. "I want to be, we all want to be . . . dazzling. Exquisite. Singular. It's our survival."

"But what if it didn't have to be?" I answer.

"What if it didn't have to be? What if the skies were made of milk? What if everyone changed their hands into flippers?" He mocks me. "God, you're annoying. I really can't stand you."

"The feeling is mutual," I answer.

Silence.

The carriage continues on. We tumble over the third bridge and, despite his obvious drunken state, Peregrine notices something out the miniature carriage window.

"Blimey." His face drops, his tin cup of quine falling beside him.

"What? What is it?" I ask him.

The carriage promptly comes to a halt and I jump to open the door, getting out to see what all the commotion is about. The warriors halt on their horses, looking up at the sight.

I follow their gazes and my knees buckle as I see it.

The tavern here is the Gray Horse Tavern, the same one where I made my daring escape. Yes, it is the same tavern, but it is not the same tavern at all. This tavern is painted black with smoke and char, burned to a crisp. Its walls are caved in and the aftermath of the fire has left it in cinders, a shell of its former raucous self.

But that is only the half of it. There, where the Gray Horse Tavern sign used to be, is strung up something else. Something unspeakable and horrifying. And yet, as I walk closer, something not wholly foreign.

It's him.

It's the gluttonous beast of a man who purchased me. The very same one. Master Gork. Except now he is not plying himself with ale or snoring away. No, no, not any of that.

For how could his mouth drink ale or issue taunts when it is stopped up with an apple, like a pig on a spit? And, just so, his wrists and ankles are tied, like a cooked boar, and he hangs from the sign in a mock kind of festive dish. And, to increase the humiliation, to my horror, his clothing appears to have been ripped to shreds and dangles there, helplessly.

All at once, seemingly on cue, the faces of the warrior women turn toward me, as does Peregrine.

"Don't look at me," I tell him. "I've got nothing to do with it."

"You *do* recognize him as the bloke I sold you to at auction?" he responds.

The warrior women listen with interest now.

"Yes, yes, but . . . I have not seen him since my escape that night, from this place, here. Right here, in fact. I distracted the driver with a fire—"

"A fire, you say?" he interrupts me.

"No, no. It was just a little fire. Of the carriage. It was my only way out." Suddenly I feel I'm on trial. "I promise, as God is my witness, I had nothing to do with this . . . barbarity."

"Do you expect me to believe that? What is this meant to be? A kind of warning for all who cross you?" He speaks a mile a minute now, suspicious, ranting.

"I swear, on everything I hold dear in my heart, on everything I love. This has nothing to do with me. I have been off at the Cliffs of Grey. They will tell you." I nod to my warrior companions, who nod back in assurance. "I have not been to this region since the night of my escape. Even so, such depravity is not in my heart."

He slows down his pace a bit, turning it over in his mind. "Yes, it does seem out of character. But as I have taught you, nothing is as it seems here, in this devilish place built out of spite."

"Built out of spite," I echo. "Why does everyone keep saying—"

"Hallo, is it you?!" A voice interrupts my thought.

I turn to the sound, and there is the young girl, the granddaughter, from the old man's cabin. The one who ushered me inside from the freezing cold, who saved me from my drenched dress and certain death by pneumonia.

"Yes! Yes, it is me!" I go to her, strangely happy to see an old friend.

"What are you doing back here?" she inquires, taking in our coterie, hesitating. "Who are your . . . friends?"

"Oh, don't be alarmed," I assure her. "These are my dear, steadfast companions. And this man here is . . . also a person with us."

Peregrine shoots me a look.

"Ah! And where are you traveling to, so far out here in the forest?" she asks.

"The Wraithen," I confide.

Her visage once again changes, now in disbelief. "Are you insane? That's a death wish. What have you gotten yourself into—"

"Don't spend a moment worrying about it, dear girl." I try to calm her.

"Well . . . I'll try not to worry, but honestly, it does sound idiotic. No offense."

"I know. Just . . . don't tell anyone we were here, or that you saw us?" I ask her.

"Who would I tell? The birds? The insects? Maybe a few curious frogs?" she jokes.

"Well, don't tell your grandfather, at least," I reply.

"Ah!" She suddenly remembers a thought. "I have a bizarre story for you, actually. It sounds fantastical, but I assure you, it's true."

"Do tell, I pray you," I ask.

"Well . . . after you left, we had a kind of . . . encounter. Yes, I suppose that's what you'd call it. Here. A frightening thing really." She looks around to ensure our safety. "Involving an ungodly amount of blackbirds."

26

COUNT PEREGRINE SEEMS to have grown tired of this encounter and wanders back to the carriage to imbibe more quine.

"Hurry it up, dear princess." He drifts away. "We don't have all day."

But I ignore him, instead choosing to listen to this curious tale.

"Now, you must promise not to think me mad," Granddaughter whispers.

I lean in farther, curious as to what could be so very outlandish.

"We had bid you goodbye not two moons earlier. As I recall . . . Grandfather was out in the field." She sets the scene. "The sun was shining and it was, quite simply, a pleasant day."

Now her voice becomes more urgent.

"Then, all of a sudden, as if out of nowhere . . ." She gestures. "The sky turned gray, as if it were about to rain. And then . . . in the very middle of the day . . . the sky turned black."

"In the middle of the day?" I ask.

"Yes! Practically noon! Astonished, I looked up to the heavens, searching for the sun . . . and instead, as God is my witness, the sky was suddenly filled with blackbirds. Not just a few; so many that it occurred to me they might, in fact, be blocking out the sun," she continues. "The screech, the sheer howl of these blackbirds, as I have never heard before and never hope to hear again," she adds. "Quite deafening."

I listen in stunned silence.

"And then, at this point it appeared as if this swarm of blackbirds were headed directly toward us, to attack us. I know it sounds a bit mad," she adds. "I *ran* into the house, gathering Grandfather, and locked the bolt as quickly as possible . . . of course, my hands were shaking horribly and we both had to do it together."

"Quite right," I say, entranced.

"And then an even stranger thing happened," she continues. "The sound of the shrieks suddenly stopped. Total and utter silence. As if you could hear a pin drop. Thinking that the blackbirds were possibly gone, I peeked out a window in the hopes that they had disappeared."

"And had they?" I ask, rapt.

"No, that's the odd thing. They were all there, hundreds of them, just perched and looking in. Just looking at the cottage, as if taking its measure. Now, you see, one blackbird alone could do little to bother . . . but hundreds of blackbirds could have torn the entire cottage apart, and all of us in it, God forbid," she confides. "We were gobsmacked. I was trembling in my shoes."

"And rightly so," I reply.

"But the blackbirds stayed stone still, as if almost . . . listening. And this went on for what seemed like a hundred winters but was probably only a few seconds," she goes on. "And before you know it, it was as if nothing had happened. All at once, the exact same second . . . they flew off. Every single one of them. Right at once."

"No," I reply, astounded.

"And then in a moment, they were gone. Nothing. No trace. Not a sound." She snaps her fingers. "Poof. Just like that. And then, if you can believe it, the sun comes out, and the black gray sky is gone . . . and suddenly it's as if nothing ever happened. Can you imagine?" she asks.

"No. Honestly, I cannot. It seems . . . well, I don't know what it seems," I answer, flummoxed.

All this time, I had not noticed Peregrine has sauntered back. Perhaps eavesdropping.

"Then, later, I thought about it," the girl continues. "And I was thinking . . . it sounded a bit like that tale I heard about Alabastrine. At the baths. Do you remember? The blackbirds killing everyone there. Except that one . . . the lone survivor."

"Yes, but perhaps that was a hyperbole of some sort . . ." I suggest.

The silence of Peregrine is now broken. He looks up, clearly unnerved.

"It's not hyperbole," he blurts out.

The two of us turn to look at him, taken aback.

"It's not?" I query. "Prithee, how would you know?"

"Because I was there," he confesses. "I was, as you so delicately put it, the *lone male survivor*."

27

WE LEAVE SOON after this elaborate tale, after Granddaughter and I have said our goodbyes. After she has kindly asked me, again, not to die.

I cannot help but ponder this preposterous account. And the even more preposterous idea that Count Peregrine was somehow involved—and was the one who survived. Of all people, Count Peregrine?

But there's not time to tarry in wonder. Keela and her army are meant to rendezvous with us by sunset tonight, before the steep climb up to the Wraithen. There is no reason to think about the auction or the Veist quite yet. There is only one terror to imagine: the Murder of Shadows. Each time I hear a new rumor about the mysterious dark entity that guards the Wraithen, I find myself chilled to the bone and then, as a kind of defense, laughing it off as simple superstition. For nothing that is real could be quite so harrowing.

Or, at least, that is what I tell myself.

By the time the sun has reached its apex, Peregrine has begun once again to dip into his quine, with his familiar self-loathing and despair.

"You might as well join me, dear princess, for tomorrow we shall die," he jests.

"I don't quite know how you have made it thus far in life with such a fatalistic, grim vision of the world. However, I refuse to take it up. Now or ever," I reply.

"Of course not, my dearest." He drinks. "You are pure as the driven snow. In mind and in body. Good on you."

"I would never assume to be either," I tell him.

"No, because you are also modest. Another annoyingly noble trait." He fills his tin cup again.

I watch him for a bit, pondering. "Did you make it up, then? That you are somehow the only man who survived this alleged attack at the baths?"

His countenance turns darker at the mention of it, and he stares into his quine.

"No, dear princess. However . . ." He furrows his brow. "I wish I had."

"It seems quite unlikely. No offense," I say. "That you, of all people, were the only one to be spared."

The sound of the carriage rolls along, continuing its monotonous churn. Outside the warrior women are quite serious, forging ahead, as if impatient to be reunited with Keela.

I suppose I am not the kind to lead them, really. They probably think me a skittish little fool who has bitten off more than she can chew. If this is the general consensus, they aren't exactly hiding it.

"Spared?" he repeats.

"Yes. Somehow you were the only man at the baths able to survive this alleged massacre of blackbirds?" I scoff. "I believe you are fantasizing or had drunk too much. As is your wont."

With that, Peregrine suddenly lunges. Now he is so close I can smell the quine on his breath.

"I assure you, dear princess, I was there. I was the one spared." He contains himself slightly. "I have no idea why, which is, quite frankly, maddening. But you needn't make light of the matter when I have the blood of men I have known my entire life on my conscience. And . . . guilt at surviving that even this drink cannot cure."

And he is so close to me now. He knows he is close and I know it, too. And there is something here, in the very small space between us, that quivers. Something like a fight, that makes me catch my breath.

He stays in this position, leaned in, and for a moment I have no idea if he's going to strangle me or devour me whole. His eyes now are the eyes of a wolf.

I realize I am holding my breath.

Quietly, as if not to disturb this spell, I meet his gaze, trying to remain cool in the face of this outburst.

"I . . . apologize," I add. "I did not mean to make light of your suffering."

He sits back on his side of the carriage, the both of us flustered.

Now he leans back, back to his cup. He pours himself another, as if to pretend this moment never happened.

But I know it happened. I know it happened and what he smelled like and what he felt like, that near to me.

This is not what that was supposed to feel like. This scoundrel. This was not meant to be felt. Him close to me. Like fireflies. Like wanting.

Like something I have never felt.

28

THE WARRIORS ON horseback see her before I do: Keela. The clearing in the forest opens up to a kind of red rock cavern, a cathedral made of stone. Behind her, divvied out in little camps, there are tents, a few campfires. In the distance, a strange, wistful song. The voice of an older man, tired and doleful. The red rocks of the canyon lit bright pink by the sinking sun.

Peregrine looks out the carriage window at the vast brigade. "What's all this, then?" he asks me.

"I told you I'd get you through to the Wraithen. They are here to help us cross the Murder of Shadows, nothing more," I lie, trying to be nonchalant.

"Why on earth would they want to help us?" he replies.

"Gold," I tell him. A lie, of course. No need to explain the vengeance we seek to Peregrine, a man devoid of conscience.

"Well, they're not getting any of my gold," he mutters.

"Of course not. I would never dream of it," I assure him.

I exit the carriage and stand, waiting for Keela to acknowledge me. She looks up, nods, and glides up to the incongruous, ludicrous white carriage to greet me. She gestures to the absurd ivory transport.

"I'm sure no one will notice this," she teases me.

"As you know, it is necessary," I remind her.

"I do hope this plan of yours actually works," she confides.

"As do I. Otherwise, we shall all be strung up at the gates of the Wraithen," I blurt out.

Keela gives me a look. "I see you've been contemplating it. Don't worry, dear girl. Worrying only makes you suffer twice."

"Or a million times, in my case, as my brain seems to be on an eternal loop," I confess.

"Yes, but remember your training. *Focus, breathe.* There is only the moment. This is the key," she reminds me. Now she turns back to see Peregrine. "So, this is the man who sold you?"

"Yes." I glance at him, simply relaxing in the carriage, enjoying a leisurely solo picnic.

"I wonder how you can stand the sight of him," she reflects. "I would slit his throat from ear to ear."

"Yes, well. I understand that impulse." I do not tell her of our strange moment in the carriage, when the air shivered.

"Let us dine well tonight, as it may be our last," she declares. "The Murder of Shadows awaits us before the next moon."

"That soon? I had thought there was longer to journey," I say, failing to hide my nerves.

"No, my dear. That is why we have met here. To bunk for the night, before the battle tomorrow." She looks out at the many little fires lit around the camp, the smell of bread and meat on a spit.

I notice the elder woman from the Azelle, Shakvi. She stands amongst the many people of the Azelle, whispering in hushed tones. As if aware of my stare, she looks up and nods, acknowledging me. She then goes back to her whispering to the large group around her, who listen intently. I notice again something minuscule in her hand. . . .

Keela follows my gaze, taking in the sight of the elder surrounded by the Azelle. "God help us."

"Yes." Yet I can't look away from Shakvi as the Azelle people stand rapt around her, hanging on her every word.

God help us, indeed.

29

PERHAPS IT'S IMPOSSIBLE to meet the Murder of Shadows in daylight. Perhaps it is nocturnal. This is what I tell myself as our army nears the cliffs before the Wraithen. The red landscape continues until the very edge of the horizon, where the rocks become black and, in the very, very distance, if you squint, you can see the spires of the Wraithen city stabbing the sky.

Peregrine seems quite content to sleep off last night's drink, as the carriage continues forward over the amber terrain. Again, he insists I accompany him in the carriage. If I am to be sold in the Wraithen, I cannot be "looking like some bedraggled peasant."

I'm certain he doesn't believe we will survive the Murder of Shadows, which is perhaps why he has informed me he will stay back in the carriage. "With the doors locked and windows shaded. I want nothing to do with it," he has informed me.

Keela's army of hundreds is an intimidating sight. And yet, something tells me the Murder of Shadows is not the kind of beast to be intimidated.

But who knows what this sinister creature may be? No one

has actually seen it. Or, I am told, no one who has seen it has lived to tell the tale.

All these thoughts are on a loop in my head as we continue on toward the perilous, mystical being. It's the not-knowing that makes it most terrifying. The riddle of what it *could* be.

The Murder of Shadows.

A ridiculous name!

As the amber rocks begin to fade, first to a kind of dusty rose, then a dusty gray, then darker . . . into a deeper charcoal . . . there begins a kind of silence I have never heard outside in nature. No sounds of birds or wind. No animals skittering about. A kind of stillness. As if the rocks themselves are bracing.

Peregrine notices it, too, his bleary-eyed countenance suddenly alert.

"Something's changed. Do you feel it?" he asks me.

"It is quiet . . . ," I whisper, trying to gauge the silence.

A shiver crawls through my veins.

And then—

"Do you hear that?" I ask him.

He shakes his head.

It's a sound, almost like a woman whispering in the distance. But the strangest thing about it . . . it's a familiar voice. A kind voice.

"That. Do you hear it?" I ask him.

He shakes his head again.

"Stop the carriage!" Suddenly, I am yelling, desperate to get out. "Stop at once!"

"Princess, what are you doing?" Peregrine tries to grab me, but

I lurch past him, out of the carriage and over the charcoal landscape, in the direction of the sound.

There it is again, that warm, familiar sound beckoning me. I run past the legions and Keela herself, who calls after me. Running over the gray and black rocks, following the voice . . .

And then I see her.

I am home! I am home! I have made it!

Who knew this perilous journey would take me right back to her!

There she stands on the other side of the cliff, reaching out to me. Her beautiful alabaster face and rosy cheeks, her wheat hair tumbling down past her ice-blue brocade dress. The most divine sight I have ever seen. A glow around her.

"Mother!" I gasp. "Mother! I have been trying to get back to you! I have missed you so!"

And she smiles now, that loving smile she reserved only for me. "My darling. My darling baby. I have missed you. I have been inconsolable without you."

She beckons to me and I hurry toward her.

"Come. Come to me! My darling girl." She reaches her arms out, the air around her shimmering. "We will go back now, back to our kind, loving world. Come, embrace me."

And I reach the edge of the cliff, breathless. My elation at seeing my mother is increased tenfold at the relief of being able to go back to my sweet world of pale pinks and baby blues. Finally, peace.

"Now, come. Come, we will go now." She beckons.

Looking down at my feet, at the hundred-foot drop into the

crevasse, I frown, puzzling over it. "But, Mother, how do I cross?"

"Simply jump," she assures me. "Jump and the two of us will return home. All will be well. All will be peace."

And now the serpent of doubt begins to weave itself around my thoughts.

"But, Mother, I'm afraid. What if I—" I hesitate.

"Don't be foolish, dear. You fell to this place. We will now fall back," she continues, her voice a soothing song.

But suddenly I am pulled backward, and there stands Keela, blocking me from the cliff and the sweet siren voice of my mother.

"Reveal yourself, trickster!" Keela stands strong, the posture of a lioness.

"Come, dear daughter . . . come to me." My mother beckons. And, again, I am drawn to my feet, toward her.

"I command thee! Reveal thyself!" Keela barks.

And now, like a slow wheel turning, the face of my mother changes from her sweet, loving countenance to one of an eerie, sinister grin . . . the eyes lose their sparkling blue and suddenly become spun over with a kind of milky glaze, the eyes of a blind man.

Her tumbling hair, too, begins to twist and wind like a thousand serpents and her ice-blue dress turns to gray and then to black. And then this pitch-black seems to take over her entire being so that she is simply a black figure there, an absence of light.

"Mother!" But it's clear now . . . this was not my mother. It never was.

And now the sinister shape begins to sink, lower and lower, until it crawls down into the cliffs, a black form, a black entity, a shadow sliding its way down the precipice. Keela and I watch as the entity slithers down the side of the opposite cliff, winding and weaving its way down, down the rocks.

And we both know where it is going.

Keela quickly grabs me and runs back toward the legions of warriors, hoping to beat the dark entity back to our brigade.

"Fall back! Fall back!" she yells out, to my surprise.

The warriors all look at one another, shocked. Keela is not one to back off from even the most daunting of enemies.

"Fall back!" she continues.

But it's too late. As the warriors hesitate, the black entity comes closer, now growing in size, still a black mass on the ground but somehow shape-shifting into a kind of black mist. And everyone it glides through, everyone it passes, is immediately transformed.

Some of the warriors instantly grow confused, standing still in a kind of stupor. I watch as their weapons drop to the ground. And then, as if being pulled by an invisible string . . . they begin walking slowly, as if in a dream, toward the edge of the cliff.

And now, as I watch in horror, they begin to simply . . . drop. They simply step off the precipice into the abyss without a sound or a word or a warning. Like lemmings, they just sleepwalk in a trance over the cliffs and fall to their deaths.

The remainder of the warriors, witnessing this, have eyes like saucers. Their horror is enough to elicit terror in me, and I begin to run. Run! Away from the Murder of Shadows, away from its ghastly enchantment.

But something else is happening, too. The warriors now begin to turn on each other, a kind of blazing madness in their eyes.

And I begin to hear them whisper, through gritted teeth and with diabolical smiles.

"Kill," they whisper. A thousand whispers, and now their weapons are raised high. Swords and axes slash the air, and blood begins to pour out, staining the ground.

Run! I have never run this fast in my life, heading God knows where, desperate to beat the ruthless dark entity and the melee it has wrought.

But the blade of an axe is raised high before me and as it comes down, the arc of it from above, I am suddenly whisked out of its trajectory and thrown backward, as if by an unseen force.

Yet it is nothing supernatural that saves me. It is none other than Peregrine. He clumsily races back to the carriage, where the driver awaits us, his eyes wild with fear and dread. The sound of the metal weapons striking flesh and bone is forever seared in my psyche.

Look one way and they are dropping off the cliffs by the hundreds; look the other and there is a massacre—the warriors' eyes as wild and hungry as wolves.

The carriage door slams quick. The wheels begin to turn fast, and soon we are racing, racing out of the tentacles of the Murder of Shadows. Yes, that is its name. That can only be its name.

The shrieks and metal clanking begin to fade as the carriage bolts farther and farther away from the desperate site.

No, I can't leave them to this obliteration.

"We have to go back!" I yell at Peregrine. There is blood spattered on his clothing, sweat dripping from his brow.

"We shall do no such thing! Are you insane?!" he replies, pulling me back from the door.

"But they'll all die!" I shout at him.

"Better them than us," he spits out, guarding the door. "And you're welcome, by the way. For saving your life."

And that's true, isn't it? A confusing thought.

"Wait . . . What is that?" I ask him, now hearing a strange sound in the distance.

"What is what?" he asks.

"Listen," I tell him.

And the two of us listen, the sounds of the metal clanking and mad shrieks now seeming to be drowned out by another sound. An eerie sound, coming from the edge of the cliffs.

"It sounds like . . ." He listens intently. "It almost sounds like . . ."

We both listen a second more, then turn to each other.

"A hum?" He says it, questioning himself.

"Perhaps, but—"

He beats me to it, peeking out the carriage window. "By all the kingdoms—"

He stops himself.

"What? What is it?" I ask him.

He turns back to me, bewildered. But his lips refuse to form the words.

"Let me see. Let me see!" I brush past him, peeking out the tiny carriage window.

But even then, even seeing it with my own eyes . . .

I can't believe it.

How to describe the scene outside this tiny window, framing the extraordinary event? In the distance, as our carriage has managed to travel a remarkable way during our escape, there is a panorama of madness.

One third of the scene consists of the suicidal warriors, dropping off the precipice into the abyss. The other third consists of the mass of blood and brutality I so narrowly escaped. But the last third, the last third is the most astonishing of all.

For there, adjacent to the cliffs and the battle, is a massive circle of gaunt, dusty creatures . . . the Azelle from the Sapphire. And they are not hurling themselves into the abyss. Nor are they stabbing each other with abandon. Instead, they are lying down. All of them. Lying on the ground, in rows and rows of concentric circles. Just content there, as if nothing is happening.

But then I realize this hum, this low hum, is coming from them.

And somehow, they are unaffected by the chaos, unaffected by the Murder of Shadows. In fact, they seem to be actually *affecting* the dark entity somehow. For, at the edge of their tranquil, seemingly submissive formation . . . the black mass hesitates, as though it has encountered a kind of mystical shield.

The Azelle continue their low, deep hum. And I begin to notice below me, the ground itself seems to be affected by this sound. Indeed, it vibrates in tandem with it. The deep, low drone continues, unabated, unbroken, and the ground continues to quiver.

Peregrine peers out beside me. "How is this possible?"

"I'm not sure. Perhaps it's an illusion," I say, not believing my words.

"Hang on, then," he says. "Who is that?"

"Who is what?" I reply.

"That figure in the middle. That old woman!" He points.

I follow his aim and see the old woman in question. It's the elder woman from the Azelle. Shakvi! She stands in the middle of the many concentric circles of tranquil, humming bodies, not a drop of fear in her, despite the terrifying battleground before her.

She remains hunched over, in the middle of the concentric circle of bodies. And, again, as last night, she is chanting to herself. But this time, it's no whisper. She spits the words and uses her whole body—the jab of an elbow, the swoop of a leg—to punctuate each sound. She is solitary in the midst of her people, and yet, she is, indeed, battling the Murder of Shadows.

"What is that she's holding?" Peregrine asks.

I marvel as the thing comes into focus.

You see, Shakvi is hunched over that very same unassuming, humble, tiny wooden box I noticed earlier.

"What is that?" Peregrine squints.

And as we watch, the miniature wooden box begins to glow, dimming and brightening as if somehow in tune with the vibration of the hum.

"Look there. Look!" Peregrine points again.

Words fail as I stare. The Murder of Shadows, this malevolent supernatural entity, appears to be somehow twisting and turning into a kind of vortex, as if it's struggling with itself, being raised against its will from the ground. The low, deep hum grows louder and more intense as the shadow is lifted off the ground. Wisps of black trail out of the battling warriors and pour into the vortex.

And as all our eyes look up to see this black swirling mist, there is an otherworldly shriek, as if it's fighting the enchantment of Shakvi and the Azelle people.

"They're—they're winning!" Peregrine marvels.

And now the shrieking grows louder, a horrible, deafening shrill, but the deep hum grows stronger still and the tiny wooden box glows as if set on fire, and then something happens that defies the laws of man and beasts.

With a bone-chilling, otherworldly howl, the enormous spinning black vortex is somehow sucked into the tiny glowing wooden box. All of it. The entirety. In a snap.

WHOOSH.

And then, as if crazed, Shakvi seals the box up in a rush. Now she begins sealing it with a kind of wax, burning a candle and continuing to chant to herself. The Azelle people, still lying down, end their hum . . . staying there, spent, exhausted to the core.

Swords and battle-axes fall to the ground. Warriors step away from the cliffs in a stupor, the entire army now taking in the hellish sight, unable to comprehend what it means or what has actually transpired.

In the distance, from within the mass of dumbfounded warriors, I see Keela emerge. She is bathed in blood. I run out of the carriage toward her and she stumbles to me.

We make our way to each other and embrace, gasping for air. "Are you hurt?" I ask. She shakes her head, tears streaming from the corners of her eyes.

Our moment of reunion is broken by a kind of jubilant outcry from the Azelle.

Keela and I turn to them, taking it in, the miracle they have performed.

I turn back to her.

"Still believe they are mad?" I ask her.

"I believe I must be mad," she answers.

"Yes, then we all must be," I reply. Now I turn my gaze to Shakvi and the strange little box. "She has, in truth, saved us. Just as she said."

Keela shakes her head in disbelief.

"It is, indeed, as if it were a dream."

30

IT IS A ghastly scene, the carnage left by the Murder of Shadows. We have lost hundreds of men and women. A quarter of our army! Dead. The rest, over the cliff's edge, lost to the abyss.

How close I came to this very same fate. If not for both Keela and Peregrine, I would be lost to the enchantment of the Murder of Shadows. Yet I cannot help but think about the mirage of my mother, how diabolical it was, this imitation. And how, even now, it fills me with longing.

But how did it know? The Murder of Shadows? How did it know my greatest weakness, my greatest desire? To be home, to rush into the arms of my mother and be back in the seat of my kingdom? And why me? Why would the Murder of Shadows choose me to enchant, rather than Keela, the clear leader of our battalion?

Keela's words echo from the past. *It has been said that the only one who can cure the spite that created this world is . . . The One Who Fell from the Sky.*

My head is heavy. My bones feel leaden.

Soon the dark will give us solace from this murderous scene.

In the morning, we will bury the bodies and honor the poor souls lost to the cliffs.

"What do you think they'll do with it?" Peregrine asks me, stretched out now on his pillowed bench in the carriage.

"Do with what?" I reply.

"The Murder of Shadows. They managed to trap it in that little box, didn't they? Now what will they do with such a diabolical weapon?" He ponders.

"Perhaps they will take it with them, back to their holy lands, to be kept out of the hands of greedy men. Mayhap Shakvi, the elder, will bury it. Somewhere no one can ever find it again."

He furrows his brow. "Let us hope so. But doesn't it seem odd, their suffering in the Sapphire Mines? When all the time they had this weapon, more powerful than even the ghastly Murder of Shadows?"

I contemplate that. "An interesting point."

"And you had no knowledge of this strange box? They just sort of . . . surprised you?"

I analyze this. "In truth, Shakvi has seemed very sure of herself. She told me quite firmly that she would save me, because she had saved me." I chuckle. "Keela was loath to even have her continue with us," I muse. "She thought Shakvi mad, the Azelle weak."

"Ah, yes!" He smiles. "Perhaps she has never been warned to not judge a book by its cover."

"You're one to talk," I admonish. "Your every thought is of outward appearances! You surround yourself with gilded facades and fine silks. You take the Sapphire to enhance your own visage!"

"Beauty . . . art, sculpture, oddities from the outermost king-doms," he confides. "These are the only escape from the tedium of life."

"And is life tedious?" I query.

"Most of the time, dear princess. Most of the time." He consid-ers. "Although there are moments . . . when something spectacular enters your sphere, shakes your foundations, and dazzles you to the core."

There's a moment of quiet now between us . . . a loud kind of quiet.

"Oh." I search for the words. "I suppose I must thank you. For saving me from that battle-axe . . . and for dragging me out of that malevolent field of chaos."

"I had to protect my merchandise," he replies.

"Yes. Of course," I answer, irked somehow. "Always the gold."

He raises his chin, a kind of strange look in his eyes.

"Don't worry. You'll be the richest man in all the kingdoms soon," I assure him.

"Yes. Good." He raises his tin cup. "Cheers."

I move to exit the carriage, turning in for the night in the camp with Keela.

"Is that all?" he asks.

This hangs in the air, in all its possible meanings.

"I'm sure I have no idea." I try to extinguish the shivering of the air. "I'll leave you to your tedium."

Part III

1

A KING'S JOURNAL

We are thankfully nearing the end of this miserable parade of princes. By the gods, every last one of them has been turned into a frog. Each one slimier than the one before. Upon their arrival, the princes flatter and jest, wanting desperately to be the chosen one. Of course, we, too, wish for each to be, as the princess must wake and marry before her birthday.

Again, time is of the essence. I have asked the old hag how long this must go on and she has merely waved a hand, saying it will all be over soon . . . once the prince "who is worthy" appears.

Balderdash!

In the meantime, it's impossible to sleep. I have taken to wandering the library, if you can believe it. Which of course you can, because you are my journal.

I seem to be agitated, carrying the weight of what I know, what the queen does not. Wanting to tell her, knowing that this is impossible.

I never assumed the event, far past, would ever amount to anything. But now, with the clock ticking, with the princess still in her relentless slumber . . . I can't help but wonder.

And how cruel that the very confidante I need, the queen . . . is the very person I cannot tell.

The effect is so infuriating that, quite frankly, I'm beginning to think this whole thing a joke.

At my expense.

Tomorrow, my consul informs me, we are to expect the last of the would-be Prince Charmings. Apparently, he's from the outer region of the provinces, fond of jousting and collecting exotic coins.

Fascinating.

If this one is Prince Charming, I'll eat my shoe.

2

IN THE MORNING, I wake with a fright, as I am being drawn on. Yes, it's true. There is a figure above me, with my arm in one hand and some sort of writing utensil in the other.

I leap out from my slumber. "What is the meaning of this?!"

As my eyes begin to focus, I see that the figure is none other than Shakvi, the Azelle elder.

"What exactly are you doing, sullying my arm in this manner?!" I blurt out.

"Oh, don't be frightened, dear. This is all for the good. All for the good," she assures me.

Nonplussed, I look down at my arm. Strange black letters lead down from the inside of my elbow to my wrist. "Will this come off?"

"Not yet. No, it mustn't," she informs me.

"But what does it say? I can barely make it out," I add.

"Nothing is as it seems," she chimes. "Nothing is as it sees. This is your name—your true name, given before you drew your first breath."

I stare at the squiggly symbols. They are utterly meaningless to my eye. "I'm not sure I understand any of this," I tell her.

She tuts. "Oh, dear girl. All will be well." She hands me a necklace. "Shall I put it on you? See, it's just like mine, nothing to fear."

And I do notice the necklace around her neck, a twine thing with a minuscule pouch.

"I'm not sure what the point is, but you did save all our lives in quite a heroic fashion just yesterday. Though I doubt my very eyes for seeing it."

"Yes, yes. Doubt your eyes, doubt your eyes!" She chuckles, tying the necklace loosely around my neck. "There."

Now she puts her hands on my shoulders. "It can only be you, dear girl."

"What do you—" I begin.

She interrupts me. "Keela has killed; she has the blood of hundreds on her hands, she is drowning in it. Do you not see? She cannot face the Veist."

"Face the Veist! Alone?" An absurd thought. "I assure you I cannot—"

"If not you, who?" She looks in my eyes.

"No, no . . . you see. I am not even truly a warrior. I'm not ready."

"If not now, when?" she asks me.

"Well, not at this moment, that's certain. I cannot begin to imagine where I would find the Veist. No one even knows—"

"Beyond the Wraithen. You have known it. You know it. You will know it," she assures me. "But it must be you. Only you. Anyone else will perish. And the blood will be on your hands. Now, that is all."

These words echo in my ears. . . . *You have known it. You*

know it. You will know it. That's it. The voice whispering in the wind . . . *I have dreamt you. I dream you. I will dream you.* The same confounding sense of time, or timelessness.

I turn to ask Shakvi but she once again shuffles over to the other side of the room, picking something up and handing it to me.

I take it, then look down, and hand it back immediately in haste. "Oh, no. No. Please. I cannot take this. I don't want this. Why would you give this to me?"

She looks down at it, the tiny, unassuming wooden box. Yes, the exact wooden box she used to capture the Murder of Shadows yesterday.

"You needed it," she tells me.

"Needed it? When?" I ask. "What in all the heavens do you mean?"

"Not in all the heavens. In this heaven. You needed it." She smiles. "You have always needed it."

I am taken aback and know not what to say.

"I must go." She quickly hurries out.

"But wait!" I implore her. "What is the meaning of—"

"What was the meaning, what is the meaning . . . you know, you will have known." She waves me off, happily going to join the rest of the Azelle.

And once again, this bewildering sense of time. Is this simply something of the Azelle? Of Shakvi? Of this place? Or is it specific to me . . . to my predicament, possibly a key?

I look out at Shakvi and the Azelle people gathered. By the looks of their packs and their horses, they are clearly prepared for a long journey. Perhaps headed back to their holy lands, as Keela surmised.

I look again at the strange black letters on my arm, unable to discern their meaning.

If anyone else were to mark me this way, I'm sure I should have been livid.

But Shakvi seems to transcend these things . . . and, indeed, all things.

Even the most terrible things.

Where we camp now, the rocks are charcoal black and there seems to be no plant life for acres around. If you squint, you can see in the distance the narrow spires of the Wraithen, growing taller as we move ever closer.

We will split up again this morning, Keela and her brigade, taking a lonely, hidden route. Peregrine, twenty warriors, and I will take the open route to the Wraithen Gates.

The warriors now have exchanged clothes with many of the Azelle people from the Sapphire Mines. It is agreed the warrior women will ride along in the barred cage behind our ivory carriage. It is a Spartan metal box with iron bars and nothing but sawdust on the bottom of it. It's unfortunate but must be done, as part of the strategy.

I make my way over to the ivory carriage, currently looking like a diamond in a dirt box.

Of course, Peregrine is grooming himself in the looking glass, which he informs me I am expected to do as well.

"We cannot have you looking like some ragamuffin from the

Cliffs of Grey, dear fake princess." He grins. "Happily, we have enough supplies to dress you up a bit. I had the brilliant foresight to bring a few extra garments, thank goodness. I really am quite clever."

"If you do say so yourself," I reply.

"Tell me, oh great fake princess, what is your diabolical plan for the Wraithen?" he asks, rather boldly.

"Why, whatever do you mean?" I answer, grinning like the cat that ate the canary.

"You can't think I'm foolish enough to actually believe you simply want me to sell you and your miscreant coterie of freaks, do you?" he points out. "I'm not quite that stupid."

"That is exactly what I'll have you believe," I respond. "What does it matter to you? As long as you get your precious gold?"

"And will I?" he asks.

"Of course you will. I have made you a promise and I intend to keep it. You shall be the richest man in the kingdoms. You should be kissing my feet for such an opportunity," I assure him.

"Yes, Your Highness." He nods.

"Excuse me?" I ask.

"Oh, nothing, dear princess. Just saying to myself how much I am looking forward to living like a royal myself," he replies.

"Yes, good. I'm sure you will fit in quite easily. For most royals I know are rogues anyway." I inform him.

"Touché, dear princess. Touché." He continues primping.

It's not until hours later, after a rather uneventful morning and afternoon in the carriage, that Peregrine and I hear it.

There is a kind of collective gasp outside our carriage, and now my sparring companion and I look out the window, to see whatever is so captivating.

As we look out, the morning fog seems to dissipate over the black landscape and now we can see closer, in great detail, the towering spires of the Wraithen, soaring up into the sky.

There's a sort of shimmering light coming off the kingdom there on its perch, as if each tower is laced with diamonds. It's a bewitching sight, the glistening black city in the sun.

"Ah, so this is what everyone is always going on about," Peregrine says, his voice filled with wonder.

And I am filled with wonder, too. It is as if the darkest genius in the universe, some extraordinary artist, had painted at once his greatest beauty and his greatest fear. A spellbinding vision, one you might take for a dream, or a nightmare.

Peregrine continues to marvel at this city of black and diamonds. "How astonishing . . . and exquisite."

I look back to see the women warriors in their metal cart jail, taking it in, a few of them agog.

"Stop! Stop the carriage!" I command, disembarking and walking over to my warrior companions.

"Do not be intimidated by this place. You have nothing to fear. Remember our plan and we shall prevail. Together," I assure them.

They look up at me and nod, a few still unconvinced.

"Everything seems impossible until it happens," I continue. "There can be nothing in there worse than the Murder of Shadows. Can there? You see, we have now reached the soft underbelly of this kingdom. And, to be true, we have on our side the element of surprise. They won't understand what we are about until it is far too late."

This begins to sink in. Slowly they return to their fierce and fearless selves again.

Back in the carriage, Peregrine contemplates me.

"Do you really believe that?" he asks.

"Believe what?" I reply.

"That we have reached the *soft underbelly* or whatever the expression was," he counters.

"Do you?" I ask.

"No," he answers simply.

"Well, then," I tell him. "I suppose I shall have to believe it for the both of us. If only you had as much faith as you do vanity."

"How do you know I am vain, and not just blindingly inse-cure?" he answers. He takes a swig from a tin flask. The Sapphire.

How often must he imbibe to retain his flawless visage? I wonder. Then I realize: We have destroyed the mines. What will happen to Peregrine when he runs out of his precious elixir?

3

THE GATES OF the Wraithen are enormous onyx works of art, as if the web of some enchanted spider was suddenly turned to pitch-black stone. A smaller, more manageable door is carved within the giant gates, one for the passing of carriages and freight.

Two guards, in dark metal armor, stand as sentries at each side of the imposing gates. As our carriage approaches, they notice us, gazing with curiosity and amusement.

Peregrine and I have dolled ourselves up to look like the king and queen of the most decadent, sumptuous kingdom in the heavens. The custom here, we're told, is not whiteface but rosy cheeks and lips. On both male and female nobles. To go without a painted face here is an indication of poverty, as it means you simply cannot afford the finer things. Our dress is brocade and silk, with lace flourishes, in icy silvers and blues, which Peregrine tells me is the current fashion.

"Halt!" one of the guards commands us, raising his hand. "Stop right there."

Peregrine and I share a look.

"Let the games begin," he whispers to me, disembarking from the carriage.

"State your name and your purpose," the other guard barks.

"I am the honorable Count Peregrine of Alabastrine. You may have heard of me . . . ?"

The guards share a look, then shake their heads.

"Or maybe not. Fine. I shan't be offended." He collects himself. "Well, if you *had* heard of me, you would know that I am the most preeminent trader in all the kingdoms. Indeed, my last sale earned me five trunks of gold."

The guards remain silent.

"And that is why I am here. To sell." He gestures toward the cage with a flourish. Behind the carriage, the women warriors, some no older than fifteen winters, sit packed together in that grisly metal compartment.

The guards note the prisoners, huddled behind their unhappy bars. "Nothing to boast about at court. Turn your carriage around, lest your head appear on these pikes." They gesture behind them and, indeed, there is quite an array of heads on pikes to behold. Just another grisly sight offered here.

"Wait! Now, wait. . . . You see, these prisoners are not the main attraction," Peregrine assures the guards. "Although once we clean them up, they will also fetch top coin."

The guards remain unmoved.

"But the jewel of the collection, the pearl of the sea, is here, in my carriage. You see, she is a princess, stolen from her kingdom. Raised with all the manners and wit of her station. And, of course, she is pure as the driven snow at first light." He beckons me. "You may show yourself, dear princess."

With this introduction, I emerge from the carriage, in all my finery. Quite frankly, I feel like a stuffed peacock.

The guards are uncertain what to make of this. Are they meant to bow? What is their station compared to mine, of royal blood but now, here, imprisoned?

I take their hesitation as my opportunity. "I prefer you not bow, as you can see it makes a mockery of my rather unfortunate situation. Prithee, let us pass, so my humiliation may not be observed by all."

The two guards share a look, still unsure. But their station is leagues below that of a princess. In their absolute world, they could be beheaded for disobeying a royal, even one being traded at auction.

Peregrine gives me a look, raising an eyebrow, apparently impressed by my regal maneuvering.

After a moment that feels like five winters, the two guards make a decision and promptly step back.

"Open the gate!" the first guard calls.

"Do you not hear, underling?" the other calls behind him. "Open the gate at once!"

"Go ahead, Princess." They bow slightly. "We hope you shall return to our fine realm one day, perhaps under better circumstances."

"One can only hope. And your kindness shall be noted," I assure them, in my most royal tone.

This is their way of covering their tracks, in case I might

happen to return one day, with both a kingdom and possibly an army. Peregrine and I return to our plush seats inside the carriage. I immediately begin fanning myself, as if to emphasize my high station.

As we pass through the gates, Peregrine looks at me and smiles a wry smile. "Are you sure you're not a con man?"

"I'm a royal; what's the difference?" I reply.

As the carriage winds its way up through the black cobblestone streets, the architecture of the Wraithen reveals itself to us, in all its dark beauty. This is a city you could almost believe was entirely imagined by a painter. A kind of masterpiece, as flabbergasting as it is inspiring. The architecture almost mirrors that of the ancients: colonnades and fountains, sculptures and spires, oil paintings faded, weathered quite beautifully, on the walls of buildings, framed by elaborate molding. All of this created with the same shimmering onyx, jewels embedded in the stones: aquamarine, emerald, and ruby.

I look over at Peregrine, who happens to be practically drooling at the prospect of the myriad riches here.

I catch his eyes with a glance. "Don't worry, my dear friend; by tomorrow this city shall be yours."

OUR ACCOMMODATIONS FOR the night are lavish, the finest in the realm, lent out for a pretty coin but in keeping with our
ruse. It is, come to think of it, the first time since I have crossed
over into this world that I have lived as royalty, as I did before in
my kingdom. Although there are no pale pinks and baby blues
here. Quite the opposite. All the tones here are dark and deep.
Intense. Forbidding.

It's really the waiting that is the sting of it tonight. Hoping
beyond hope that our plan actually works, that we will not all end
up dead with our heads on a pike just outside the city gates. Such
a fate would be entirely my fault, of course, as this entire charade
is my scheme in the first place.

My bedroom chamber, the size of two of Grandfather's cabins,
sits next to the chamber of Peregrine. I can even hear him inside,
his restless feet pacing the floorboards, until he stops suddenly
and I hear a knock at my door.

"Who is it?" I sing out, knowing exactly who it is.

"It's me and you know it's me," he answers, vaguely annoyed.

"Me? I don't know a 'me,'" I tease. "Me who?"

"Me, Count Peregrine of Alabastrine, etcetera, etcetera, etcetera . . . ," he quips.

"Ah." I open the door and there he stands, leaning up against the archway.

"As this is our last night before we are all murdered, I thought we perhaps could have a nice meal," he explains.

"The last time you offered to take me to a nice meal, you sold me to a dangerous drunkard," I reply.

"Touché. Yet things are different now." He sighs. "The least you could do is sit down and watch me dine while you insult me."

"Well, that does sound fun. How I love to hurl injuries your way," I jest. "Tell me, what kind of fanciful dining experiences does this diabolical place offer?"

"Legendary ones, I've heard," he tells me. "Be sure to wear your finest, or the finest I've lent you. I hear fashion is akin to religion here. We mustn't embarrass ourselves."

"I suppose. But absolutely no tricks and shenanigans," I warn him.

"Tricks, no. Shenanigans, mayhap," he replies. "Meet me down in the entry hall before I change my mind and decide to go on a bender."

I shut the door in his face.

Infuriating.

5

IT LOOKS LIKE this: a place of fountains and falls, in blacks and bruised plum, with hanging gardens and vines lit up by candle-light. Although it is a place of dining, we are set far apart from the hoi polloi, on a kind of stone terrace, overlooking the king-dom below. The light hitting the flowering vines and the myriad foliage, the waterfalls somehow both inside and outside, are daz-zling, a testament to whomever invented this place. As with all things in the Wraithen, it seems to hang somewhere between fantasy and delusion, as if it couldn't possibly exist at all.

"I wasn't prepared for it," I tell him, looking around me.

"For what?" he replies, eyeing a papyrus scroll where is written down tonight's feast.

"For the beauty of it. Of this kingdom," I confide. "I had heard such sinister words about the realm of the Wraithen.... I had never imagined how ravishing it would be. How strange and sublime."

"Yes, it is peculiar, isn't it?" He looks around. "Almost as if it doesn't exist at all."

"Yes, that's exactly it," I reply. "I feel as if I am somehow sus-pended between realms ... ever since we crossed the black cliffs."

He ponders. "Perhaps we died by the Murder of Shadows but don't know it yet."

"What a horrible thought! You certainly are deranged," I answer. "But if so, I wonder if this would be considered heaven or hell . . . ?"

"Well, you're in it. So, obviously, hell," he jokes.

"Very amusing." I pretend to slap him with my napkin. "And how is it that I could possibly belong in the same one of those as you?"

"That I cannot answer." Now he changes the subject. "Fake princess, you have your own royal keep and, hopefully, you shall earn a hearty one for me."

"Oh, you shall have your gold. Don't worry," I answer, perturbed.

"I shall need every coin." He reflects. "Now that everyone's running out of the Sapphire . . . thanks, I'm sure, to your little stunt in the mines."

"Stunt?" I chide. "Is that what you'd call it?"

"Fine, fine." He gestures. "Liberation, what have you. But the end result is that I am running out of Sapphire, which means I shall be turning ugly, too, which I find . . . distressing."

"Oh, stop that. You must be fishing for compliments. Again, as I told you, you actually look better. Distinguished. Intriguing."

"Ah!" He smiles. "And are you intrigued?"

We are interrupted by the attendants, in black silk, arranging the feast before us and pouring yet another glass of quine for my companion.

"Why do you imbibe so much?" I ask him.

"Why do you imbibe so little?" he answers.

"It seems I don't quite get as much out of it as you do," I suggest.

"If you were wiser . . . you would. Now you are simple, sweet, and optimistic. And you have no idea how terrible the world is." He raises his goblet for emphasis.

Even his goblet is an elaborate thing, of tinted purple color with gold etchings, the glass itself a work of art.

"I believe I encountered the perils of our journey just as equally as you did. They were . . . petrifying . . . even to a grizzled, worldly person such as yourself," I point out.

"True." He drinks, thinking out loud. "I wonder if you will die tomorrow?"

"Would you shed a tear?" I ask.

"Why, I would be devastated," he quips.

"Well, if I am, I'll simply have to haunt you until I drive you mad," I respond.

"My dear, you have already driven me mad."

It comes out before he can stop it.

It stays there in the air, and he can't take it back.

I don't quite know what to say to this. Perhaps this is more to do with the copious amount of quine he's been drinking.

We are both silent now. Feeling foolish. As if each of us is somehow off-kilter. As if each of us is not used to being so.

But the attendants come back with more quine, brandy, sweets, and an exotic collection of rare cheese, enumerated to us in great detail. This cheese from this region of so-and-so, this other cheese from that region of something something. While the lengthy origins and pedigree of each distinctive cheese is recited, Peregrine gives me a funny, bored look across the table.

I stifle a laugh in the midst of the gravitas of the cheese ceremony. The attendants look a bit nonplussed and this, of course, makes us have to stifle our laughs even more, which is obviously impossible.

Above us, the night sky is clear now; the moon is full. The man in the moon looks down at us, stifling a laugh with us, too, hung at the very top of the canopy of stars.

I suddenly remember the words of Shakvi, that the stars stare at us from the past.

Now we walk back along the black cobblestone path, winding even farther up, to our luxurious château. Peregrine keeps his focus on the constellations above us, pointing. "You see, there, that one is Orion's Belt. One of the easier ones to recognize. And over there, see, that arch there . . . that is Scorpio. The arch is what gives it away."

"Suddenly you are a professor of astronomy?" I tease.

"Yes, I have spent many nights under the stars, with only their light to shelter me," he replies, his thoughts now somewhere far away.

But now I surprise him with my knowledge of the constellations. "There are the seven sisters of the Pleiades. There is Ursa Major. And Ursa Minor, of course. That one there, you see. That is the North Star, formally known as Polaris." I point to it. "That's the one to follow if you're ever lost. Which, knowing you, you will be."

"Very amusing," he replies.

"Wait . . . Where are we, exactly?"

The paths here are narrow and winding, easy to get lost on. I suddenly have a fear we will tarry and lose track of the grand event tomorrow.

"Never fear, dear princess, never fear," he assures me, sensing my nervousness.

It is a few turns and twists until we reach our luxurious oasis, far away from the riffraff. Through the lush entry we go, the moonlight shining down through the great dome above. It's an odd thing; in this place, you never really know if you're in the interior or the exterior. The hanging gardens and vines seem ever-present, confusing the issue.

We ascend the grand, swirling staircase in silence, neither of us quite knowing what to say. The air thick between us.

Now we are at my chamber door and I turn to say good night.

He gives a perfunctory bow. "I do hope you enjoyed your dinner tonight, Your Highness. I had no idea they took their cheeses so seriously."

I let out a laugh. I feel light.

"Good night, sweet princess." He smiles. "Sweet princess, good night."

"Yes," I add. "I will see you in the morning."

The moonlight comes down through the leaves of the hanging gardens, the beveled window beside us offering a view as if we are now the ancients, looking down from our kingdom in the clouds.

And the night air around us warm, a breeze in it.

A thought comes over me and, before I can help myself, I blurt it out. "Do you ever wish you could be someone else? Or think about all the things you might do . . . ? If you could?"

"If I could, I would—" He stops himself, suddenly caught. "But that would not profit."

Something in his eyes, his hesitance, turns my knees to jelly.

And I would almost tumble over. But luckily, I am able to shut the door behind me before any of that can happen.

6

———◆———

THE MORNING OF the much-awaited auction, I am awakened by a stranger. He is a lithe man, with deep, calculating eyes. Yet his manner is one of a man without a care in the world.

Before I have even opened the door in full, he steps in, bringing his entourage along with him. Each member seems to be strewn with an entire closet of clothes, headdresses, jewelry, shoes, and feathers. They barrel in as if this is their home.

"Excuse me, but—" I try to get his attention.

He waves me off. "No arguing, dear princess. I am here to dress you and time is of the essence!"

He claps his hands together and points, ordering one of his minions to the side. He commands each of them with snaps and claps, like a dog trainer.

"No, you see, there must be some mistake—" I go on.

"No mistake, dear. You are the first princess ever to be sold at auction in the Wraithen Kingdom. And, therefore, the one who dresses you—if they get it right, of course, which, obviously, I will—will henceforth be asked to dress only the highest nobles in the kingdom, for only the highest occasion, for only the highest coin. So, you see, it can only be me," he explains, as if all of this should be obvious.

"No, you see," I explain. "I already have a dress."

This stops him, amused, he turns to his underlings. "She already has . . . a *dress*."

They all laugh in tandem, as if this were the funniest joke in the world.

"I'm not sure I understand . . . ," I politely reply.

"It is more than a *dress*, my dear befuddled princess," he adds. "Much, much more than a dress."

"Well, why don't I show you what I was told I would be wearing . . . and then you can scurry off to wherever it is you usually scurry off to," I chide.

"Very well, then." He accepts my challenge. "Let's see it."

"But of course." I smile sweetly, making my way over to the wardrobe. "Just so you realize, Count Peregrine will not be happy about this."

"My dear, who do you think hired me?" he replies. "Or do you think I just go around barging into princesses' bedchambers for the fun of it?"

His gallery of servants chuckles.

"No, need to snicker, underlings. He'll disdain you nonetheless," I inform them. This shuts them up.

He smirks at my insolence, but there is a bit of respect there behind it. As if he recognizes me now.

I pull out the light blue and periwinkle brocade dress I was given for the occasion, holding it up.

"You see, quite appropriate," I inform him.

There is a silence in the room. I'm not sure what kind of silence this is. . . .

"No," he replies.

"Excuse me?"

"No. It is not appropriate. Not quite, for you, dear princess," he adds. "You see, you must be . . . legendary."

He waves his arm in a grand gesture, as if painting the picture. "The fallen yet beautiful, the royal yet fated to be sullied . . . a tantalizing, exotic, singular prize."

He begins pacing around the room, thinking out loud. "It must be something . . . they haven't seen before . . . something beyond their wildest imagination."

Now he turns to look at me. "Let me see your legs."

"Insolent—"

"I am an artist, woman! Have you never heard of the great Seballine? Never mind, it doesn't matter. Quite frankly, you are the canvas. And I am the painter, the master of the masterpiece, if you will. And you will." He seems very proud of himself.

"Why should I show you my legs?" I ask.

"My dear, you shall have to show me all of it," he informs me. "For I need to know the shape of my canvas, my clay, rather. How to mold thee, how to mold . . ."

"I shall not show you all of anything. Other than the door," I retort.

"Don't worry, dear. I assure you I am not interested. This is clearly an aesthetic arrangement. Now calm down and stop being so . . . princessy," he commands.

"Fine."

"Fine," he repeats, continuing his contemplation. "It should be something . . . regal, astounding . . . yet . . . disheveled. As if you've just been snatched off the throne and thrown into the arena . . . to the lions."

"Ummm." I ponder, noticing his minions, hanging on his every word. "May I at least have some tea?"

"Never!" He turns to silence me. "Oh, all right. But nothing more than that; you shall have to fit into your corset."

He gestures to his servants. "You heard her! Tea! Chop, chop!"

They scramble out, as if fearful of the whip.

"You do know you don't have to treat your servants so?" I inform him.

"And why not?" he replies.

"Because it's . . . low. And not good business for you, mon ami. No royal wants to have to stand by while you abuse your underlings," I say, trying to enlighten him. "It's depressing."

"Humph." He thinks about it. "Mayhap where you come from, audacious princess, but here it is a mark of pride. And anyway, stop interrupting me. I need to think."

He continues pacing around the room, muttering to himself. Finally, after the tray of tea has been deposited, poured, and drunk . . . he snaps his fingers as if awakened from a trance.

"I've got it!" he bellows to the ceiling.

7

IT'S A COLOSSEUM of sorts, where the auction is to take place. Apparently, this is a monthly tradition, but by the looks of it you would think it was a once-in-a-lifetime event. The colonnade down to the arena is a wide path of onyx flagstone, less bumpy and more suited for a parade. And, indeed, it feels as if one is on parade, each side of the road populated by the curious multitudes; some wave, some drink, some laugh and cheer.

The sky is gray this late morning, dawdling between sunshine and rain, unsure of itself. Across from me, in the carriage, sits Peregrine, seemingly lost in thought.

"You didn't have to hire that . . . gentleman to dress me," I admonish him, wishing for something. Not sure exactly what— perhaps an apology.

"Oh, but I think I did." He raises his chin, feigning a kind of inspection. "He did a fine job."

"Is that all? Fine?" All morning long I have been primped and preened over as if today is my wedding day. Seems like quite a bit for just . . . *fine*.

"Honestly?" he asks.

"Yes. Honestly. I know it's not your natural state, but you could try it every once in a while," I reply.

"Honestly." He pretends to look out the tiny window, at the carousing masses. Now he looks back at me. "It makes me think . . . I shouldn't sell you at all. That I should keep you for myself."

"Keep me!" I scoff. "What makes you think I would want to stay with you? What evidence have you provided that would support such a ludicrous idea?"

"So you *do* want me to sell you. Good. Now I don't have to feel guilty," he replies, miffed.

"Oh, it's all very simple, isn't it? Sell or don't sell. Profit or don't profit," I quip.

"My dear princess, this was your idea, remember?" he points out. "You are the one who came to me with this ludicrous plan and promise of riches. I should have just kicked you out, then and there."

"Well, I'll be gone soon enough," I reply, irked and incapable of understanding exactly why.

He continues to brood while the hoots and hollers from outside fill the silence. There is even a concert of trumpets along the route. There, at the head of the entrance. So much pomp and ceremony. And for what? The auction of souls. It's a vicious kind of jubilation.

Our carriage comes to a halt within the gates of the colosseum, in a sort of hidden staging area. I peek out through the little window, trying to gauge the crowd. It is no use; we are in the damp stone underbelly, unable to see, waiting for our debut.

"Stay here. No one is to see you before the event," he commands me, opening the door and disembarking.

The noise of the throng makes me feel as if the entirety of all the kingdoms is gathered here today.

I open the carriage door just a wee bit, to assess the warrior women behind me. Each one is dressed as a kind of "wild savage" from the Cliffs of Grey. Animal prints abound as if the warriors are tigers or cheetahs or anything "other." Certainly not human. No, never that.

They look up at me and we share a look.

A nod.

It's now or never.

8

———◆◆◆———

THE REVELRY AND commotion of the raucous audience in the colosseum continues. I am now brought to a kind of staging area behind an ornate velvet curtain by the great Seballine, who is preening me along the way. His subordinates flurry around me with great meticulousness, touching up my hair and makeup, straightening my dress, taking a fastidious look at my face and then touching it up again.

Out of the corner of my eye, I spot Peregrine, standing in the alcove. His hands on the back of a chair, he stares intently at the floor beneath him. Then, restless, he walks a few paces here and there, then back to the chair, where his hands continue to tap tap tap. It's difficult to see what exactly is happening over there, but why should I care? This is my plot, and it is about to begin.

In front of me, the warrior women of the Cliffs of Grey, dressed in their ridiculous "barbarian" attire, are auctioned, one by one. I can hear the sound and commotion of the bidding, but have yet to see the interior of the arena, as I am last on the bill. "The spectacle they have all come to see," I am told.

Before me is carried a great gold-gilded looking glass and, when I look into it, I hardly recognize myself. The face looking back at me, the entire body, all the skin on this figure in the glass, is a rose gold. Shining and metallic. The dress itself, a brocade and embroidered thing, is also in hues of rose gold. The corset sucks me into unhealthy proportions, and the skirt of the thing, more like an ocean, puffs out, first in brocade and then in a kind of chiffon, so that I feel a bit like a wedding cake.

"Hold still," the great Seballine commands me.

Now he ceremoniously pins an enormous tiara atop my head, which seems at once a crown and the backside of a peacock. This is also in hues of rose and gold. But here, as in the dress and the bodice, the tiara headdress is set with a hundred sparkling stones, all in different shades of rose and amber. It's a spectacular work of art, indubitably. Even though I find my dresser to be persnickety, he is certainly correct in that he is an artist, as insolent as he is talented.

Now the underlings come and begin hanging my neck with more and more rose and amber strings of jewels, a cascade dripping down my neck, a waterfall of shimmering stones.

The proud Seballine steps back and peruses his work.

"It's . . . almost . . . perfect." He tilts his head one way.

"No offense," he adds, a cursory nod to me.

There is a kind of beautiful, suspenseful music from the arena, heralding in the next act.

"Ah! That's our cue!" Seballine jumps up with excitement, leading me forward.

As we near the screen, I hear the sound of a drum, contrapuntal to the mysterious, melodious sound of the music. The drums, vibrating like a storm approaching, as if something spectacular and death-defying is about to happen.

As we reach the final moment, as the drums come to a crescendo, my elbow is taken and I am pulled aside.

Baffled, I look up to see the face of Peregrine, there beside me, intense. This moment must only last a second, but it feels like a hundred moons. And his eyes, now sans the Sapphire . . . faltering. Changing. No longer in perfect symmetry. His left eyelid droops a bit, and there is a small scar that bisects his right eyebrow. It is a singular feature, imperfect and . . . beautiful.

I reach out and graze it with my fingertips. "How did you come to have such a wound? What tale is behind its making?"

Peregrine steps forward.

"What are you doing?!" I hear the great Seballine yelp, baffled.

But then a strange thing happens, before I know it is happening. . . .

The lips of Peregrine are on mine, kissing me as if we will both die this very moment.

I am a princess and he is a rogue. He is a liar, and perhaps a thief. I should strike him. I should scream. But that's not what's happening.

No, what's happening is that I am lost in this moment, my stomach fills with a swarm of butterflies and my feet are somehow off the ground. The drums grow louder still, and my heart beats along with them, hard enough it would seem to jump out of my chest.

The kiss stops and he looks at me, his hands upon my shoulders.

He whispers, fervent, "Don't go out there. This is madness. Stay with me. Stay here with me."

I falter.

The great Seballine looks on in astonishment.

There is a flourish of trumpets and before I know it, I am being carried out, by Seballine and his underlings. The curtain shielding me from the view of the audience parts.

9

LOOKING OUT ACROSS the great, gilded arena is a sight
unlike any I have ever dreamt. More exquisite than the pharaohs
of the ancients. It is overflowing with the multitudes of the kingdom. Yet each and every one of these ostentatious attendees is
wearing a mask. Some gold gilded, some lush velvet, some beaded
or in rows of peacock feathers and scarlet plume. The servants,
too, all don masks, albeit less elaborate ones, shades of gray, beige,
and dun.

But that's not quite the worst part. Underneath their masks,
servant and noble alike bear hideous fangs, filed down into
sharpened daggers, white knives in a row, ready to tear apart the
throat of anyone displeasing. It's terrifying.

To wit, the very best seats are centered in private boxes, each
one a luxurious, decadent chamber. Each of these extravagant
chambers is decorated as if Midas himself footed the bill. Each
in their own style, with toile or silk walls, brocade curtains,
flowering plants, and plush velvet seats for the sumptuous, vain
nobles. And, standing there next to each of them . . . their masked
servants, fanning them with giant palms. Grand feasts adorn

the carved wooden tables before them: grapes, olives, figs, a pig stuffed with an apple in its mouth, eyes still wide open, as if shot in the entry hall. I shudder as I remember the dreadful scene at the Gray Horse Tavern, Gork there, burned on a spit, apple in his mouth.

But there they are! In many of the lavish private boxes, my fellow warrior women, standing tall, purchased . . . a trophy for each master. Each one of them now in a scarlet velvet mask. Perhaps that is the costume here, to show a kind of newly won ownership. There in the bottom of the arena, down near the front, an opulently dressed, gold-fanged man holds court. He seems to be the only one in the entire amphitheater devoid of a mask. Perhaps his gold fangs are his tribute to this circus. Behind him rest trunks upon trunks of gold, silver, and diamonds. This silly, unmasked man is a kind of barker, standing directly in front of the overflowing chests of treasure, announcing this and that to the audience, making jokes and singing bawdy tunes.

The warrior women look at me, their faces masked. I keep my face blank, too, regal and indifferent.

The drums have now stopped abruptly, mid-note. The silence in the colosseum is palpable, as the faces, the hundreds of sets of masked eyes, stare flabbergasted at the spectacle . . . of . . . me.

Then, as if it's a collective thought, they all spontaneously come to their feet and begin to applaud madly. Delighted, they whistle and yell out, "Bravo! Bravo!"

The great Seballine steps out to my side and, feigning modesty, takes a humble, flattered bow. Then he steps back, and now the thunderous applause begins to die down.

I attempt to catch a glimpse of Peregrine, but it's impossible. He's somewhere behind me, backstage, in the damp stone shadows.

Now the festooned barker, feeling the audience, glides charmingly in my direction.

"Ah, yes. Ah, yes! Here she is . . . the one we have all come to see." He takes his hat off, offering me a dramatic bow. "The great spectacle, the enchanting sight, does not disappoint."

I stand still as stone, unimpressed and aloof.

"Does she not sparkle with the royal blood of a princess? Does she not sparkle with the highness of her station? Do those eyes, as shimmering as the ocean, not stand in defiance of what is to come? And who would not want to see such innocent defiance . . . if not to break it." The barker slides around me, making his case.

The audience stands rapt.

"These bonny long locks, this bonny mouth?"

He tantalizes the audience, a director of sorts.

He does not touch me, but he is pointing to each feature as he goes, waving his hands just so.

The entire colosseum is in his hands.

But I am in my head. Steeling myself for this moment, wondering if it's possible that I have just led my fellow warrior women and myself to our deaths. Perhaps I am a fool. Perhaps Peregrine was right. Perhaps this is suicide.

"Yes." The gold fangs glisten. The barker eats it up, reveling in their reaction. "Yes. These gold-gilded ankles . . ."

"Ten thousand coin!" It's barked out, from a squat, feather-masked noble, in his ostentatious private box near the front.

"Ah! So the bidding has begun? I thought you would at least let me finish." He smiles, drawing a laugh from the audience. "Well, I suppose if you must, then you must . . . let it be known, the bidding starts at ten thousand coin—"

I brace myself. This is it.

"Before you settle this," I interrupt, "I feel I must comprehensively prove my worth."

He turns to me, intrigued. "Truly . . . ? And how will you do that, Princess?"

"I would like to show you," I demur.

He gauges the audience.

The throngs yell out, one over here, one over there, "Yes, yes! Show us! Let us see, let us see!"

The carnival barker now turns to the audience, excited by the prospect. "Would you enjoy that, ladies and gentlemen?"

They hoot and holler behind their disguises.

"Very well." I turn to the semicircle of musicians. "Please play that song from earlier, although . . ." I think a moment.

I then glide over to the composer and whisper into his ear. He looks at me, his eyes widening.

The entire arena is silent with anticipation.

I give a minor sort of curtsy.

And now the music begins.

10

THE LANGUOROUS SOUND of the music slithers its way up through the arena. Beginning slow and low, building . . .

I direct my gaze to the warrior women, each in her own lavish private box, poised like masked statues for their new masters to boast about and ogle.

But now it starts.

Slowly, as the shivering notes tantalize, I creep. Slowly at first. Easing from one side of the stage to the other, fluid as water, silent as night.

The theatrical barker stares at me, his eyes ablaze. Yes, this will play, he is thinking. This will do just fine.

The audience lets out a little gasp of excitement as, one by one now, the warrior women also start to creep. Slowly, ever so slowly, they mimic the dance. They slither through the ostentatious private realms of their new masters.

The throngs stare, enraptured, as the enchantment continues.

I now nod to the composer. He begins to pick up the tempo a bit.

The rhythm quickens, and I manage to steal a look at Peregrine. He stands there, unlike the entirety of the colosseum, curious. As if he's certain there must be a trick coming. He ever so slightly raises an eyebrow. A look of wry amusement.

And I reflect it back to him, as if he has read me.

Now the drums louder. Now the drums faster. A crescendo into fever. A delusional fugue!

And, just as it reaches its apex, a mad squeal, a visceral frenzy . . .

The warrior women slip their knives out from the places they were concealed in their costumes.

They slide the knives under each and every noble's mask. . . .

In the bat of an eye.

The festooned nobles crumple to the ground, their fanged teeth spattered in blood.

But now . . . in this aftershock, the guests of the slain nobles realize, in horror, what has just occurred. They each look up to find the warrior women, scarlet-masked, covered in blood, standing above them.

I turn to the dastardly barker, a knife in my own hand now. "Leave this place. Hurry now, before they kill you."

He stands frozen.

"Go!" I command. "Before I change my mind."

He bows out, stepping backward.

And then he turns and runs.

The colosseum is pandemonium now. The remaining nobles are screeching, clawing, elbowing each other out of the way to reach the exits. No use; the warrior women are agile and spry.

The felled nobles collapse backward into their piles of gold, weighted down by blood and treasure.

The chaos continues and the familiar figure of Count Peregrine emerges from the shadows.

He steps before me.

"Is this my fate, dear princess?" he asks. "If so, I desire the blade to be yours."

I meet his gaze.

"This one shall be spared!" I call out, gesturing to Peregrine, my voice echoing around the colosseum.

"There, you see. You saved me from the Murder of Shadows. *Now* we are even," I say.

He nods.

"By night, everyone here will be dead," I inform him. "If I were you, I'd hide."

"I see," he replies.

"Oh, and, of course, your treasure. I told you you'd be the richest man in all the kingdoms. I am good for my word." I gesture toward the overflowing trunks of gold and jewels, the bloodied treasures piled up in the royal boxes. "You may have to clean it up a bit. But you and I both know gold has always been dirty."

He looks up at the plethora of gold, diamonds, and coin treasure. Yes, he will be the wealthiest man in all the kingdoms, perhaps even in the history of the kingdoms. No matter the price of what Sapphire is left, Peregrine will avail himself of it, never needing to worry about imperfections. Such is the life he's chosen.

I choose differently. I choose to see the beauty in the flawed and the broken. And for a moment, Peregrine was beautiful.

"You see, you got what you wanted," I tell him, turning to join my fellow warriors. Heading toward them over the dirt of the arena floor, I steel myself for this day of battle.

But suddenly a hand is on my arm.

Peregrine steps beside me in the middle of the bedlam.

I look up at him, his rugged new face, his real face, his desperate eyes.

He whispers, "Did you not feel what I felt when I kissed you just then?"

And the truth is, I felt this and beyond. I felt the moon, teetering above the stars.

He senses my hesitation. "Come with me. We can be rich! Happy. I will spoil you. I will live to spoil you. It will be positively embarrassing how spoiled you will be."

The warrior women are shrieking now, giddy with revenge for their brethren slaughtered at the Cliffs of Grey.

"Look around you, Princess," he pleads. "This is beneath you."

My parents, the king and queen, would be appalled by my current situation. They, too, would consider it beneath me. Yet I remember—the injustice, the carnage, the cruelty that has plagued this realm and cost the lives of too many of the families in the cliffs, and in the mines, while these nobles led their decadent lives, their feet pressing on the necks of all those beneath them.

A fleeting thought: Is Roix any different, in the end?

But I am not there. I am here. And I cannot forget what I have seen.

"This is not beneath me. We cannot just stand by as entire

villages are slaughtered. As the wretched and destitute are carted off to the mines." I turn to leave, but stop and twirl toward him one last time. "And what of you? Do you not think you, too, will be carted off one day? When the Sapphire runs out? When you, too, are wretched? Carted off to some terrible dungeon to end your days with your head on a pike?"

He wraps his fingers around my arm, holds tight. "You cannot go to the Veist. She is the source of all the pain of this world. You will die . . . you understand?"

But I shake my head gently and wrest out of his grasp. "Knowing that I had the chance to stop her, and instead doing nothing . . . I could not live."

I turn while I still have the courage, and march to join the warrior women, signaling them to join me.

I don't look back.

11

THROUGH THE WRAITHEN streets we advance, toward the gate to the city. The streets are anarchy now, nobles scampering, shrieking, and ducking into whatever nook or cranny they can find. The sight of our brigade, drenched in blood, daggers in hand, clears a path for us down to the doors of the kingdom.

My two warrior companions come upon a stable and nod to each other. They steal a palomino and a mustang. I wrangle a black stallion, with raven hair almost blue. The three of us, now on horseback, charge down to the front gate.

I know what their plan is before they say it, watching them jump up to stand on their horses in perfect balance, an astonishing sight. Forthwith the nobles disperse, even more panicked, leaving the street before us empty. It's a wide avenue now, down to the imposing front gate. All the better for our brigade to gallop through the path at full speed.

The two gate guards turn to ascertain the source of the noise, the horses' hooves thundering through the streets. Their eyes turn to saucers as they see my two companions on horseback, arrows drawn. Quickly, they open the behemoth contraption.

Slowly, the gates begin to give way, the onyx doors and then the iron grid portcullis. Outside, at the head of the legions, Keela sits, steeled, on her horse. The battalion is behind her, hundreds of fierce men and women from the Cliffs of Grey, enveloping the black landscape.

Most have no armor. Many of them don't even have a horse. But the cliff warriors are capable of a kind of dexterity, instinct, and blitz. Their enemies often meet death in bafflement, still piecing together their own demise.

Keela then gives me a knowing nod, breathes in, and lets out a thunderous battle cry. A remarkable sound—a kind of high-pitched shriek with a million tongues in it. The warriors answer her with the same shrill wail, and they're off.

Into the Wraithen Kingdom they gallop, to avenge the deaths at the Cliffs of Grey, as well as all the slings and arrows dealt to them by these rotting, decadent nobles, drunk on power and high with gold. The powers that allow all the elders to be sent off to their deaths in the Sapphire.

I watch the legions pass, led by Keela, who gives me a solemn nod. The army is now in its entirety, reunited, to take the Wraithen by storm. I wonder, in this moment, if I will ever see Keela alive again.

And I wonder, too, if ever she shall see me so.

12

THE LAST THING I would expect to see here, in the nether realm of the Wraithen, is what lies before me. In the center of the glittering onyx city there is a steep, charcoal path of first cobblestones, then gravel, then dirt. It winds down into a kind of hidden valley below. The quiet here is what's truly unnerving. Not the usual sounds found in nature, birdsong or a thrush through the fields. It is as if the landscape itself is frozen, or perhaps lying in wait. I shudder to think of what it might be awaiting.

I stop a moment, taking note of the slight mist in the air. It hangs as if there is no direction in which to go, as if this place is some kind of blank purgatory, neither here nor there. The silence is absolute—and deafening.

The elder, Shakvi, had told me I would know how to find my way here to the center. And yet, I am surrounded by what is quickly becoming a thick fog, with no real sense of direction or bearing.

A moment of panic sets over me as it begins to dawn on me how naive I am to be here. What in all the heavens was I thinking?

"I'm a fool." It comes out as a sigh, a realization.

The fog is thick as pea soup now around me . . . but the silence is broken by what sounds like a sort of birdsong, a gentle melody, reaching out through the mist. I follow the lilting song, hearing now the sound of a babbling brook, equally tranquil. The pleasant rushing of the water leads me through the fog.

And now I am in a placid scene: a clearing, long green grass all around, wildflowers painting the field, surrounded on the outskirts by lush weeping willows and cherry blossoms in full bloom, the flowers quivering in the slight breeze.

But how can this be? This place beyond the Wraithen is spoken of as a dark, dying, terrifying place. And yet, standing here . . . I might as well be home in the most sumptuous gardens of all the fairy kingdoms. The verdant scene, the scent of jasmine, nearly brings tears to my eyes. For it has been so long that I have seen anything, really, but cruelty, blood, and depravity.

Yet this clearing is as if sent by the ancient gods, by Artemis herself, to delight and please the eye.

There is a thought here, but I cannot grasp it . . . it stays just out of reach, an arm's length from my mind, so that I might not take it in and contemplate. I try once more to bring the thought in . . . but it tarries there, unable to make the last part of its journey.

Instead, a very different thought replaces it: how very tired I am. Yes, of course, I've been traveling for days. Why shouldn't I be tired? Yes, yes, of course. I must rest here. I must lay my head down on this delicate green grass, in the middle of this bucolic scene; I must lay down my body, smell the green of the grass and the cherry blossoms, feel the warmth of the sun on my face, hear the babbling brook as it lulls me to sleep. . . .

To sleep, ah, perchance, to dream.

To slumber away in this enchanting place, not a care in the world. . . .

And now it is that all is forgotten, all the tasks and words and advice given me . . . it begins to drift softly, pleasantly away, leaving me light. Light as a feather, light as a cloud, my eyes close and the thought I was trying to grab, an arm's length away . . . will never reach me.

Something about the ancients, this garden, sent by the gods . . .

Something about sent by the gods . . .

To please the eye . . .

The eye.

. . .

That's it.

Wait.

What was it she said, Shakvi? Nothing is as it seems. Nothing is as it sees.

Doubt your eyes.

I open my eyes and grab this thought before it can flap its wings away from me and fly off into the sunlight.

Nothing is as it seems, as it sees.

Doubt your eyes.

I begin to unfocus my eyes, to see in a way as if my whole vision is blurry. A kind of surrender of sight.

And as I do that . . . the green grass below me begins to wind and wriggle. The jasmine scent begins to foul. As the garden around me begins to reveal itself, to transform, I jump up in horror at what had been deceiving me.

Below me, the green grass, the fields, had been nothing but a pit of vipers, of snakes. Snakes that I had lain on, that I had lain in . . . asps, cobras, king snakes, with stripes of red, yellow, black. I gasp, running now in terror, over the thousands upon thousands of snakes, seeing the brook now, not a gentle thing but a rolling ooze of sludge, seeing the weeping willows and cherry blossoms now as they are . . . barren, black, and dead. The air now rotten, the smell of sulfur.

What a cruel trick!

A terrible trick, and as I run farther and farther toward the edge of the clearing . . . it almost seems like, but mayhap it's my imagination running away even further . . . it almost seems like from somewhere, almost as if from up above, from beyond the clouds . . . there is the sound of laughter. Or not exactly that.

But the sound of someone laughing at me.

13

---·◆·---

THERE WAS ONLY one path, between two incredibly steep black cliffs, out of the snake mirage or garden of vipers or whatever I choose to call it, which I am refusing to decide on, as I prefer not to think of it. If my mind can imagine such beauty in such revolting things, then my mind can surely forget ugliness.

This is what I tell myself as the path between these two towering cliffs appears to grow tighter and tighter. At last, the path seems to come to a kind of conclusion, and I find myself standing there, leaning against the steep rock wall, breathing heavily from the exertion and wondering if there is any way around these soaring cliffs.

Am I lost?

But upon further inspection, I see there is a slight opening between the two towering rock faces. I peer inside and see that there is, surprisingly, an extremely large cavern.

I contemplate the route behind me.

No, I cannot go back. How could I? Back to the pit of vipers and God knows what else lying in wait there in the fog.

I close my eyes and inhale, steeling myself for whatever awaits me here in this mysterious cavern below.

It's a tight squeeze in between these rocks, but once through, there is space enough in this gorge for an entire kingdom.

High up above, through some of the ebony rock formations, the sunlight streams in, illuminating the cavern below, almost a kind of earthen cathedral. As I creep to the sides of the cave, steadying myself on the way down, I begin to notice something fracturing the light ahead, sending it to and fro.

And there I see it: down below is a vast lake—the size of which one could not hope to swim across in a day, unless one was the best swimmer in all the kingdoms, which I most certainly am not.

On either side of the cavern, there is room enough to carefully navigate adjacent to the water. I let out a sigh of relief as I begin to balance myself, creeping down toward the narrow path below.

This is exactly the moment I notice the tide within the lake. Or not a tide exactly . . . but a current. A current that now twists and twists upon itself, creating a kind of swirl in the midst of the great cavern lake. As I stand there, the current seems to grow more and more violent, and I wonder, in a panic, if there is some way that the whirlpool will suddenly crash its waves against the rocks, dragging me down to a watery grave.

I hurry my way down, down now, as fast as humanly possible, to the little path at the edge of the water.

I am just about to step onto the path when I see it.

There, now, gliding down from the top of the rocks, serpentine, as if lying in wait, is the hideous thing. No, it's not feigning beauty like the garden. No, it's not raging within itself like the whirlpool.

The thing before me, the creature, is a kind of gorgon with the scaled body of a reptile leading around to its top of more than a hundred heads, undulating in and out, fluctuating, poking forward and then back. Each of these heads is slightly distinct, some deep green, some black, all terrifying, with teeth the size of daggers. The entity itself is the size of the giants in the tales of the ancients, there standing before me, guarding the narrow, wet path to the other side.

The Veist.

I stand stupefied, looking first to the swirling rapids below, then to the hideous creature above. Drowning rapids, stabbing creature.

Maybe this will be the end of it.

Maybe this is supposed to be the end of it.

Perhaps if I plunge myself into the crashing water and am dragged down into the rapids below . . . perhaps that is the gentlest of deaths to be found today.

The light of the water refracts on the multiheaded gorgon and I realize that, of course, it is coming closer. The rays from above shine a quick spotlight on its razor teeth.

Yes, I will hurl myself.

I will hurl myself into these crashing waves.

I take a deep breath and quite literally lose my balance as I stop just in time to not fall immediately into the whirlpool below.

The whirlpool of churning water reminds me of the vortex

of the Murder of Shadows, both seemingly made from the same diabolical master's hand. A coincidence?

Wait.

The Murder of Shadows.

The box.

The tiny wooden box.

Will this work?

Once released, won't the Murder of Shadows kill me? Yes, it will kill me. Most likely.

But what choice do I have?

I just nearly slipped to my death mere seconds ago.

Quite simply, I have nothing to lose.

I reach into the folds of this stupid rose-gold dress, now torn to ribbons, and find the tiny wooden box where I placed it, sewn tightly into the lining. I fumble, hands shaking, to extract it.

The slithering beast makes its way closer, closer still, over the slippery rocks, the waves crashing at its talons.

Please oh please find it oh hurry.

And now I have it.

Please please please, I pray to the heavens above.

And now, without hesitating, I take the two sides of the box in each hand and break open the wax used to seal it.

If I die in this moment, please God, let me die quickly.

And the box is opened.

14

WHAT HAPPENS NEXT is a moment of suspension.

The creature, oddly, seems to realize that something is afoot. Its animal instinct, perhaps, aware of something otherworldly, something unnatural.

But this hesitation is momentary and then, as if now spurred by a new enemy, the gorgon attacks.

The long slithering necks of the creature are now upon me, and as I look up . . . its many heads, its many mouths, its hundreds of teeth glisten, ready to tear the flesh from my bones.

I am doomed.

One of the hundreds of teeth catches my tattered dress and I am whipped off-balance, now prone on my side, ready to be devoured.

I close my eyes, not wanting the last thing I see to be those slimy razor teeth.

But then, suddenly, my hair begins to stand on end, and I can feel it . . . the cold. Goose bumps. The chill that came in the moment before the Murder of Shadows.

I open my eyes to see the black nothingness as it creeps its way out of the box, and serpentines up the body of the gorgon, up the tangle of necks and mouths and heads.

And as the jaws of the beast are upon me, so close I can smell its rancid breath, its neck violently snaps off, the head falling with a thud beside me.

And now I am covered in its insides.

I look up in horror as the hundreds of remaining heads above me, the hundreds of necks and thousands of teeth, begin snapping forward and snapping back, this way and that, careening and chomping, as each head rips each of its other heads to pieces. Each mouth tearing at the hundreds of necks beside it. The flesh coming off the bone now, devoured, shredded to pieces, cascading down into the crashing waters below. Down, down into the vortex, a monster devouring itself. The shrieks and sound of flesh, harrowing. I cover my ears and watch as this thousand-stone creature mutilates itself, each of its heads, each of its minds, turning on the other one.

The rocks above the cavern begin to fall from above, the force of the giant creature fighting itself shaking the very ground.

It dawns on me that I could be trapped in here, entombed in this place, if the cavern collapses in on itself, which, as the rocks continue to fall and the beast obliterates itself, seems certain. The slithering, self-annihilating creature twists and turns, violently staggering this way and that.

In a blind bolt I catapult myself through, between its talons, underneath it and toward the narrow path, rushing over to the other side of the lake. The rocks are falling in droves now and the beast seems to have nearly eviscerated itself. It moves slowly, as if the life is draining quickly out of it. The black mist of the Murder of Shadows seems to cling to it, twisting and turning itself with every stab of the wounded gorgon's teeth.

But this is not the time to observe. The rocks are coming down as big as boulders and, as the decimated body of the thousand-stone creature is finally extinguished, it lands on the foot of the cavern with a resounding thud.

There is an avalanche of boulders as I begin to run, the dust and stones pummeling me from above. I cover my head with my arms and run blindly forward, away from the final death knell of the gorgon. Then I hear the very last thing: a colossal splash. And I realize, the creature's body has now been sent with the rest of it, down into the watery vortex below.

The avalanche continues unabated, seeming to multiply itself as it goes, careening toward me in dust and stone. My feet seem to have taken over my thinking process now, as somehow I am able to stay harrowingly close, but just ahead of the explosive grit and rocks.

Mercifully, the avalanche begins to abate, having made its point. As I finally reach a safe enough distance, I wipe the dust and dirt out of my ears and eyes and turn to look back down at the panorama below.

There is nothing now but a pile of rocks and boulders. No sign of the lake, no sign of the cavern, no sign of the gorgon. No, not even a sign of the Murder of Shadows.

My eyes search for any opening in the rocks, waiting for the sinister black shape of the Murder of Shadows to come winding its way out from the minuscule cracks between the boulders . . .

but there is only dust swirling, nonchalant.

I collapse now in exhaustion . . . dusty, delirious, soaked with the waves from the lake.

I contemplate the sky, fading to lavender, the sun setting itself down for the day.

It's a laugh now, a loud cackle.

I hear it first . . . before I realize it's coming from me.

15

SOMEWHERE UNDER THE night sky, I wake with a start.

It takes a moment to realize I'm in the exact spot where I collapsed, having simply passed out from exhaustion.

The sky above me appears purple and bruised, as if readying itself for a great downfall.

I remember the thought I had, just before apparently going to sleep. . . . It was the thought that the Murder of Shadows had not affected me. And how could that be? Then a second thought had replaced that, which was something about the necklace. Ah, yes . . . that the necklace, the one I had almost scoffed at when given to me by Shakvi . . . that it must have had something to do with it.

Unconsciously, my hand touches the necklace there at my collarbone.

Yes. Yes, this must be true.

But how could Shakvi have known of such a thing?

I hear the low rumble of thunder far off in the distance. Yes, this is not a good time to lie around contemplating the past.

I get up and survey my surroundings.

From where I am standing, the slope of the hill reaches upward.

I dust myself off, although this is pointless, really. I'm sure I look as if I've just been hurled out of a volcano.

As I begin to climb the hill, I notice what looks like a thousand steps, it seems, heading up to the pinnacle. There, a countless array of spires shoot up from the darkened sky, each one somehow more foreboding than the next. Knives tearing through the sky, now a kind of deep plum, deciding finally on a tempest.

First a drop, nothing more. Then another. Then one more. And now they come, the drops in agreement. Yes, we will rain down now. Yes, it's time.

By the time I make it to the top of the slope, I realize what it is that I'm staring at.

This is a palace. And it can belong to only one being. The gorgon was not my foe. My foe has yet to be confronted, for this is the palace of the Veist.

The rain continues to come down steadily.

It would be tempting to end my little foray here, turning back and blaming the storm. But, of course, there's no escaping the task at hand.

As I move closer to the onyx walls of the palace, I see it is covered with climbing ivy. I touch the vines tentatively, wanting to be certain this is not actually a wall of vipers.

Normally, I would not attempt to climb a straight vertical drop with my bare hands . . . it's certainly not something I would have even thought about in Roix.

Or is it?

I recall the way in which I escaped many a tiresome situation at the castle—the creeping method I would use, hurling myself from the drawbridge to the portcullis back home.

Home.

The thought of it like a kick in the chest.

Now twisting myself up through the ivy, using the spindly tendrils as a rope, catching the stems with my hands and feet, using them as a kind of ladder, I somehow manage to wind myself high enough to ascend to the apex of the palace walls. I grasp at the slippery ivy, winding it around my hands, and catapult myself up, over, and onto the roof.

I tarry a moment there on the roof, catching my breath. Down below, I see the ground covered with a fine mist, as if clearing itself, disguising itself. Never to be seen again.

I begin creeping over the roof, shielded by the hanging foliage, and find my way to a kind of turret. There, I begin to make out a curious sound to hear at present, the soothing sound of a fountain, tranquil and harmonious. As if the whole world has stopped for a moment of pleasure and respite. I will not make the same mistake twice. I will not let down my guard.

I peer through the ivy and see spread out below the most elaborate confluence of baths imaginable. There's an enormous reflecting pool, adorned with fountains and marble sculptures, each made with a kind of uncanny knowledge of the human form. Each statue the picture of movement, as if somehow caught in motion. At the end of this lush, bewitching landscape, almost invisible due to the steam coming off the water, is a kind of spring. A mineral spring, with a distinctive scent.

I creep my way down through the hanging gardens, where I hide behind a marble sculpture of a man. It's a bit peculiar. There is not a single guard. Not a single soul. Yet there's something else about this absence. Something ominous. As if I'm being watched. Yes, that's the feeling. And yet, each time I turn, there is nothing, no one. Only the fountains and statues to accompany me. The rain has worn itself out for now. The night is deadly still, the feeling of the eye of the storm.

But now, there. There is the sound of a voice, soft, and I startle, looking around for its source.

It's a man's voice, but in a whisper, melancholy. I know not what it says.

I hold still, hoping to catch the voice again, to locate it.

Another mumble, and now I realize the voice is actually right there next to me, and I jump, turning to see whence it came.

And there it is in ebony marble, there at my side the entire time, the sight of it too astonishing to believe. My eyes make their way up the onyx statue and I realize, to my horror, that this is not a statue at all.

That, instead, this sculpture is not a sculpture at all but is actually . . .

Svan.

16

FOR A MOMENT, I stand gobsmacked at the "statue" of Svan before me. His eyes are nearly closed and his mouth is frozen, gripped. His voice is more of a muttered exhale than the voice of a man. To see this wiry, gallant warrior, the man who saved me from certain death in the swamp, now in such a pitiable state, is like a dagger to the heart.

"Svan . . . What has happened? What is this foul enchantment? What monster could have cast it?" My words flying out on top of themselves.

"V-Veist," he stutters.

And now, it seems, he is entirely depleted. His eyes shut, as if from exhaustion, and he appears to go back into a kind of standing slumber. His sculpture one of battle, one of motion, his sword out, ready to slay, but his countenance now asleep, in peace.

I stand there, bewildered and overtaken with grief. How far he has come from his majestic fire dancing, now here, frozen in stone.

But there is also fear. If the ominous Veist can do *this* to Svan, what in heaven's name can the Veist do to me?

There is also the small circumstance of not a single person knowing quite exactly what the Veist *is*.

The dulcet tones of the fountain carry away my thoughts and, as I turn, I realize that every one of these statues is an actual person, turned into a kind of living, eternally suffering testament. Their eyes sometimes open ever so slightly; in moments, their countenance transforms, in subtle ways . . . as if a thought washes over them.

This, too, is a stupefying realization. Will I, too, be turned to a living sculpture, only to spend the rest of my days here in this cruel, mocking place, posed like a puppet?

To my astonishment, I recognize two more statues at the foot of the waters, one to each side, a kind of herald to the baths. I draw closer and inhale, covering my mouth as I realize this new horror. You see, it is the two enchanting girls from the Cliffs of Grey.

Their faces are frozen in a kind of sunken grace, and as I walk in closer, I see something too pitiable for words. It's a tear there, a single tear. Just one. Rolling down the cheek of one of the girl statues. Before I know exactly what I'm doing, I am embracing the statue, tears rolling down my face.

"No, no. Don't worry. I will get you out of here. Never fear," I continue. "This will never be the end of your story. This is just a moment. Just a moment in time. But soon it will be the past. I promise."

But this moment is interrupted as I began to notice the sound of rustling, just a hint from the wind, or possibly the leaves hanging down from the vines. I look up and catch a blackbird, there, atop a spire. Now I look around and begin to notice more black-birds. There, one on the turret. There, one on the tower. Two over there. Three over there.

And now more.

One by one, they arrive at this netherworld. Setting down, each one, with purpose and seeming to set their gaze on me.

And now more.

Setting.

Staring.

Hundreds of blackbirds perched in a circle around me.

They make not a single noise. They just sit atop there, pondering me. I try not to gulp or to move, not sure quite what they are capable of but feeling that whatever it might be, it's diabolical.

Just wait now. This is not unlike the story told by the old man at the cabin. A hundred blackbirds, all at once. And then, too . . . the story of the baths at Alabastrine. A swarm of blackbirds—

As this thought is forming itself in my memory, the blackbirds do not bother to wait for its completion.

Instead, they fly together, in a mass high upward, turning into a kind of living thing, sinewy, an entity weaving and swirling in the night sky. The bruised, mean clouds behind them showcase the formation in silhouette. The temperature now, something in the air, suddenly dropping. My breath comes out as frost. Chills up my spine.

And now the form, the myriad blackbirds, steadies its dance and manifests itself at the foot of the steaming mineral springs, so that it's difficult to tell what is occurring at all. I squint into the fog, able to make out nothing.

But then it appears, out of the mist of the springs. A coal-black figure, tall and spindly, svelte and hovering somehow.

I attempt to move my feet, to scuttle toward some form of cover, but it's no matter. Somehow the sinister entity has entrapped me.

It glides in closer, closer still, taking its time.

And I realize, of course.

That I am staring at . . .

The Veist.

17

———◆———

SUSPENDED AND SHIMMERING, the nebulous figure of the
Veist nears me.

"So this is the little girl who can move mountains." The words
come out as a kind of melody, glistening.

Suddenly, the face of the Veist becomes exposed. The skin,
the eyes, the lips. An unexpected revelation. This shimmering
visage, somehow here and yet not here . . . is actually ravishing.
Devastating. As if the ancients themselves constructed such a
countenance to fill the gods with jealousy.

Just as the Wraithen seemed somehow drawn from the
dreams of an obsessed artist, so does the appearance of the
Veist. A beauty beyond earthly constraints. Somehow both
transcendent . . . and yet vastly sinister.

"Do you like the sculpture of your companion?" The Veist
gestures to the ebony statue of Svan, his eyes closed now, in
his bewitched slumber. "Or how about these two girls from the
cliffs?"

"No, I do—"

"I knew how much you admired them." She sneers. "They are a present to you."

I am utterly dumbfounded, unable to understand in any way, shape, or form how the Veist could know of such faraway things.

"You have kno—"

"Knowledge of your journey here? You think I cannot possibly understand about the creatures of the swamp, or your flight from the Cliffs of Grey? Your auction in Alabastrine? Your sweet little cabin in the woods?" The Veist relishes these revelations, her delight growing with each utterance.

I stand, perplexed.

"How you gave yourself to, what should we call it, the *cause*? How did you put it? Justice? Liberation? Something about innocent villages and wretches in the dirt?" Her intangible form glides, serpentine, quivering in and out of this plane. I shake my head, as if to clear it of confusion.

"But you can't possibly know of such—"

"I know everything, my dear. Why do you think you are here before me? My darling, wasn't it a bit easy . . . The cleaving of the Sapphire Mines? Your foray into the Wraithen? Finding your way here? To me? Wasn't it all . . . just a bit too easy?" she conjectures.

I contemplate this, parsing it out.

"It is wonderful to have your enemies vanquished, isn't it?" And now she takes pleasure in this reveal. "To have the women who kidnapped you strung up atop the gates of the Alabastrine?"

I bristle at the image.

"Or the bloviating boor who bought you? Wasn't it just a treat to see him hanging there, like a pig on a spit?" She smiles now, truly proud. "The apple in the mouth was inspired, don't you think? It really is the small touches that count."

"I do not derive pleasure from the suffering of others," I inform her, trying to find my bearings in this fugue.

"Of course you don't, dear princess. You were not raised so. You were raised to smile and nod and say just the right thing at just the right moment. But never too much, mind you." She takes on the voice of a mock governess. "Never too much. You must keep your voice quiet and demure. You must never say anything to offend or to challenge. You must marry whatever revolting slob you are given. And you must *like* it. . . . Tell me, why is it you miss your life divvied up in teaspoons back in your precious kingdom of Roix?"

This last part lands like a punch.

"How do you know I—"

"Ah, the kingdom of pale pinks and baby blues . . . how graceful, how pretty, how polite and sweet and shining. What a lovely place to smile and nod. What a lovely place to watch as your life . . . goes slowly by . . . your voice . . . taken away. Your thoughts . . . taken away. Your control over your very body . . . taken away as they stuff you into whichever shape they find most pleasing and gift you to the highest bidder." This is all delivered in a soothing, slow, sultry tone. A kind of alluring persuasion.

I stand transfixed.

"Tell me, dear girl, why *do* you want to go back?" she inquires. "When here, here you have grown strong, slain every enemy. Forged your own path. Planned a campaign with your own mind and conscience, and emerged victorious? Yes, I may have helped at the start—but these are *your* achievements. Manifested by *your* thoughts. Your soul. You are no longer a shadow trailing behind all the fatuous, bloviating idiots of the ages, men who dictate every rule. Whose reign depends on your pledge to smile and nod and *just be pleasant*."

"I have not defeated every enemy," I interrupt. "Not quite. The man who betrayed me, who sold me, lives on quite happily."

She tilts her head in amusement. "Ah, your dearest Count Peregrine. Did he not save you from the Murder of Shadows . . . ?"

"Yes, but how could you know it when—"

"My dear, everything has already happened. And everything will happen again," she adds, an afterthought. "You are here. You have been here. You will be here."

"Who . . . what are you?" I reply, stunned.

"I am the creator and the destroyer of worlds," she coos.

As if to demonstrate, the rain now begins to fall in buckets, the night sky finally opening up.

The Veist continues to shiver in and out of a kind of spectral plane.

"Observe." She directs me toward the reflecting pond beneath us. "Can you see that?"

At first, there is nothing to see, but then, before my eyes, I begin to recognize the kingdom of the Wraithen in a kind of motion. Not a picture or a painting but an image moving in the water. As if I am watching from the skies.

"That is the beautiful sight of your dear friends collapsing to their deaths. The very picture of failure. It was a nice try. A noble one, particularly for a princess. Quite frankly, it had nothing to do with you."

And, as if somehow amplified by the Veist, the agony of the scene below seems to crescendo.

"They will lose, of course." She slinks beside me. "Pity, it was a fun game. Serfs and Nobles. I shall have to remember it."

"It is not a game. It is the life of the people. It is the suffering of the people," I reply.

"So adorable how simple your mind is." She floats above, just so. "Oh, I think you will enjoy this part. My dear, look closer."

And there, before me in the waters, we seem to fly down even closer to the scenes of the Wraithen. And then I recognize with horror exactly what I am looking at. I am looking at Keela. There she is, shimmering down below, trapped, it seems, in a cul-de-sac, surrounded by soldiers in black armor.

"This is truly a magnificent moment," the Veist purrs. "Such pathos."

And now the surrounding soldiers are upon her, all in a throng. And I watch as she is buried in swords and soldiers.

"Keela!" I cry out, watching from above as her life is extinguished.

But now the waters grow still and the vision fades.

"So dramatic," the Veist teases.

"You are a foul, horrid creature," I spit out, slinging the words at her. "Depraved and beyond redemption."

"Ah, redemption." She ponders. "Yet . . . you haven't wondered why, exactly, I would manifest this place, and all in it? Dear princess. Aren't you curious?"

"What do you mean by this?" I shriek. "What have you *manifested*? What I see and feel are true! I am here, as you are." But even as the words leave my lips, the image of the Veist quivers before me, sowing doubt.

"Look around you," she continues. "Do you not admire what I've built here? My exquisite dream come to life? A refracted image of your world, created out of spite."

This sends a shudder through me.

The cacophonous sound of the battle in the kingdom below grows stronger and I turn, wondering if it's possible to save them.

"Do not bother, my dear." She feigns kindness. "It's hopeless, you see."

"Nothing is hopeless," I reply, wishing I could believe it.

Now she shimmers in front of me, suddenly making herself as strange and beautiful as all the stars in the midnight heavens.

"Join me, Princess . . . you can rule in this place forever. Ships will sail at your command. Armies retreat. You can resurrect your warrior friends, or leave them to the dust," she lures me. "Whatever you desire, you can be. A river of diamonds, an ocean of gold."

I stand there, bewildered, unable to comprehend this fever dream.

"I would rather die than sit at your right hand in this cursed place," I tell her. "I want only to go home."

"So . . . ," she replies. "That is what you want, yes? To return to your meek, subservient, pathetic little life in Fairyland?"

"Yes," I answer softly.

"Why?" she prods me.

"I want to be with my mother and my family and all I know," I confide.

"And you're sure of this? Absolutely sure?" she queries, contemplating.

"Yes," I answer. "I have never been so sure of anything in my entire life."

There is a stillness here, interrupted by the thunder sounding off in the distance. Now the beginning of lightning, in fits and starts. One here. One over there. The thunder and lightning seem to come closer, as if making their way only to the two of us.

"Very well." She turns away, seeming to sink somehow. "Then you must die."

She whips around and immediately I feel my body suspended in a sort of invisible clutch. She reaches out her glimmering hands and fingers to cast her diabolical enchantment on me. Now I am to be a statue.

Higher, higher up she lifts me, until the fountains and statues sink far below, like tiny little toys waiting to be placed at the feet of a toddler.

And I realize, in this moment, that the Veist does not wish to turn me into a statue. No. She wishes to destroy me altogether.

It is as if the lightning is pulsing through me now, the sparks from her fingers enveloping me, a sort of blue light in it.

And that is it.

I am done now.

It's over.

I will never see my beloved mother again. I will never see my stately father or my kingdom of pale pinks and baby blues.

I could have died there at the swamp and it would have been simpler.

I wish I had.

My eyes begin to close as the Veist sends this blue lightning through me, as I surrender to my fate. Yes, this is the way it would always end. I was a fool not to see it.

Not to see it.

I gaze down and catch sight of my arm. The strange forms still written there in black ink. But they are no longer black. They pulse with blue lightning. They burn. And I shriek with pain. As the sound echoes around us, the forms seem to shift and change— to remake themselves. The forms become letters on my arm. . . . I finally begin to discern them.

The sparks are running through them, yet I can barely make the letters out. . . .

M . . .

A . . .

A flash of lightning, pulsing through me.

R . . . A . . . N . . .

Another bolt, scorching me from within.

In agony, I rush to read the rest . . . A . . . T . . . H . . . A.

The inside of my body, burning up, my veins, feeling as if they're about to burst.

M-A-R-A-N-A-T-H-A.

And now I whisper it.

"Maranatha."

And now, somehow, a kind of strength in it.

"MARANATHA."

And now, something strange happens . . . the Veist seems to sink down from our great height, carrying me down with her. And the lightning continues, but no longer from her outstretched hands. For her hands are not shimmering anymore. In fact, they have suddenly become just normal, merely mortal hands, alabaster and no longer quivering.

"MaaRaaaNaaaTHaa . . ."

The Veist appears to be flickering in and out of the spectral plane, of her spectral self, into a common human form of flesh and blood.

"No," she whispers to herself. "No no no . . ."

I continue, now stronger, seeing how the Veist is weakening.

"MaaaRaaaNaaaTHaa . . ."

The sound of my voice, almost a prayer, affecting the Veist, turning her into nothing but a mere mortal. Only flesh, only blood.

THWAP.

She grabs me by the neck, mad with rage, dragging me down to the vast reflecting pool. Here, now, next to the statue of my dear piteous companion Svan, still at slumber.

"MaaaRaaaNaaaTHaa . . ."

The thunder and lightning crash above, now a crescendo. Lightning like madness itself, pummeling the waters. Thunder joining in, shaking the stones beneath our feet.

"You will not suffer! You will not have to be weak, subjugated, violated, abused!" The Veist is in a kind of frenzy now, possessed. "I will spare you that! This, *this* will be my blessing!"

"MaaaRaaaNaaaTHaa . . . ," I continue, beckoning.

"I will save you, dear princess. You will not have to be deceived and sullied and crushed. I will spare you the unlucky fate of your curse—of being born a princess!" And with that, the Veist plunges my head into the reflecting pond.

The water rushes over my head, the strangle grip of her hold choking me. Now my hair in the pool, like tendrils, seaweed, wrapping itself around my neck. My lungs, so meager, unwarned, unable to take a breath before being plunged down into the pond. My brain now asunder, thinking of all the things I could have done, thinking of how I should simply have let myself be devoured in that swamp, let myself be sold, let myself drop off the precipice of the black cliffs.

The Veist may only be in mortal form now, but that does not make her weak. She continues to rant and rave, crazed, as she holds my head under the water.

Oh, how easy it would be, if I had been born a boy.

An ash-haired boy like Keela's son at the Cliffs of Grey. Conducting experiments with buckets and frogs.

Yes, buckets and frogs, rods, and—

Lightning!

I make my head go limp in the water. Still. The Veist waits and then, ever so slightly, loosens her grip. Having defeated me.

And that is the moment I hurl myself out of the pool, whipping the Veist into the water. She falls, and before she can recover from the shock . . . I grab the sword off the statue of Svan. Out of his grip and down into the water. Into the great, vast reflecting pool, a magnet for lightning.

A frog in a bucket.

"MARANATHA!" I shriek.

The Veist struggles to wrest herself out before the—

FLASH!

And then the crash of thunder.

The metal sword draws in the lightning bolts. One and then two, and then three. The lightning, electrifying, flowing through the veins of the Veist now, through her mere mortal body of flesh and blood, raising her up like a macabre marionette . . . she dances there suspended over the water, convulsing and shaking with each new strike of lightning.

It is a hideous sight, but it is a breathtaking sight.

As if the gods themselves are punishing the Veist, unforgiving in their ire. Perhaps she has flown too close to the sun.

After an eternity of this astonishing sight, the Veist finally collapses into the water, slain, limp, the reflecting pool collecting her body like a floating doll.

Yet now there is a voice, a last gasp.

I lean in toward her.

She strains, the life draining out of her.

I come in closer.

"It was that you . . . belonged to me. My sweet . . . Maranatha."

And now the light in her eyes snuffs itself out, and the breath trails away . . . up into the midnight sky, the rain coming down in droves. Her body wading now, a black-festooned corpse adrift in the fateful reflecting pool.

I stand frozen, as if I had, indeed, been turned into a statue. I stare at the dead figure of the Veist, the alpha and the omega, the maker and destroyer of all things, who created this world out of spite.

But it's as if the thought can't be embraced, the thought can't catch up to itself, because as I stand there . . . I begin to notice a kind of falling off.

A kind of quivering.

A kind of flickering in and out of . . . matter. An erasure. Of each of the statues. Of the spires. Of the hanging gardens and the palace itself. And now everything beyond. In fits and starts, the clouds, the rain, the canopy of stars above . . . begin to disappear.

And the lands beyond the Veist, the landscape . . . that, too, the black rocks, the cliffs, everything out to the end of the horizon, quivering and then dimming off.

Vanished.

Until all that is left is the wading corpse of the Veist there in the reflecting pool and the shimmer of that, too. Her lifeless body and even the water now, oscillating, flickering in and out of the spectral plane, into . . .

Nothing.

And that's the last I remember.

18

LATER ON, THEY will tell me I emerged with a gasp as if coming up from the bottom of the ocean. They will tell me I was in a slumber for a matter of weeks. They will tell me the soothsayers informed them I was lost forever. Then they will excitedly tell me about a dotty old woman who came to the castle. That she had an idea. They will tell me her idea was that they would have to search and search throughout all the kingdoms for the only prince who could break the spell. Prince Charming.

But in this moment, here, as I open my eyes only to see a circle of astonished faces staring down at me, they do not say any of those things. Too astonished, I suppose, to utter a word. And, as I look around, I begin to notice that I am surrounded by about twenty naked men, looking very embarrassed and attempting, badly, to cover themselves up with the shards of what look like very small leaves from the water lilies in our reflecting pond.

"What in the name of God—"

But I do not finish my sentence.

In an instant, my mother is upon me, embracing me in a way she has never done before, unable to let go, her eyes welling up with tears. My father, too, shows a side of him foreign to me, leaning over and kissing me on the forehead.

"Who are all these naked men?" I ask.

"What? Oh . . . them. No, don't worry about them." He turns to them, gesturing for them to make their exit. The mortified men seem more than happy to oblige, scurrying out. "My dear, sweet princess! You have frightened us all to death. Look at your poor mother, she has been inconsolable."

My mother, still clutching me in her embrace, lets out a laugh more like a breath. "It's true, my darling Bitsy. I haven't slept in weeks."

Then . . . the both of them turn to a chestnut-haired stranger standing there, and thank him.

"Oh, my dear prince. You have given us new life!" my mother exclaims.

"Yes, noble Prince Charming, you have saved the day! You shall be handsomely rewarded," my father corrects himself.

The chestnut-haired man bows graciously. "Your Highness, King Roix, as you know, it is all the reward I should ever desire. Your daughter, the princess, shall be the happiest bride on earth."

My mother gives me an uncomfortable glance. "Yes, yes. Let us talk about that later. Right now, we have to celebrate the return of the most precious daughter in all the lands. Dear little itsy Bitsy, I am giddy with love!"

"Yes, yes, of course." My father nods in agreement. "We shall have a banquet like no other, a celebration to plunge all the other kingdoms into a jealous rage!"

He pats this so-called Prince Charming on the back. "And,

my dear prince, that is when we shall make our announcement. Oh, happy day!"

The chestnut-haired prince gives me a fond look. "My dear Elizabeth, I promise to make you the happiest princess in all the kingdoms. And one day, queen, of course. Our two kingdoms, now forever entwined, shall flourish in wealth and happiness."

My face must register a kind of shock, because he suddenly looks a bit self-conscious, at which point he politely bows out of the garden.

"Oh, Mother, I have had the most amazing dream." I grasp her hand.

"Yes, dear. I cannot wait to hear all about it. But, for the moment, let us go and get you bathed and dressed; tonight will be a night of jubilation never to be forgotten. The night the princess came back to us!"

She pats my hand.

My father agrees. "Yes, now get her dressed and make her pretty; there will be guests from all around! Nobles, dukes, counts, and countesses. Approximately twenty irate princes. But never mind, dear. . . . We will not let any of that dampen the mood!"

With this, he makes his exit, whistling like a carefree schoolboy.

"What is the rush, Mother? I'm still in a bit of a daze, you see—"

"Oh, darling princess, my little moppet . . . I have the most exciting news. We shall make the announcement tonight of the royal nuptials. You and the Prince Charming!" she adds. "You'll love him. He enjoys jousting and collecting exotic coins. And, of course, he's the one who saved you!"

"But he did not save me, I saved—"

"Of course he saved you, darling! You've been in a deep slumber for weeks!" she interrupts. "He kissed you and now you're here! Thank God above! Now, let the maids take you down to bathe and eat, not too much, of course, as you will have to fit into your corset, and then they shall have you gorgeously dressed for the forthcoming banquet. You will be the most beautiful girl in the kingdom!"

With that, she makes her exit, nodding to the maidens to prepare me.

Rose and Suzette step forward.

"Oh, we could dance a jig!" Rose exclaims.

"So happy you made it back to us!" Suzette embraces me.

"Well, then, Your Highness. Are you ready to be pretty?"

19

THEY'VE SAT PRINCE Charming beside me at the head of the banquet feast. Everywhere, there are garlands and flowers and wreaths. Before us now, Prissy and Bolanda, dressed as if this celebration is clearly for them, having dazzled us with a troupe of contortionists, acrobats, jugglers, and even a pig with the ability to read minds, introduce the fifth bit of entertainment: a gaunt sword-swallower from the outer reaches of the kingdom.

As he performs each of his death-defying feats, Prince Charming expresses a giddy kind of excitement, clapping madly, like a boy at his birthday party. Every once in a while, my mother catches my eye and reminds me to smile. Which, of course, I do. There have been speeches upon speeches. So many speeches. And I have smiled and nodded through all of them.

There was even a fabled magician, performing the introductory skit, who requested I come forward in order to release a cage of doves for his illusion. Everyone gasped when I accepted his request, particularly Prissy and Bolanda, who whispered furiously behind their respective fans. My betrothed, Prince Charming, leaned in at that moment and urged me not to participate in this heretical and low entertainment. My mother also gave me a look of chiding as I left the stage to return to my seat, front and center, with Prince Charming.

Somewhere in the middle of the fourth sword-swallowing, I notice a strange, grisly old woman, hunched over in the archway behind the stage. I have never seen this particular woman and am a bit surprised to see such a frightful sight at the banquet. Unusual for the king to allow it.

"Mother," I whisper to her, beside me. "Do you see that woman over there? The extremely old woman, hunched over there, in the arch?"

My mother follows my gaze and lets out an embarrassed little smile. "Yes, my dear, I know she is a fright, but that is actually the old lady who saved your life. Can you believe it? And though she's hideous, she brought you back to me, so as far as I'm concerned, she's the most beautiful woman in the world."

"Ah, I see," I reply.

"Now do try to engage the prince in some pleasant conversation, will you, dear?" she urges me.

"Mother, I have. All he wants to talk about are rare coins. Whether they are bronze, gold, or silver. Which magistrate adorns them. How that relates to their value. Etcetera, etcetera, etcetera," I reply.

"Yes, dear, I know it may not be scintillating conversation exactly. But you shall be hearing much, much more about such things for many moons to come." She bops me gently on the nose with her finger. "Boop. So, you might as well get used to it."

I smile, warmed by simply the sound of her voice.

I notice a bit of movement out of the corner of my eye. Turning toward it, I realize it's the old, cloaked woman, who now disappears down the hallway. I'm not sure quite why, but I have the urge to follow her, perhaps to thank her for her troubles.

I excuse myself and, before my mother can stop me, make my way behind the tables to the archway where the old woman had appeared. Yes, I will follow her. It's the right thing to do. I shall be gracious. But there is something else propelling me. . . .

The hunched figure scurries away through the castle, at lightning speed, much quicker than you would think a woman of her age could possibly travel. This, of course, piques my interest even more, and I find myself following her down, around, this way and that, through the stone labyrinth of the castle.

Finally, she stops in a stone room down a winding corridor, and I catch her there. Strangely, it is I who am out of breath.

I call out to her. "Wait! Wait, please! I have yet to thank you."

She whips around, still with her face hidden underneath the black cloak, strange yet agile.

"You've not to thank me, dear princess." Her raspy voice comes out from beneath the shadowy cloak.

"Oh, but I do," I answer.

But now, she takes the black cloak down with purpose and I stifle a gasp. Her face is pockmarked and crinkled, almost unrecognizable as human. A kind of beast, hideous to look at.

"Ah." She catches me. "Even you cannot escape the chains of this place. Frightened of my ghastly face, are you?"

"No, I j-just—" I stammer. "I apologize. I did not mean to offend."

"You'll be surprised to know, deary, that I was beautiful once. Yes . . ." She thinks, takes her time, relishes the moment. "Beautiful enough for your father to fall in love with me. . . ."

She trails off. I find myself confounded, unable to wrap my fingers around this thought.

"Of course, that was before the pox, you see." She turns to me, and now there's something familiar in her eyes, something mischievous. "Before I became so hideous, so ugly I might as well die."

"I'm very sorry. That is quite unjust," I respond. "Cruel."

"Cruel. Yes. Your father was cruel, then, wasn't he?" She ponders this. "Leaving me to rot away, uncared for, thrown out like yesterday's scraps."

"Forgive me, kind woman. But I cannot imagine my father would do such a thing," I add. "He must have not been informed—"

"Not been informed . . ." She cackles, shaking her head. "Ah, to be so young and naive! Not been informed, you say . . . of the baby in my gut, the baby he gave to me, the baby he stole from me."

"A lie," I reply.

"I cursed your father, my dear," she confides. "He is to give that sweet baby up if she's not married by her eighteenth birthday. He is to give her to me."

And now her old, haggard face begins to quiver slightly and transform. Now it is a few winters younger. Now twenty winters, now thirty. And the pockmarked skin of her face begins to heal itself, turning from wrinkled to smooth ivory alabaster. And now the face begins to reveal itself.

Ravishing.

And I gasp as I realize . . .

It is the face of the Veist.

I step backward in terror.

"You will again be mine, my darling Maranatha." The stunning face of the Veist brings itself into the light.

"No . . . it can't be." I try to comprehend this.

And now she begins to shimmer again, to quiver in the moonlight. "I dream you. I have dreamt you. I will dream you."

Those very words!

The same voice, whispering from the wind . . .

"But why . . . and how could you—"

"My darling girl, I answered your plea. *'Do not force me into a life in a gilded cage, please free me of this fate . . .'*? I did hear your prayer. I dreamt an entire world for you."

"No. It cannot be. Your imagination . . . your dream—" I fumble for the words.

"Oh . . . and why not?"

"Because . . . because—" And then the image of Shakvi, the tiny wooden box, the black ink letters written on my wrist. "How could you have enemies in your own creation? Your own dream?"

But the Veist only laughs at this. And now her face transforms once again . . . into the ancient, withered face of Shakvi, a twinkle in her eye.

"We all have aspects of ourselves that we cannot control. I was a different person . . . before your father stole my light."

And now her visage morphs again, from old and kind to young

and sinister. The ivory skin of the Veist almost aglow, her raven hair billowing. "You have shown yourself to be more powerful than I could ever have imagined. Than *you* could ever have imagined. You could stay here." She taunts me. "Lead a life of smiles and nods. But you have tasted freedom, and power . . . are you really content to sit politely next to your Prince Charming? Is that all there is for you? Is that all you were born to do?"

I stand there, stunned by these revelations.

"The choice is yours, my darling girl." And now she is before me, her pale hand reaching out to touch my cheek. "There is nothing, no dream I wouldn't dream for you, no kingdom I wouldn't conquer for you. But now . . . the dream is yours."

And with that, she begins to transform again . . . into a hundred ravens. The onyx wings, blue-black, fluttering.

Now these hundred blackbirds are flying up up up, to the top of the turret and into the moonlight streaming in from the high windows above. And now I realize . . . I recognize this room as the exact same room from the moment just before my journey: the turret, the tiny windows high above, the floor covered in sawdust.

And my eyes follow the hundred ravens flying out through the tall turret windows high above, the moon shining in. I then lower my gaze back down to the empty stone room.

I pause, a thought circling.

And there, in the middle of the sawdust-covered floor, a thing I hadn't noticed before.

There, in the middle of the room. Do you see it?

And it is like the thought circling in my head, the realization, the possibility, is claiming my limbs and pushing me, moving me, forward toward it. . . .

Toward . . .

The spindle.

The End

Acknowledgments

There are so many sages around to thank! It's hard to know where to start.

First, I must thank Kristen Pettit, for her stewardship in this and all things. Tara Weikum, for putting up with my annoyingly absent-minded nature. My agent, Rosemary Stimola, who is always wise and savvy. My husband, Sandy Tolan, who puts up with my strangeness, odd habits, and mercurial spirit. My son, Wyatt, who is my universe.

And, of course, all the people who have believed in me along the way. My mother, Nancy Kuhnel. My father, Dr. Alejandro Portes. My siblings, Charles de Portes and Lisa Portes. David Michaels, Mira Crisp, Andrew Zinn, Mark Lord, Sally Van Haitsma, Fred Ramey, Dan Smetanka. Thank you for pushing me to believe in myself and for accepting me, despite my strange ways.